FIRST ANNUAL
BDSM WRITERS CON
ANTHOLOGY

FOREWORD BY
DR. CHARLEY FERRER
EDITED BY **LORI PERKINS**

First Annual BDSM Writers Con Anthology © 2014 by BDSM Writers Con

All Rights Reserved. No part of this book may be reproduced or transmitted in any form or by any means, electronic or mechanical, including photocopying, without permission in writing from the publisher.

For more information contact:
Riverdale Avenue Books
5676 Riverdale Avenue
Riverdale, NY 10471.

www.riverdaleavebooks.com

Design by www.formatting4U.com
Cover illustration of Fetish Fine Art by CapturedErotica.com

Digital ISBN 978-1-62601-104-5
Print ISBN 978-1-62601-105-2

First Edition August 2014

Table of Contents

Foreword by Dr. Charley Ferrer	1
Roman's To-Do List by Jennifer Kacey	5
When Restraint Set Me Free by Cris Anson	15
Full Surrender by Debra Hyde	19
Dirty Girls Have All the Fun by Lise Horton	29
Silken Desires by Laci Paige	37
Learning My Lesson by Jessica Lust	40
Paris Light by Leya Wolfgang	51
Retrograde by Scarlet Hawthorne	62
Caro's Fantasy by Marie Tuhart	79
Point of No Return by Kestra Gravier	91
A Virgin Again by Helena Stone	110
You're Mine by Gray Dixon	118
A Hart for Talia by Roz Lee	132
Psychology and Misconceptions of the Roles in BDSM by Dr. Charley Ferrer	140
…How I Feel? by Cara Downey	156
Sloane's Threesome by Paige Matthews	166
All of the Above by Cassandra Park	176
Puppy Gets Her Medicine by Corrine A. Silver	184
Employment Benefits by Carrie Anne Ward	187
My Princess by Mia Koutras	192
That's Harsh by Laura Antoniou	206
Editor's Note by Lori Perkins	233
About the Authors	234

Foreword
By Dr. Charley Ferrer

I was kinky before kinky was a word and definitely before it was ever popular!

I remember as a child, I loved to wrestle with the boys and pin them down. As we grew older and they grew stronger, my wrestling days ended—it was no longer fun for me as the thrill of controlling them was gone. Thus began my drawing days. By fifteen, I found myself compelled to draw pictures on my walls…and not just small ones you could hide behind a picture frame or poster…but the big live sized murals which made my mother angry.

My first painting was of a man and a woman kissing. It wasn't so much that I'd drawn on the wall instead of on paper that caused an uproar and earned me the whispered title of "the troubled child." It was how I'd depicted the couple. In my painting, the man was nude and the woman was dressed in a long gown. To me, the painting portrayed an openness in the man; his willingness to be completely exposed to the woman. And though I didn't quite understand all the nuances to that particular thought at the time, I knew it was crucial. That painting led to several others and by the time I was seventeen years old, I drew my masterpiece. It consisted of a naked man tied to a post while two women in short shorts whipped him.

I sat before that painting for hours wondering why I was so drawn to it. It wasn't the sexual undertones which really spoke to me so much as the spiritual and emotional ones. I was drawn to the raw power of the drawing. The vulnerability of the male. His surrender and sacrifice. The control of the women. As I sat there staring at what I'd drawn, the world disappeared, the voices around me quieted, and everything seemed as it should be. Unfortunately, for a Spanish girl mired in machismo, my drawings were blasphemous. I went from being the "troubled child" to the child who should be committed.

Throughout my life, I had only ever seen negative depictions of individuals who had similar desires. I had no one to turn to to answer my questions. I couldn't trust the family with my thoughts and the few friends I did reveal my desires to declared my desires were strange and unnatural. One close friend actually implored me to pray to be rid of them. Another felt I hated men and wanted to emasculate them when the truth was far from it. I quickly learned to hide my desires and buried them from those I dated and cared for lest I find myself forever alone.

It wasn't until I was in my thirties that I discovered I wasn't alone in my yearnings. There was an entire community of men and women who embraced these same cravings, the same emotional and sexual identities, and they didn't think I was abnormal or perverted. And joy of joys, there were many strong confident men who would gladly take their place in helping me make my drawings a reality.

From the moment I discovered the BDSM lifestyle community, I immersed myself in learning all I could. Finally I was home…I belonged…I wasn't weird nor demented nor in need of psychiatric assistance. I was normal and whole!

As the years went by, I wanted to help others feel that same sense of wholeness…of belonging…I'd discovered. To let men and women know that there was nothing wrong with the way they expressed their love and affection; it was merely different. After a few years of lecturing throughout the US, I began lecturing to the medical and psychiatric community as well. In 2005, I spoke before the World Association of Sexual Health in Canada and before the International Latino Association of Physicians in Venezuela about the need for medical providers and mental health workers to learn the truths about Dominance and submission to enable them to provide better health care and support for their patients. I quickly earned the title of America's BDSM Expert. In 2013, I was one of a handful of Sexologists around the world invited to speak before the Chinese Sexology Association, the first time the Chinese opened their doors to collaboration with "outsiders."

In 2011, I came out of the *Leather Closet*, in my books *BDSM The Naked Truth* and *BDSM for Writers*. In them, I admitted to being

BDSM Anthology

a Dominant and embracing sadomasochistic desires in my relationships. This was a major turning point in my life as I could no longer hide behind the guise of being a Clinical Sexologist and Psychotherapist who was speaking objectively. I found many colleagues drawn to me, wanting to learn more, while others shunned me. One colleague in particular, whom I admired for her work in addiction recovery treatment, condemned me for coming out. She felt it was inappropriate for me to "encourage" patients to accept their desires when I should be "treating" them for it.

Instead of discouraging me, she inspired me to do more. To find other avenues where I could educate the populace. That's when I turned to writers. BDMS writers in particular. I figured, if I could teach authors the various nuances of the power exchange and help them understand the emotional and psychological connections men and women make in this highly erotic and often misrepresented lifestyle, they could pass along that knowledge to their readers; thus in essence, helping me reach more men and women.

In 2012, I created *BDSM for Writers 3-Day Intensive Workshop* which provided three days of lectures and a night out at a BDSM Club. It quickly became clear readers also wanted in on the workshops. By our third year, my 3-Day Intensive morphed into a four-day **BDSM Writers Con** bringing together many more participants who wanted to write about or exploring the world of Dominance and submission. I changed the format a bit to include even more aspects of Dominance and submission including live demonstrations conducted by friends who are BDSM Experts.

Because I wanted to stay true to my original intent, I created two tracks for the conference. One for authors where they could enhance their skills and attend workshops which addressed their particular writing and publishing needs in this genre, and a second track for everyone (writers and readers) which focused on various aspects of this wondrous and extremely diverse world.

I also joined forces with Lori Perkins from Riverdale Avenue Books to bring you the *Between The Covers Erotica Reading Series* held during our newly included BDSM Book Fair on the last day of the conference. Plus, Lori had the inspirational idea to create an Anthology for the conference and offered to publish it for us. Our *First Annual BDSM Writers Con Anthology* holds stories from many of our Featured Authors, some of whom may be your favorites; as well as several stories from our contest Finalists, several of whom are making their writing debut. We're sure they'll soon be added to your list of must read authors.

I have so much more I want to say and share with you that I could fill a thousand pages and still not have shared it all. So I'll stop for now, invite you to join us for our next annual BDSM Writers Con and answer the question that was recently posed to me:

In a nutshell, what is BDSM?

My Answer: It's a healthy normal way to love and show your affection for another.

Live with passion,
Dr. Charley Ferrer

Roman's To-Do List
By Jennifer Kacey

"You made me what? Wife?"

Roman's displeasure dripped from every word and Joslin turned away to hide her smile.

"A to-do list."

Silence. "On a Saturday." Definitely a statement through his gritted teeth instead of a question.

She swallowed the giggle threatening to bubble out of her at any moment and bit her lip. Out of the corner of her eye she caught his spanking hand twitch and the cheeks of her rear heated with phantom warmth. Straightening a pile of mail before continuing gave her an opportunity to regain her composure.

"Yes, Sir. It's rather lengthy too, but you don't have to do it all today if you're not *up* for it." Her grin widened so she pulled her blonde ponytail over her shoulder to hide her delight.

The wave of frustration he left in his wake nearly knocked her over as he strode to the mudroom and grabbed his leather chaps.

Blood and adrenaline raced in her veins as he buckled them in place around his jeans-covered thighs.

He threw sunglasses on, covering up his mocha brown eyes and his jaw flexed as he clenched it tight.

He snatched the piece of paper off the granite without looking at it, then yanked his keys off the peg by the back door. "A to-do list. My one Saturday off from the shop this month and this is how you want to spend it. After turning me down this morning for sex. Only time since we've been together..." He opened the back door, grumbling the whole time. He didn't exactly slam it. That wasn't his style. But he definitely closed it firmly.

Joslin twisted around and walked to the island to wait. It wouldn't take him long to figure it out.

She heard the engine on his Harley rev to life and in no time he was out of the garage and the sound of the bike faded away.

Roman owned an extremely successful machine shop in Arcadia, Kansas. He worked long hours to support both of them while she finished med school. To say he was her rock since they'd been married didn't even come close, and she wanted to do something to give back to him.

The to-do list he held wasn't a normal list.

It didn't have errands to run.

Oh no.

Each bullet point listed something to do with sex.

And Roman was a lot like her.

If a list existed, things needed to be dealt with, handled, finished and crossed off. She couldn't wait to get started. Some of the things on the list they loved to do. Other items they hadn't tried yet. And a few they hadn't even discussed from a sex position app a friend of hers told her about from The Library. Jenna was full of deliciously dirty tidbits of info.

Joslin thought about surprising him with lingerie and a sexy dinner but either one of them could be called away and she didn't want to chance missing an opportunity for them to be intimate. Make love. Fuck like rabbits. Or all of the above depending on his mood.

He was a grade-A, card-carrying Dom and member of The Library, the private BDSM club they belonged to, catering to people just like them. Individuals, couples, and poly groups free to explore every dirty and decadent fantasy they could imagine in a safe oasis.

A secret place where they could discover their happily ever after.

Pain. Pleasure. Both.

Two sides of the same coin.

Joslin reached up and ran her fingers over the small lock and metal chain that circled her throat. It hadn't left her body since the moment he put it on her in a collaring ceremony shortly before they were married.

For almost two years, she'd submitted her power to him. Freely gave it to him when it came to anything sexual. She'd found her place with him, on her knees, from the very beginning and had never been happier.

The rumble of Roman's bike in the distance made her pussy clench. It grew louder as he came closer.

As he came home.

She removed her shorts and tank top, not having to worry about any undergarments since she'd refrained from putting any on when they'd gotten up that morning.

Taunting him as she made breakfast had just been an added bonus.

The clip holding her ponytail in place came next and she stacked her clothes on one of the bar stools slid beneath the counter.

She climbed up on the cleared island and shivered at the cold granite against her palms and lower legs. It didn't take her long to move to the far edge of the empty space. She stopped with her knees against the edge to be as close to him as possible when he came inside.

The sound of the bike moving into the garage had never turned her on more. She sat back on her haunches, spread her legs wide and placed her hands, palm up, on the tops of her thighs.

Her submissive pose was his favorite. He'd taught her years ago what he liked, and she lived to make him happy.

The back door swung open and bounced off the side wall, and there he stood, backlit by the sun pouring in as if he were an avenging archangel.

Sexy.

Dominant.

She shivered as he closed the door, hung up his keys and stalked closer.

"That's some list you have there, little girl." He placed the crumpled half sheet of paper on the counter next to one of her knees and finally took off his sunglasses. His deep brown irises pegged her with more intensity than she'd seen in weeks.

Biting her lip, drew his attention and then he focused on her eyes again.

"Did you like it, Sir?"

One side of his mouth curled up into a smirk. "Fuck. Yes." He circled the skin on one of her knees with his thumb.

His hands were one of the sexiest things on his body. They were rough. A working-man's hands.

They could bring her immeasurable pleasure or bring her to tears, strapped to a cross, with nothing but a whip as a tool to play her.

She shivered as he looked down and focused on her bare pussy.

He gazed at her face again and raised an eyebrow.

The giggle she'd had to hide earlier slipped out. "I had her waxed for you yesterday."

"And not the time of the month obviously. I knew the timing was off." He ran his knuckles along the side swell of one of her breasts, making her nipples tighten and bead. "Been planning this for a little while, wife of mine? Hands behind your back."

Her muscles responded with barely a flicker of cognitive reasoning from her head. He was her Master in every sense of the word.

Pain and adrenaline shot into her system as he latched onto both of her nipples. She gritted her teeth, panting. Her hips swiveling in time to the beat of her heart as she processed the pain.

He pinched harder.

"Sir?" she shrieked.

He let go and her abdomen contracted a handful of times as the blood rushed back into the tight tips of her breasts. Slowly, he rolled them between his thumb and first finger. "So. Pretty."

Joslin caught the scent of his shampoo as he leaned over and licked one of her nipples. "Mmmm," was the only sound she could make as he kissed and nibbled and tongued first one breast, and then the second. She dug her fingernails into each opposite forearm, reminding herself not to reach for him.

Burying her fingers in his shaggy dark hair sounded very nice but she wanted his approval even more.

With one more lick to each nipple he straightened, towering over her once again.

The look in his eyes.

Fuck.

Dominance came off him in waves, sinking into her pores, her dreams.

She ran her tongue across her bottom lip as she eyed his mouth. "Want a kiss?"

Her eyes flicked up to his for a second and then they settled on his lips again as she smiled. "Yes Sir."

"Then you'll have to earn it for lying to me earlier."

"But..." She sucked in a breath to argue before she thought better of it, but he cocked an eyebrow at her one more time. She closed her lips, sucking them in past her teeth and she clamped them shut. Nodding seemed the best answer.

He tugged her bottom lip free where she nibbled on it and slid two of his thick digits into her mouth. "Suck them."

The flavor of his skin exploded across her taste buds and she moaned, closing her eyes to revel in his possession. He tasted like liquid arousal and leather.

Wetness slid from her core, coating the lips of her sex as she licked and sucked on his fingers. He gripped one of her thighs with his free hand, moving her legs farther apart.

Vulnerability urged her to close her legs, but she wanted what he offered even more.

She sucked hard on his fingers as he pulled them from her mouth.

He reached beneath her body, slid them along both sides of her clit and filled her weeping sex with them.

Her eyes closed and her head fell forward in bliss.

"Look at me," he growled as he fisted her hair, yanking her head up to stare at him again.

She panted and arched her back as he filled her pussy over and over.

"I'm going to make you come and I want to see every emotion flit across your face. Your eyes." He added his thumb to the mix, moving it in her wetness, then he rubbed her clit in tight, hard circles she couldn't fight.

Sensation and heat filled her pelvis and expanded up her torso, her head.

Warmth spread across her chest and her cheeks as an orgasm coiled inside her.

"Please Sir?" She clenched her teeth as his pulse raced at his throat.

"Not yet. Not. Yet." He didn't slow down. He didn't pause so she could stave off her orgasm.

No.

He picked up his pace, curling his fingers as he pulled them out each time so he could drag them across her G-spot.

"Come when I count to five." He growled the words out and his nostrils flared as a rush of pussy juice coated his fingers.

"One, my beautiful whore."

She trembled at his deliciously naughty nickname for her.

"Two." He licked her jaw, making her shiver.

"Three."

She moaned in distress as the walls of her pussy fluttered in the first vestiges of climax.

"Four, my little slut. Sucking my fingers into that wet snatch of yours. Who's pussy is this? Who does it belong to?"

"You, Sir. I belong to you." It was an oath, a pledge, a prayer even. All rolled into one as she stared at the man who was her everything.

His fist tightened in her hair and her entire body tensed with it.

So close to release.

So.

Close.

"Five!" He shouted it and wrenched her head to the side to bite her throat.

"Fuuuuck," spilled from between her lips as she came for him. Shockwaves of ecstasy jolted her body as pleasure pulsed through her veins, rocking her hips while she jerked in the cage of his ownership.

He bit her again on her shoulder and growled against her flesh. "Mine."

Before she knew what happened he flipped her over onto her stomach with her hips against the side of the island.

"Eeek," jerked out of her as parts of her chest hit warmth from where she'd been sitting and other parts chilled her naked flesh.

The sound of his zipper snicking downward blew her mind into a million pieces. He jabbed his cock against the opening of her pussy and plunged inside while her orgasm still rippled through her muscles.

Did he take off his pants?

No.

His chaps?

No.

"Thank. You. Sir. Thank. You." She breathed each word out as he thrust inside her again and again. Her toes almost touched the ground each time he pulled out but she had no leverage. No ability to control even an ounce of the situation she now found herself in.

Nothing turned her on more than that.

His control.

His complete domination of her mind and body.

He grabbed her wrists which she'd lost control of when he'd flipped her over. He crossed them at her lower back again and used them to his advantage. His cock jerked inside her, making her toes curl.

The rattle of the contents in a drawer drew her out of her sexual haze.

She flipped her head and hair to the other side just in time to see him pull several long garbage bag ties out. In no time her wrists were bound behind her back in the same position they started when he was going to put her in rope.

Just the thought of rope made her lay her head on the island and twerk her hips on each plunge of his cock.

Several more things jangled in the drawer to his side but she couldn't see.

The whack of a metal spatula on her bare ass made her suck in a sharp breath. "Thank you, Sir."

His rumble of approval shot into her veins as if it were a 470 volt electrical current.

He spanked the other cheek, harder, back and forth and back and forth until she gasped. She jumped when the spatula clattered onto the island. He grabbed her ass, making her moan and fucked her hard and frantic.

"So. Damn. Sexy," he snarled as he leaned over and filled her pussy with his thick shaft. Her entire body was alive with sensation. "What do you like more? Being bound? Or the metal on your naked ass?"

"Your chaps, Sir. The leather. And jeans. Hitting my sore backside. That. You. Huhhhh…" She trailed off as he grabbed her shoulder and ground his hips against her tender skin.

"Mine." He latched onto a handful of her hair, using her own body to take her. To own her. To love her.

BDSM Anthology

He let go of her shoulder and reached beneath the edge of the island, somehow finding her clit with his strong fingers. Stroking her, pleasuring her, owning her body because it belonged to him.

"Huh, huh, huh," she panted as all of the sensation coalesced into the need to come again for him. "Please, can I come, Sir? Please, let me come. Please." She shook her head in his grasp and he pinched her clit.

"Come. Now."

She screamed her pleasure into the intimate space they shared.

Roman's hips lurched forward as he buried himself to the hilt inside her clenching core, coming inside her. With her. "Sexy. Wife." His whole body shuddered above hers and he licked the skin of her shoulder.

Her pussy clenched down on him as tiny explosions of joy burst along her spine, traveling to the edge of perfection and beyond because he was with her.

"Love you, Sir."

Instead of replying he pulled out of her and hoisted her off the island and down to her knees in front of him. His still semi-hard erection twitched by her mouth. "Lick me clean."

She smiled up at him, loving it when he got dirty. Her pussy contracted and his semen leaked down the insides of her thighs.

He tasted like cum, both of theirs, and she followed his orders, loving it when he hissed. He finally moved back, tucking himself back into his jeans and watching her as she licked her lips.

"You missed a spot."

She peeked at his crotch and then back up at him with a question clearly written all over her face.

He smiled, glancing down to the ground.

Joslin followed the length of his body until she found was he spoke about.

His boot.

It had a drop of cum on it.

Hers.

His.

Didn't matter.

"I'm waiting." He grabbed her hair, shoving her down to his boot.

That scent.

Freshly polished leather. She'd done them herself less than twenty-four hours before. The fragrance did something to her. She sank into her submission and licked his boot clean, placing her forehead on it when she was done.

"Thank you, Sir. Thank you so much."

He knelt down with her, petting her hair, her back. It gave her enough time to settle just enough so she wasn't riding so high on her adrenaline. She could process a little of what they'd done and she moved her head against his boot.

"My beautiful whore," he whispered and pulled her to stand, palming her cheeks as he stared inside her. "Beautiful." His head dipped and his lips brushed against hers. He kissed her lips, licking them softly until she opened for him.

Nothing compared to his kisses. Soft or hard, something primal lived inside him, and his urgency fed her somewhere deep inside as he tasted her.

"You earned it. No doubt, you earned it."

He rubbed his nose along hers and hugged her close, releasing the ties on her wrists. His laugh rumbled through her as she wrapped her arms around his waist, snuggling into his chest.

"My handsome, Sir."

He held her tightly for a second more, then tipped her chin up for another kiss. "I'm pretty sure we get to cross off at least three now." He chuckled but his nostrils flared as he wiped a drop of semen from her breast and gave it to her to lick off.

"Three, Sir?" she asked as she swallowed another piece of him inside.

After steadying her, he grabbed the piece of paper and his sunglasses which had fallen to the floor at some point. "Fuck wife on island. Use kitchen utensils during a scene. Make wife lick cum off my boot." He closed his eyes and adjusted his cock behind the fly of his jeans. He pegged her with an intense gaze. "That one was exceptional. So yes. Definitely a few to mark off."

She leaned against the counter as he walked to the refrigerator, in search of a pen. "I think the rules state somewhere we can only cross off one at a time. Sir." She bit her lip, reveling in the blazing ardor that crossed the distance between them.

"Is that right?"

"I think so. I saw it on the internet which means it has to be true."

He smiled, eyeing her all the way to the floor and back up.

She stared at him, loving the man in front of her more than life itself as he grabbed a pen out of a magnetized basket on the side of the stainless-steel appliance.

He hung the list up on the top of one of the doors of the fridge by a little magnet that said, *Good girl.* He read it for a few seconds and then marked one off.

"Which did you mark off, Sir?"

He tossed the pen back in the tiny basket and slid his glasses onto the island. "Fuck wife in shower."

"But we didn't do that."

He scooped her up into his arms and took off with her across the kitchen, eating up the distance through the living room into their bedroom. "Guess we'll need to fix that immediately then. Don't you think? The list doesn't lie."

She smiled against his chest, hugging him close.

"Best to-do list, ever."

When Restraint Set Me Free
By Cris Anson

Of course you'd give me more. We both knew that our first session was merely a prelude, a "getting to know you" flogging. You knew before that scene was over how much I craved the touch of your expertise. And I knew you fed off my reactions, because you told me so. This time you wanted to break down all my inhibitions, wanted me to let loose and let go and become one with your flogger.

And so you showed me how.

The first time, you started with what I later called "cotton candy" floggers, the softest leather kissing my shoulders then being slowly dragged down my back. Maybe ten minutes later you paused to inquire as to my well being.

More, I responded. After all, I had barely felt anything but a breeze, had hardly started breathing hard.

You stroked my arms, nuzzled my neck, murmured soft words of encouragement, then stepped back to switch to a progression of increasingly heavier floggers with more bite. I was pretty sure I wasn't the subspace type and you zeroed in on that. When you paused, it was to fondle and arouse, not soothe and hypnotize. The bite of pain from a pinched nipple soon turned to exquisite pleasure and my mantra remained, "More".

I held myself down to stifled grunts and moans—not of pain but of arousal—because a tiny corner of my mind was still aware of those who might be watching in that spacious dungeon and I was, after all, still a neophyte with all the insecurities and hesitations that come with it. I could not, however, keep my squirming body still as it reached for the bite of leather, the increasingly forceful touch of your hands, the fist roughly grabbing handfuls of my hair to position my head for an aggressive kiss.

At one such pause you plastered your fully clothed body against my naked back and butt as your arms encircled me, and I released my hold on the cross to grab at your head, wanting you to nuzzle me, nip my earlobe, anything for closer contact, more sensation. But you did the Dom thing and repositioned my hands on the wood so all I could do was thrust my butt out to you in silent supplication.

You did not disappoint.

One last sensual block of time squirming and gyrating, then all too soon you were gently embracing me and turning me toward the sofa. I felt the soft flannel of a blanket on my skin and knew my flogging lesson had ended.

This time it was in a more intimate setting, the basement of a hundred-year-old urban townhouse accessed by a steep, narrow stairway, a fitting location for a dungeon. A St. Andrew's cross bolted to one side of the original stone foundation walls, the sturdy two-by-ten beams in the ceiling holding myriad rings for restraint, the uneven cement floor, a three-foot-deep pit in one corner complete with padded bench, a smaller room behind the stairwell containing other, unfamiliar-to-me implements awaiting action.

You started with someone else, this play partner new to the lifestyle receiving your introduction to flogging and me as your assistant handing over your implements as required. Naked, she was a beauty, slender with beautiful breasts, younger and more petite than I, and yet I felt no jealousy, only envy that she was first on the cross. But I knew first wasn't necessarily best, and I thank you for eventually proving me right. Because I fed off your energy and it spiked my own.

She had known she'd be a sub, and she went into subspace halfway through the same regimen I recognized from my own initiation. Ten minutes of the soft flogger, pause and stroke and murmur, ten minutes of a coarser-textured implement and its twin, another pause to check on her well being, and so on. I couldn't help but time it because I was curious and wondered—hoped—that my second treatment would last longer than her 45 minutes of play followed by at least 20 minutes of aftercare (note to self: repeat after me: "I was not jealous!") followed by a half hour or more for your recuperation, snacking on carbohydrates and rehydrating yourself in the tiny kitchen.

Our gazes connected. *It's time*, we both agreed without words.

The three of us, with the newly minted sub to be our assistant, descended only to find the cross and other stations occupied and, from the looks of things, would be so for quite a while. We investigated the empty smaller room to see what could substitute for the cross to keep me anchored. We discovered an array of sturdy fur-lined cuffs of thick black leather and you buckled me into a set several inches wide and constructed so that ancillary straps rode up my palms for extra support when I would stand restrained and vulnerable and searching for a handhold to reality.

Unlike the first experience, when you directed me to disrobe, you made a ritual of slowly removing one garment at a time, whispering delicious obscenities all the while. This made me realize that your prior action was a ploy to make me take the deliberate step of offering my nakedness to you while nonetheless hiding behind the euphemism of "research." And now you were declaring your desire for me by undressing me. So I didn't blink when the thong came off as well, leaving me clad in nothing but need.

When you raised my arms and hooked my cuffs to one of those ceiling rings in that dimly lit dungeon room, you began to teach me about myself.

What I learned: I'm stronger and sturdier than I thought. Louder, hornier, more passionate, determined to leap tall buildings if that's what it took to get closer to you, to claim more from you.

I learned that pain and pleasure are so inextricably intertwined, the mind cannot separate the components: the pinch of the nipple, the thrust of the finger, the pull of my hair leading to a demand for more ravagement, all morphing into exquisite pleasure. I accepted—no, drank in—more of the lash, more of the sting, with each stroke, the outpouring of endorphins mitigating the pain and creating instead an ever-ascending high.

I learned how to express myself in wordless gyration, demanding the exploring touch of your hand, your demonic mouth, the rasp of your chest hair on my back— thank you for finally removing your shirt to let me feel your body on mine.

I learned the heady sense of empowerment that comes from being the center of your focus, that your entire being was dedicated to my pleasure while ignoring your own, that you were incredibly attuned to my slightest unspoken wish, reading my body language when my ability to articulate escaped me. Even if your arms ached and slackened from the force and stamina required to wield, with increasing velocity, two floggers for over an hour, you found the strength to give me what I demanded. Yet again when my knees fairly collapsed and I had to call a barely audible "red" in order to breathe, you mustered the energy to lead me to a chair and continued ministering to me. If you had blue balls or a Dom high, you nonetheless sublimated them to my needs.

I learned that some primal yearnings transcend a lifetime of strictures and don'ts, and if an avid audience ogled me, so be it as long as I reached that plateau off which I jumped time and time again under your inspired tutelage. I learned that being restrained made the evening a more profound experience, allowed me to break free of all my boundaries and soar unfettered.

I learned that age doesn't matter, so sue me if people think I'm too old to be sexy. To be insatiable. To seduce you as you seduced me. Weeks later I still vibrate with the memory of more than an hour of what was too powerful to be called simply "play" or "scene".

But life goes on. I know you have your path, as I have mine. Whether or not lightning strikes again, know that I treasure the experience and I thank you for it from the deepest part of my being.

And I still silently yearn.

Full Surrender
By Debra Hyde

Chad had his ways. He displayed no male bravado nor was he at all bombastic. In fact, he had not demanded Adele's submission even though they both knew that's what she wanted—and that he stood expertly poised to give it to her. Instead, he chose more subtle means, preferring to woo and coax, to dangle enticements rather than issuing ultimatums. Bringing Adele to submission, he believed, should be a tango of teasing seduction.

This night, he insisted on a relaxing evening with an old movie, *The Palm Beach Story,* a crazy romantic comedy from the 1940s. "You'll love it," he assured Adele. "It's a screwball classic. Marriage gone haywire; hilarity ensues." But when she saw the opening scene, she turned to Chad, mock accusation in her expression.

Because Claudette Colbert's character appeared, bound and gagged in a closet. And then, in the next shot, in a wedding dress.

Chad bellowed, laughing. "I swear I forgot that!" He raised his hands in surrender. Then his expression softened. "Although the two do go rather nice together." He was more than pleased about his accidental oversight.

"Don't get any ideas." Adele play-punched him in the arm. "We don't know each other that well yet." Then she followed suit. "At least not yet."

The married couple of Gerry and Tom Jeffers—Claudette Colbert and Joel McCrea, respectively—hadn't known each other well enough either. Both belonged to separate sets of identical twins, and both wanted to steal their respective twin at the altar. Which meant that, upon succeeding, they married each other by mistake.

The film was filled with screwball mishaps, but its basic

message was very simple: chemistry always wins out. In one scene, tipsy from drinking, Gerry couldn't unzip the back of her dress without Tom's help. He pulled her onto his lap, kindling her. "You don't think this is a little intimate, do you? Doesn't mean anything to you anymore to sit on my lap, huh? What if I kiss you there? Or there?"

She shudders, but admits nothing. "It's nothing."

But she surrenders when he pulls her on the couch, asking, "Doesn't mean anything to you anymore?"

"Almost nothing," she breathlessly counters while Tom carried her upstairs to their bedroom.

Chad kissed Adele's shoulder. "I like that scene," he admitted softly. An overwhelming shiver raked Adele, running from her shoulder, up her neck and shooting to the top of her head, It was so forceful it nearly hurt. Whether the product of his kiss or his words, Adele didn't care. Eyes closed, she relished the sensation until it was utterly spent.

Then Gerry ran from Tom in the movie, believing that, when it came to seeking his fortune, he'd be better off without her, and through several machinations, she falls into the rich and kindly clutches of one J. D. Hackensacker III.

Chad returned to watching Gerry's escapades, especially with Rudy Vallee playing Hackensacker. Adele was not pleased by his sudden about-face. "Are you all chase and no catch?" she asked. Her body was in revolt against Chad's sudden neglect.

"No way. Where's the fun in that?" Chad answered, grinning. "I have every intention of going for the catch."

"And the chase?"

His expression turned sly. "Well, a good pursuit can be exciting."

"Really?" Adele challenged. "Then why didn't you take me with that last kiss?"

His slyness took on a devilish look. "Because keeping you on edge, keeping you wanting makes for a much better chase."

Caught between two men, Gerry continued to resist Tom, claiming until the last that she knew what was best. That whenever she tried to do what he wanted, she always messed up, leaving a disaster in their laps. But at the threshold of her bedroom suite under

Hackensacker's roof, she buckled under and allowed Tom a goodnight kiss. Her willpower weakened.

And then faltered completely.

With a full orchestra serenading Gerry with *Good Night, Sweetheart* from the garden, Gerry struggled to unzip the back of her strapless dress yet again. Frustration got the best of her, sending her to seek Tom for help.

"I can't open this blasted dress," she complained. She sat on Tom's knees as he fussed with the dress' fastener and, with he serenade in full swing, she collapsed in his arms. By song's end, Tom has seduced Gerry to his bed.

Chad returned the stroke of his finger to Adele's shoulder, the one she found indulgent and irresistible. A light kiss followed. And another. Still more trailed their way to her neck where, planted in its sweet spot, Adele gasped as another shiver ripped through her. His kisses kept her breathless. Adele heard the movie reach its big reveal, sensed Gerry's and Tom's ultimate reconciliation, but they floated through her awareness as Chad's mouth found hers.

She lost herself in that kiss, thinking only of Chad's soft lips, his knowing tongue, his tender but promising embrace. The kiss grew vigorous, Chad's lips pressing against hers, his tongue guiding hers. Their breathing became sympathetically paced, their hearts, too, and when Chad tapered the kiss to its end, he asked, rubbing his nose lightly against hers, "So are you my Gerry?"

"That depends,' she murmured. "Are you my Tom or my Hackensacker?"

He chuckled. "When you choose to come to me, maybe you'll find out.

Adele undressed in her bedroom and stood naked before its full-length mirror. She thought of Gerry and Tom and how, no matter how funny the film, that in this day and age, they'd be seen as fools of the highest sort for putting each other through such crap. But she did like how, when logic failed her, Gerry gave herself over to her emotions, to what was really in her heart.

Adele turned to the side and assessed her figure. She wasn't size-0 slim, but so what. Plenty of men like a bit of meat on the bone—Chad had certainly made no complaints. And one thing she knew for certain: she wanted to yield to him. Now. Tonight.

She was ready to find out if he was a Tom or a Hackensacker.

She pinned her hair up—maybe Chad would like undoing it—stared at herself in the mirror one last time and took a fortifying breath. She tiptoed downstairs and across the house to Chad's bedroom, flinching as old floorboards moaned underfoot. At its threshold, she took another deep breath.

The door stood ajar. It squeaked as she opened it, the threshold board, too. Adele grimaced; there'd be no surprising Chad tonight.

"If you intend to place yourself in my bed, then kneel and ask for my permission."

Chad sounded implacable, a tone she had not before heard in his voice. But its commanding tenor woke her body and, like Gerry in her unzipped dress, she feel sway to it.

Adele knelt. "I have made my decision," she said, her voice barely above a whisper. "I have come to you. Please, will you allow me into your bed?"

It would probably sound corny, this response she had invented, if she were on the outside looking in, but she could not help her reverence. It wasn't just Chad's tone or his bidding; it was years of postponing this moment, of never fully acknowledging what she needed, of never actually seeking it. Something about Chad made it safe, even right, for her to take this step and she knew she'd forever loathe herself if she didn't.

"You may."

After all her years of denial, permission came in a mere two words. Adele felt her body swell with want, with need, alive and ready for the passion Chad offered. She rose and, crawling into his bed, found her way to him.

His arms enfolded her, his warmth surrounded her. He nuzzled her, his nose against her cheek.

Until his lips found hers and his hands found her hair. His kiss was fierce and his hands quick, undoing the pins in her hand and grabbing her tresses as they fell free. His fingers burrowed into her hair, their hold as strong as prison chains. Chad devoured her.

"Is this the real thing?" she asked when he allowed her air.

He chuckled, his tone unchanged and in charge. "It's always been real," he told her. "But now we're heading for the deep end of the pool."

Adele whimpered—she couldn't help it; she had always avoided the unknown and its risks.

"Don't worry," Chad assured her. "I won't let you drown. I won't let harm come to you."

He kisses her again. A hand trailed from her neck to her breasts. There, it grasped and kneaded, took her fullness into it. Chad moaned, taken by the exquisite feel of her flesh and, ending his kiss, dipped his mouth to her nipple.

His tongue darting about Adele's pebbled hardness, its teasing telegraphing wanton sensation to points throughout her body. She began to ache with need, wanting him, and pressed his head hard against her breast.

But Chad pulled away. "Oh no you don't," he warned. "It's not yours to say what comes next." Like a wrestler making for his final move, he stretched out atop her, pinning her in place with the full length and weight of his body. One hand grabbed hers, pulled it up over her head where it meet his other hand—and a wrist cuff.

Chad had the ropes and cuffs in place, awaiting her. The cuff closed around her wrist and Chad tightened it. He went for her other hand, the other cuff. Adele thought briefly of calling out, stopping it, but if she did, she would shatter Chad's trust in her.

Trust in her. She didn't realize until just then that Chad depended on her trust every bit as she depended on his. His weight lifted from her, leaving her panting in its absence. He was at her feet now, cuffing them into place, returning her to that spread eagle position he had introduced her to at first play. But now the stakes were higher.

She lifted her head and found him kneeling between her legs—staring at the space between her thighs. Staring at her.

"You're beautiful when you're wet," he said.

It should've struck her as a compliment, and it very nearly did. But no one had ever uttered those words to her before, never pointed out her own lust to her.

"You pussy lips, your pubic hair—you're drenched."

He spread her legs with his hands.

"Even the insides of your thighs are wet."

Adele groaned. It was too much—too obvious, too embarrassing. Her eyes rolled back, her eyelids fluttered shut. Somehow, she felt safer this way, as if it distanced her from Chad's lurid observations.

"I bet your cunt could swallow me whole."

She tried to ignore his obscene enjoyment of her, and Chad apparently would let her. He rose from the bed, claiming he needed the bathroom. She expected a reprieve from his blatant pronouncements, but no. Her body would not allow it. Her nipples ached for more of Chad, her pussy, too, throbbing as if to call him back. It surprised her that Chad already had such a hold over her body. She wondered if her soul would be next.

Chad slid back onto the bed, crawling up its length. He could take her right there, she realized. Adele flexed in the bondage, pulled on the wrist restraints and, if not for her toes curling in anticipation, one might wonder whether she was trying to escape. But when Chad made contact, sliding over her with his naked skin against hers, her whole body shuddered. His body felt hard against her softness, sure against her naivety. And, never having felt such contact—never being held down and having her focus so narrowed—Adele moaned.

She felt his cock brush between her thighs and, reality hitting home, she lurched. Still, she kept her eyes closed.

"Not to worry," he whispered as he brought a hand to her cheek, "I'm wearing a condom."

His lips came to rest on her neck, soft and enticing. His kisses played there, knowing already where they could most easily torment Adele. Unable to hold Chad—unable, really, to move in any significant way—Adele did the only instinctive thing available to her: she opened herself further to Chad.

She stretched herself into the spread eagle, her body begging where her voice could not. She spread her legs at the thighs, scoring success when Chad's hips fell between her, when his hard cock met her labia. She arched her back, desperate to meld her body to his, desperate for the claiming she had consented to.

"Tell me," he said. "Tell me what you want."

Adele whimpered, words failing her.

"Tell me why you're here, in my bed."

She knew she had to answer him. All of their introductory play had gone this route, too.

"I want you to fuck me," she said, her voice hoarse with effort and desire. "I came to your bed to give my consent to what I want."

"And to what you need."

"To what I need, yes," she acknowledged.

She felt his arms scoop under her shoulders and his hands come to rest atop them. She arched herself again, so willing, so wanting.

"Open your eyes," Chad commanded.

Adele did as she was told and found a determined Chad—a man unwilling to turn back. The sight of him burrowed into her, weakened her, and her eyes began to flutter shut.

Until he commanded otherwise.

"Keep them open."

She felt his cock throb against her. Then he moved, angling himself.

"Don't take your eyes off of me."

He stared at her as his cock parted her labia, as it found purchase at her threshold. Adele gasped. No man had ever felt so real, poised there. Then again, no man had ever made her anticipate him as Chad had, keeping her attuned to every aching sensation his dominance awoke in her.

Chad pushed into her, once, twice, his eyes never leaving her. He watched her struggle to keep her eyes open, watched her expression as he breeched her.

He drove home on the third push.

The gleam in his eye was too much for Adele. Her head lolled back against the pillow, eyes snapping shut, as he took her. For an instant, she thought she could escape him this way but when he began that inevitable rhythm, she had to watch. She gazed at him, at his body in motion, driving into her and claiming every inch possible. She wallowed in the feel of him, of his cock raking her, her cunt rippling against him as he pulled out, then welcomed him every time he pushed back in.

The more he fucked her, the hollower her body became. It needed his complete and unrelenting fullness. It needed his hammering, his drive. It needed conquering.

Adele needed conquering. She would remain hollow without it.

Chad held her tight, his breath swift and rough. Now and again, he shuddered, unable to resist Adele's wet, plush perfection. At first, he savored her delicious pull and focused himself there, but all too soon he gave way to the inevitable.

He stepped up his pace, pounding Adele towards senselessness.

His own orgasm, still buried in the depths of his body, made itself known, first as a spreading tingle, then, suddenly, like a torrential surge. His balls tightened, his cock swelled—close, he was so achingly close.

That final rush upon him, Chad grabbed Adele by the hair, pulling hard, and bellowed, "You're mine!"

Adele flailed, cried out, shocked by his words, his grip, the pain ripping through hair. Chad's orgasm overpowered her. He roared in her ear, pummeling and grunting like a rutting beast driven to expend itself until it had nothing left to give. As he slowed, as Adele's senses attuned themselves to the sound and feel of Chad's climax—of her *master's* climax—she felt him throb within her. And imagined how magnificent he would feel without a condom in the way.

Chad buried his forehead in the crook of her neck, panting. His breath felt like steam, blowing across her but dissipating before it reached her breast. Its nipple sat taut, still engorged, and as Chad's hand came to rest there and languidly cup her breast, she realized Chad might be sated, but she wasn't.

Adele remained afire.

Chad rolled off of her, resting to one side. His fingers wandered from her breast, journeying down her body. He knew she was still aroused.

Which only inflamed her further. Adele arched her hips, seeking Chad's touch where it would do the greatest good. Had she the freedom of her hands, she would've grabbed him and shoved his hand between her legs, submission be damned!

"You need to come," he said.

"Yes."

His fingers teased about her pubic hair.

"Fucking wasn't enough for you."

But he kept clear of her labia and, worse, her clitoris—her all-too-neglected clitoris.

"No."

She wanted to scream at him, to tell him to just get it over with.

"I could fuck you again and I bet it still wouldn't be enough."

Adele groaned. Would his torture never end? His words had such a hold over her, something she never considered possible. But then she never believed a man might come along who could either.

"No. Please!" Her own words were both acknowledgement and plea, and both were urgent and desperate.

Chad ignored her and rose from the bed. Adele watched him peel off the condom, knot it and, head to the bathroom for its disposal. She could do nothing except flop her head back on the bed and strain against the bondage. Chad clearly enjoyed teasing her, keeping her aroused and waiting.

He returned and, sitting at the end of the bed, ran his hand up her leg. "Seems to me I have a decision to make. Should I make you come or should I keep you wanting? The former would be the merciful thing to do. But the latter? Well, I can't help but wonder what you would be like if I kept you bound to my bed all night—have you sleep next to me, unappeased and suffering." His fingers returned to her pubic hair. "What do you think, Adele? Should I or shouldn't I?"

His final question wasn't rhetorical. Where the others were taunts, this one was sincere. He wanted to know what she needed. He wanted her consent.

"Should," she answered. "Please, should." Was this what it felt like to be the fly, caught in a web and waiting for the spider?

"Please," Adele repeated. Desperation clouded her. All she could think of—all her body would let her think of—was the possibility of coming. And coming hard.

"I'm going to be generous," Chad decided. "It's too soon to kiss you with the taste of cruelty. So I'm going to kiss you in a way you've never been kissed before."

Her entire body quaked at the touch of his lips between her legs. She couldn't control it, couldn't stop it, she was so primed for any carnal attention. His tongue searched her valley, touching and tasting every inch of her. Skimming her labia sent her moaning and squirming, her legs widening and inviting more.

"Please," she implored. "There, please!" She couldn't wait a moment longer.

Chad granted her appeal, circling low and long, tending that place where all points met and were most sensitive. Adele longed to reach for Chad's hair, to push him into that spot. To have his tongue penetrate her. But she couldn't, and Chad knew he could keep her fever-pitched by denying her that pleasure.

Denying her—that's what much of this was. It was a matter of one wish granted, but another held overhead, waiting for her to scream in frustration before lowering that prize. And Adele loved it.

Still Chad did not penetrate her but, his taunting guiltlessly full and unforgiving, he brought a finger to her clitoris. Adele lurched and cried out—the prize now hers.

Chad circled, tongue and finger in tandem. His tongue coursed over her, keeping all sensitivity there ablaze. His finger plied her, seeking that one miniscule spot in that hard tangle of nerves that said, "Oh yes, there."

But *oh yes, there* came in a wave of shuddering, staccato gasps. Throbbing jolts pelted her, a tight tingling took hold, gripping from within—a sudden pinch and she was there. Release was hers.

It came in cascading pulses—pleasure rippling ever outward like the rings of a water droplet striking a puddle. Finally, Adele was spent. She was hollow no more.

For a time, Adele could not think, could barely move. Everything Chad had done had left her vapid, stupid with spent lust. But when he released her from the cuffs and gathered her into his arms and kissed her neck, she found the wherewithal to mutter, "Tom. Not Hackensacker. Tom."

Dirty Girls Have All the Fun
By Lise Horton

I was feeling naughty. In fact, I was feeling downright slutty. I wanted to get down and dirty with some guy and wipe all the aggravation of the day away in the euphoria of a heavy-handed, intense scene. I craved some nice paddling pain, and all I had to do was find the right Dom for the job.

I dressed in a trampy outfit of a short, black and blue plaid skirt (appropriate, no?) and a black lace bustier with white thigh highs that looked wonderfully whorish – in that nasty, Lolita kind of way – with black, fuck-me Mary Jane pumps. I piled my red hair up with clips, all tousled like I just got fucked hard. I let a few curls dangle down –I had a curl on my forehead and intended on being very, very bad. Just like that horrid little girl in the old nursery rhyme. Last, I put on lots of makeup, including the fire engine red lipstick that a guy always liked to see smeared all over my face after a nice, long cock sucking.

Now I ask you, what nasty man could resist me?

I sauntered into the club around midnight and things were well underway. Too early and you ended up with the poseurs and the first-timers. It can get old in a hurry, fending off all those needy guys and girls who can't tell a fellow sub from a Domme. I knew most of the players – the same girls who liked to get their asses paddled, the boys who wanted a tough Mistress to strap up their balls – and the mad, bad Masters – the men who sought out submissives to cater to their particular, kinky needs. I always got a tingle down below looking those men over. Dominant, aggressive, alpha – one hard look from one of those guys and you knew he had no problem taking a dirty little girl and making her very, very sorry she'd been bad.

Saturday night was "Anything Goes" night. Newbies were

warned, told the fun and games were intense, and if they came to play, they'd better have their safe word handy.

I glanced around. Most of the Masters I knew had already made their choices and were leading their subs for the night off to the various private play rooms. A few remained in the public areas because the excitement of performing in front of the crowd upped the raunch factor.

Personally, I didn't care one way or the other. Sometimes the guy who chose me wanted to punish me publicly – the better to rub my naughty face in my subby faux pas. But I would just as soon be humiliated privately. It was being dominated that revved my engine, not the audience.

As I glanced around, I spotted one particular man in the corner. He was tall, and broad-chested, with long black hair in a braid, a full beard, and he was dressed in black jeans and a black leather vest – the better for me to admire his manly chest. Just my type. He looked like a pirate and I wanted to be his captive. But he'd be an Edward "Blackbeard" Teach kind of pirate, not the suave Errol Flynn type. No swashbuckling involved. He'd just get me naked, tie me to the mast and make me scream. He also wore heavy black boots – the better for a little slut sub to feel on her neck.

He looked me over, and I met his eyes. He stood a little straighter, smiled a promising, evil smile and strode toward me. He held a collar and leash in his hand and when he approached me and held it out, I merely bowed my head. He fastened it on and things south started swelling and dripping. It was a thick, heavy leather collar, with lots of studs and rings. The kind he could use to jerk me around. A serious Master's collar. An ownership collar. My cunt was tingling with anticipation and when he fastened it nice and tight, I knew tonight was going to be something extra special. Once he'd hooked the leash, he turned and led me to the back of the club, toward the dungeon rooms filled with a hard-core sadist's special selection of toys and props for all the dirty games played there. Only serious players came back here, where no holes were barred, and edge play wrung screams from willing slaves. I'd never been to these rooms before, but right now, more than anything in the world, I wanted to be inside one of them with this big, raw man.

When the door closed behind us with an ominous bang, my new

Master pulled off his vest and I had a minute to drool over the strength in his chest and arms. Muscles bulged, but that wasn't all that was bulging.

"Come here slut."

He didn't ask. He commanded me by tugging hard on the thick chain leash. When I reached him, he dropped the leash, then undid my bustier and pulled it off. He smiled at my big boobs, and hard nipples, and pinched one tightly in each hand. Wrenching at them.

"You've been a bad little girl. Look how horny you are." He squeezed my nipples harder, twisting them, and laughed when I groaned and grimaced. But, God it felt good. I'm a proud pain slut and when I say "hurts so good," I mean it!

"Before I decide what your punishment's going be, I'm going to make sure you understand who you belong to. All your holes. These tits. That ass. All mine."

He let go of my nipples and undid his pants and pulled out his cock. It was long, and hard. Made my mouth water. He was thick, too, and his dick stood straight up, pointing north, almost to his navel. It was a monster and it was going to feel so lovely shoved in all my orifices.

I wondered which one he'd take first?

"On your knees, my little slut. Time to suck Master's cock."

I was delighted to get on my knees, but his heavy hand on my head felt oh, so good as he pushed me down. Forced me to kneel. I leaned forward, lips parted, showing him I was ready for my Master to fuck my face.

"Now be sure to take Master's cock all the way down – or you will be very, very sorry."

"Yes, Master." I licked my lips and opened wide as he guided the thick, purple head toward my waiting mouth. He slid between my lips, stretching them wide, and pushed deep into my mouth, until I gagged a bit, before relaxing my throat as best as I could. I was in dirty girl heaven. I loved the taste of him, all salty, musky and dark. Like a fallen angel. And as he pumped slowly into my mouth, each thrust going a little deeper, I was spiraling down into that great headspace. A slut on her knees, her Master's cock rammed down her throat.

Bliss!

"You'd better start sucking, or Master will be very angry."

I began to suck, wiggling my tongue against the massive organ filling my mouth. My cheeks hollowed as I got to work and he grunted in satisfaction, then proceeded to really fuck my face.

Sucking as hard as I could, when he'd pull out a bit, I'd swipe the tip of my tongue against the underside of the head, swirl around the top, and then swallow his meat when he shoved back into my throat. Before long it wasn't a matter of sucking or licking or wiggling, but just taking his cock down my throat as he pumped harder and faster.

"That's right you little cocksucker, take it deep. I want to gag you. I want to see you choking on cock. You're just a hole for me to fuck, so take it all. Your Master is enjoying his little cocksucker and will reward you later. Now, have some more."

He was thrusting deep and fast, and I was struggling to get it down as he surged forward. I had to fight to breathe through my nose, wallowing in the absolute debauchery of having this man fuck my mouth. After an especially deep thrust, he grabbed my hair. He yanked my head to his groin, forcing his cock completely down my throat. His pubes tickled my nose as I gagged around him, and he held me there for interminable seconds, before pulling out and letting me gasp for air.

"I'm very pleased with my little slut sucker. I was going to make you swallow your Master's cum, but I have a better idea. Stand up."

I climbed to my feet, gasping, with drool running down my chin. My lipstick was no doubt smeared all over my face. My Master's cock was certainly smeared red.

"I like seeing your little slut mouth all smeared. Your lipstick looks good on my cock, no?" I nodded eagerly, getting hotter by the second at the glint of dominant sadism in his eyes.

I wanted more. I love a challenge, and this guy clearly knew I was no shrinking violet sub. He looked me up and down, smacked my breasts, one after the other, until they ached. Grinned when I moaned.

"I want my slut naked. Get that off." He stepped back and pulled off his vest, as he watched me unzip my naughty little Lolita skirt. Sometimes I wear nice white panties underneath. They get a horny Master all worked up to paddle my naughty ass and explain why slutty schoolgirls need punishment.

Not tonight though.

I was naked and bare, but I stood there in my little white thigh highs and heeled Mary Janes, and my Master got that lecherous look anyway.

"Shame on you. Naked pussy under that skirt? Tsk, tsk. I'm going to have to punish you for that, before we got down to some serious fucking."

He grabbed hold of the collar and pulled me with him to the big, scary spanking bench. It had legs at an angle, like a sawhorse – the better to restrain your sub for punishment – which he did, with chains around my ankles, after spreading my legs good and wide. Then he bent me over and pushed me down, until I was lying flat on my stomach. He grabbed my hands and pulled them over my head, stretching them in front of me so he could chain them, too. I was all spread out and helpless. He could do anything he wanted to me.

"All righty then, dirty girl, let the good times roll."

I had no idea what he planned to punish me with. Belt? Paddle? His hand? A tawes or flogger or whip? So many things to beat me with, so little time!

Anticipation had me dripping.

He shoved his fingers between my legs, then stuck them in my mouth.

"That's right, you horny slut. See how much you get off on this nasty business? You need a stern Master to keep you in line, don't you? A firm hand to make you behave?" He wiped his fingers down my cheek.

"Yes, Master."

"Let's see if I'm the guy for the job."

The tingling thrill of fearful expectation made my skin twitch. That feeling that makes you want it – even if you don't know what it's going to be – even if you don't think you can take it.

Then the waiting was over.

Whistle, snap – fire on my ass!

The cane.

The firm kind. The kind that always caused agony. Bad, harsh, sometimes leaving bloody stripes across my cheeks. The kind that felt like a flame-thrower crisscrossing my ass, over and over until my legs give out and I'm screaming.

I was screaming then.

"Are you sorry yet, little slut?"

I opened my mouth, then closed it.

"Apparently not."

Now the swish, and the white-hot flare of pain between my legs.
He caned my pussy.
Hard.
Over and over again.
I screamed some more.
A couple more hard strokes and he tossed away the cane.

He rubbed his rough palm across my ass; slid it between my legs and smacked my pussy.

"There. I think I've made my point." One last stinging swat, and he laughed as I squealed.

Now my knees trembled. Pleasure/pain. And that darkest lust overriding all other emotions. I wanted to feel his cock deep inside me. I wanted him to give it to me hard. See, I'd always loved the bad boys. The bigger, the more dominant, the raunchier – the better. And when they looked as bad as this man? So dark and devilish and sinful? He could do any nasty thing he wanted to me, and I'd love every minute.

I knew if he was looking deep into my eyes, he'd read my ravenous hunger. I knew, too, behind me he was no doubt smiling broadly, his teeth white in his black pirate's beard.

"Now it's time for some fun. Master wants to play some more with his naughty little slut. And Master's cock wants ... let's see, which nice tight hole should we try? Eeenie, meanie, miney ... yep, that's the perfect choice." He grabbed me by the hair and yanked my head up from the spanking bench. "I'm going to fuck that tight ass until you can't walk."

He slathered lube across my asshole and shoved a couple of fingers deep inside. I moaned loud and long.

"Get used to it, slut. Master's cock is going to be in there soon." After lubing me deep with his fingers for a minute, he shoved a dildo up my ass. I groaned louder now, the burning pinch and the sudden shock of being filled full of dildo unbearably good. Of course, I wanted something more than plastic filling me up. He slammed the dildo in and out for a few minutes. Rough. Hard.

Perfect.

"I knew my little slut wanted to take it up the ass. You have that dirty little smile that tells me you love having your ass reamed. Don't you?"

"Yes Master, I love getting fucked up the ass, Sir,"
"I bet you like a really hard ass fucking, don't you?"
"Yes Sir, I love a hard ass fucking."

"Then this is your lucky day." He yanked the dildo from my ass and squirted more lube into my hole. Then he was pushing his thick cock inside me. It stretched me wide, wider than I'd ever felt, until I whimpered at the burning pain. But I wanted it to hurt. Wanted all of him. He slid in slow and steady. There was no time to adapt, to get used to being stuffed full. He forced his way in, further and further until he was all the way in, his cock stretching my ass to capacity, his balls jammed against my pussy. He grunted as my moans rose and fell with the sensation.

"All right, my little ass slut. Time to get fucked hard." And he pulled all the way out with a pop, before ramming in again, deep and rough. He began to pump steadily in and out of my ass, until he had me squealing, begging, pleading, groaning.

My own special way of urging him on.

"Master, please fuck my ass hard."

"Oh, Master is going to fuck your ass good and hard. My slut has a nice tight ass hole. It needs a good hard fucking. You like my big cock up your ass, don't you?"

"It's so big, Sir! It hurts!"

"It's supposed to hurt. What fun is it if I can't make you squeal? And you love it, don't you?"

"Yes, please Sir, fuck my ass!" and then I was coming hard as he reamed me. The orgasms rolling through me, wave after wave. My ass was clenching on his cock until he came, too. I felt the flood of his hot cum surge into me, heating my ass. He pounded in once, twice, three last good strokes before he pulled out. He shot the last of his cum into my stretched hole and on my blistered cheeks, as the last of his orgasm wrung him out.

For a moment the air was filled with the rasp of the two of us panting. I was in a dreamy state of submissive euphoria. My ass was burning and throbbing, and my orgasm throbbed in my flesh like a raunchy heartbeat.

"Look at that. My cum filling your hole. That's my kind of nasty, dirty girl. Master believes he'll keep this little slut slave for his very own." His growl in my ear almost made me come again. Nothing else mattered now but that rough, husky sound. The feel of a huge cock pounding my ass, being chained tight, strong hands holding me down, cum dripping out of me. Those feelings were more real than anything else in my world.

"Yes, Master, this slut wants to be yours and yours alone."

"It doesn't really matter, though, does it, slut, because you'll do anything I demand, won't you?"

"Yes, Master, anything."

"The perfect answer. We'll have lots of fun, won't we slut?"

"Yes, Sir. We'll have lots of fun."

Beneath him, I smiled.

* * * * *

Later that night, I rolled over in bed and snuggled against the big bear of a man beside me. His arms were wrapped around me, holding me tight, and my ass was tucked against his groin. I smiled at the feel of his hard cock at my cheeks. It appeared he hadn't gotten enough of me. Maybe I had another masterful ass fucking in store? Or maybe he'd put me on my hands and knees and take a turn in my cunt?

I breathed deeply of his scent, and felt a calmness deep in my soul being in his arms. Commanded. Protected. Loved.

His voice whispered in the night.

"Happy Anniversary, little slut."

"Happy Anniversary, Master."

"Do you like you gift, dirty girl?"

I peered across the room at the new spanking bench sitting in the moonlight. It had been waiting for me in the bedroom when we got home. He'd insisted we break it in that very evening and my ass still burned from the spanking and paddling he'd given me on top of the caning.

"Oh, yes Master, I love my gift! Thank you, Sir."

"You are very welcome, little slave. Love you." He bit my neck, then kissed it and made it all better.

"Love you too, Master."

I smiled as I closed my eyes.

Sometimes dirty girls have all the fun.

Silken Desires
(An excerpt)
By Laci Paige

Opening the door to her apartment Roxi could hear a noise coming from across the hall, but Jake and Kristy hadn't returned yet. It came from Jake's *special* room, his kinky playroom of sorts. It doubled as his private gym and he equipped it with exercise machines rigged with bondage implements. Quietly pushing the door open an inch more, so she could peek in, her breath caught in her throat.

Jonathan, wearing only his jeans and looking as sexy as he was dangerous, threw a bullwhip toward a punching bag. He looked torn, furious, and gorgeous all at the same time. His hand wrapped around the thick handle as he moved with a grace only he could possess. She watched mesmerized as the two bellied-braid of the leather thong snaked back and forth through the air looking for purchase. She jumped unexpectedly as the nylon popper made a cracking sound that she knew all too well.

Jonathan's body looked firmer and his muscles more defined than she'd ever seen before. He planted his bare feet on the floor, bending at the knees. Throwing the whip forward, from the bottom of his soles following through with his whole body, he made the bullwhip look like an extension of himself. The repetitive popping noises made her remember a time that she tried to block from her memories, but the invisible burn of her scars wouldn't allow it.

The most painful of the memories became clearer in her mind as she remembered the day she decided to leave Jonathan. The first day he used a whip on her. A shiver ran down her spine, her heart rate increased, and her breathing came quicker. She wasn't afraid, not at all. In fact, quite the opposite, she was turned on, and that's what scared her into leaving him in the first place. She never told anyone of this, and kept it bottled up inside of her all this time. Even Jonathan didn't know.

Her body hummed with anticipation, watching the whip flow through the air. Each time it hit the target, her body zinged, practically crying out for the burning sting she could imagine it leaving behind.

Jonathan needed to know the truth. He was unattached, worked the whip like a pro, and he was there for her. Each resounding crack called to her. She needed it badly, and needed it now. What she never got the chance to tell Jonathan in words, she'd gratefully show him now.

Roxi disrobed in the hall and slipped into the playroom undetected. Kneeling in submission at the door, she waited. The cracking sounds went quiet and she heard Jonathan breathing heavily from across the room. She heard movement, but refused to look.

"What the fuck?" His bare feet appeared in her vision. "Roxi get up!"

"Permission to speak, Sir."

"Roxi, we aren't playing."

She lifted her head slightly and looked at him through her lashes. "I *need* this, I *want* this." Her voice waivered, almost into sobs, as her body uncontrollably shook like a junkie needing a fix.

His mouth popped open and he gapped at her. "What are you saying, Roxi?" He knelt as tears formed in her eyes. He placed his hand on her cheek. "Talk to me."

"There's something I should've told you a long time ago." She sniffled.

Friends since childhood and lovers as adults, Roxi leaves Jonathan without explanation. He assumes it's due to his changing lifestyle; venturing deep into the world of BDSM, but she has a deeper secret that has her running away.

After a life-changing year in hiding, Roxi comes home a new woman, a sub with masochistic needs. When she confides her secret to him, Jonathan realizes that to keep her safe from harm, he must be her Dom, and help her obtain the physical peak she needs. Love cannot be a part of the equation. Jonathan has to protect his heart and guard his soul.

As he finds himself falling for another woman, Roxi admits she wants more from Jonathan. She wants his heart and soul along with his perfect domination. She wants a life with him, but can he risk loving Roxi again?

Also available at other fine online retailers.

Learning My Lesson
By Jessica Lust

Your words lingered in the silence.

I couldn't bear to look into your expressive eyes a moment longer. I knew I had disappointed you. My heart felt heavy with it. I saw not only anger and disappointment over what I'd done, but I also saw the traces of sadness along your mouth. I lowered my head to your chest, unable to meet your gaze a second longer. Your heartbeat was the only sound in my world as it echoed in my ear.

I was pleased the *Beast* had been sheathed as I didn't think I could bear to meet his eyes further. The *Beast* terrified me...hurt me....I...I...hated the *Beast* within you and didn't ever want to see him again.

The water was cool by the time you raised from the tub and lifted me up in your arms. Agilely you stepped out of the tub and set my feet on the floor. You grabbed the big fluffy towel and began to dry me with it. I felt the color rise to my cheeks as you ran the towel between my thighs. I drew back from you, startled, embarrassed, noticing my nudity and yours as if for the first time.

"There is nothing you will keep from me, girl. Everything you are is mine." You pressed your hands between my thighs once more and swiped the towel along my pussy lips, taking the drops of water with it. "I thought to wait another year before I began your training, but since you've decided to become a whore..." You shrugged and let the words hang in the air between us and continued drying me, your hands rougher with each passing second.

"I am not a whore! Not until you made me into one." My voice dripped venom. My eyes narrowed in anger. I lifted my chin higher and stood before you defiantly. My hands balled into tiny fists. I trembled slightly as my own anger surfaced.

I cried out as the full impact of the back of your hand struck against my cheek and I tasted the blood from my cracked lip on my tongue. My brown eyes were huge as I stared at you in disbelief.

"You bastard!" I lunged at you, seeing red before my eyes at your actions. Never before this day had you ever treated me so cruelly—so sadistically. I was a fighter and that's what you'd drawn out of me.

You easily side-stepped out of my path, your hand connecting with the small of my back, keeping my momentum going. The next instant, I banged into the wall and felt you pin me against it, your body flush against mine. I braced my hands against the wall trying to push from it but you grabbed one of my wrists in each of your large calloused hands and yanked them behind me, forcing my back to arch, my large breasts squashed against the wall.

I cursed as you lifted my hands higher behind my back, causing pain to shoot through my arms, effectively keeping me pinned to the wall. One of your large hands easily covered both of mine, holding them together as you reached for something in the bathroom cabinet just to the right of me. I shivered as I felt the metal handcuffs clasp close against one wrist, then the other, in quick succession and renewed my struggles in earnest. I yanked hard at my hands to free them but merely caused the metal to bite harder into my wrists.

"Let me go this instant, you bastard!" I screamed at the top of my lungs, my words echoing over the bathroom walls. My heart slammed in my chest and skipped a few beats as I struggled against you to no avail. You reached for the cabinet once more and I seized my chance to escape and thrust my head back hard. I whimpered as I felt the back of my head connect with your chin and your oath joined mine.

"Stop it, Master. Stop it!" I could hear the growing panic in my own words. Felt my heart slam against my chest, heard the sound of my heartbeat pounding in my ears. I wondered if I could survive more punishment when I'd yet to recover from the last one. And though I knew my words were merely fueling the *Beast* within you, I couldn't stop myself from uttering them. "Release me now, you fuck!"

Your hand tightened painfully in my hair. With a cruel yank, you drew me away from the wall and dragged me down to the floor, eliciting a scream from my lips as my knees slammed hard against the tile floor. My own struggles added to my pain as you released me and grabbed for my ankles. I kicked out at you several times before my foot connected with your broad chest, pushing you away. I heard you swear once more, then

your hands grabbed at my ankles and yanked them up roughly, pitching my entire body forward. I hit the floor hard as my face and breasts took the full impact. In a flash, you tied a rope around my ankles effectively stifling this part of my struggles, but as I kicked out with my now bound legs once more, you knew it was useless to try and keep me from the harsher side of what was about to come.

You grabbed the back of my hair and yanked me back up by it, making me scream out in pain as you brought me back to my knees and quickly wrapped the remaining length of rope around my throat, then looped it once more around my ankles, effectively binding my throat to my ankles then stepping away. The rope held me arched precariously, making it extremely uncomfortable to kneel quite straight.

My eyes widened in horror as I felt the rope tighten about my neck when I kicked out at you once more. My mouth opened in fear as the air was robbed from my lungs by my wild actions. It was fear which made me cease my struggles as I knelt before you, anxiously trying to calm down and waiting for what would befall me next.

You had bound me, then stepped away and stood across from me, leaning against the wall, your eyes watchful. Your arms crossed in front of your chest. Not saying a word. Your eyes took in every detail—no matter how minute. The way my large breasts jutted out from having my back arched. The way I nervously licked at my full red lips as I pleaded for you to release me. The panic showing in my large brown eyes turned them an even darker shade of brown till they appeared almost black.

It seemed an eternity before you straightened from the wall and approached me. My heart skipped a beat as I dared hope you would release me. I knew you saw it in my eyes. But instead of being released, I felt the sting of your hand across my cheek once more. The force of the slap sent my head reeling to the side from its impact. I didn't need to look into a mirror to know I would wear the imprint of your fingers upon my cheek, the burning over my tender flesh confirmed that for me. I stared at you in shock, in complete disbelief of your actions, only to feel your hand slap me just as hard on the other cheek causing tears to spring to my eyes.

"I will tolerate much from you, girl, as we begin your training..." Your voice was low and menacing as you began. Your normally warm loving eyes harsh. A cruel glint in their depths, as they locked with mine. The stern set of your jaw, your mouth, left no doubt as to the serious conviction of your words. "...but I will not tolerate your disrespect. For that, I will punish you severely, each time it crops up. Do I make myself clear, girl?"

"Release me, you bas..." I didn't get the chance to finish my plea before I felt your backhand land once more against my already burning cheek. This time, there was no doubt you'd meant for it to leave its mark. Tears streamed down my face, making it sting even further as pain and humiliation mingled into one.

"Focus!"

The hairs stood up at the back of my neck as I heard you shout. Panic raced through me, making me shiver. My eyes widened, locking with yours. I blinked to see you more clearly through my tears. I swallowed the lump in my throat and became even more aware of the rope tied about my slender neck as it restricted my ability to swallow. I couldn't help but swallow once more to assure myself this was really happening and not merely a nightmare.

"You belong to me, girl. I alone decide what to do and when. I control whether you breath or not—whether you live or not." To emphasize your words you stepped closer and covered my mouth and nose with your large hand, then reached for the center of the rope and yanked it back with your right hand, tightening the rope about my throat.

My eyes darted to yours, frantic, as the air escaped my lungs. My mouth opened wide against your palm sucking against it, as if I could get the precious puffs of air I desperately needed from your flesh as seconds turned into minutes. My face turned red from lack of oxygen as time ticked by and still you restricted my breath. Your hand followed my movements as I began to panic and struggle against your hold keeping a tight seal over my mouth and nose. Your right hand snaked into my hair, thrusting my head back, forcing my windpipe open increasing my need for air. Your eyes glued to my face, watching my every expression as I went from disbelief, to panic, to outright terror.

You noticed every nuance of my struggle for breath. My eyes were wild with terror when you finally released me, leaving me coughing and panting for air. My heart pounding.

"Tell me what you've learned, girl?" You whispered against my ear crouching down beside me, your voice softly compelling as opposed to its harsh cruelty just moments before. I felt your breath against my ear. "Show Master what a smart little girl he has."

"I learned….I learned that you own me." My words were a hoarse whisper as I turn my face into the crook of your neck, tears rolling down my cheeks, sobbing against you. I needed the comfort of your arms once more as my sheltered world has suddenly turned upside down and hell now reigned in its place.

You drew my head back by my hair, controlling me that way once more. Your eyes locked with mine and you shook your head making my heart race once more at having gotten it wrong. Immediately, new fears set in anew as I wonder what would happen next.

"No, girl. You've yet to learn my ownership, but you will…you will, soon enough." There was a wicked gleam in your eyes as you uttered those words before continuing. "Now tell me what did you learn today?"

I wracked my brain but I couldn't think of anything else. I trembled with fear at what would happen next if I angered you further. My ass, thighs, and back already burned from the leather belt and my ass…oooh gawd…I could swear I still felt drops of your cum oozing from my hole. I felt the pain from having to accommodate your thick cock as you thrust inside me, taking me like a whore, showing me "what horny men wanted." That's it!

"I learned what men want from me." I shouted the words; the sound seemed to echo in the small room.

Your wicked grin was my first clue that I was on the right track. "What else did you learn, girl?"

"I learned…I learned…" I couldn't help but shiver at having to say the words, fearing they would only fuel the anger you had under control at the moment. "I learned your rule about not allowing other men to touch me should never be broken." I rushed to add. "And I'll never break it again, Master. Never! I'll never let another man touch me. Not Tommy or Jake or Stev...." I bit my lower lip realizing too late I had poured more fuel over the fire than I'd intended to with my confession.

"How many others have there been, girl? How many others have touched you like Tommy did?"

I shook my head in denial but it was too late. I had ratted on myself in my zest to make you proud of me and revealed more than I had intended to share. As I knelt before you, I saw for the first time how much my innocent curiosity had affected you; how my revelation tarnished the trust you had in me. I tried to rectify my mistake, to reassure you, gasping when I leaned toward you, needing to touch you in some way, only to feel the rope tighten against my throat, choking me. "I never did more than touch, Master. I swear. I just wanted to touch them. To feel them touch me too. I just wanted to know what it was like. But I didn't like their hands on me, Master. I didn't...I didn't want them."

"You're nothing but a whore!" Your voice dripped contempt. The words so low, I strained to hear them. I shook my head adamantly in denial but you were no longer listening. "A dirty lying whore! And to think, all those times I trusted you." There was disgust in your voice as you spit the words out at me. Your words felt like daggers piercing my heart.

"No, Master, it's not like that. I didn't..."

"Did you spread your legs for them as well?" There was venom in your voice which you didn't bother to conceal as the *Beast* within raised its head once more. I could only stare up at you, my face bright red from your accusations.

"I guess I won't know until I fuck you there myself, huh?" I cried out as your foot deliberately slapped against the tender flesh of my pussy when you took a step forward, towering over me.

"And what about this mouth of yours, girl, did you suck their cocks with it? Did you wrap your lips around them? Taste them?" Your fingers gripped my face, squeezing my cheeks mercilessly, forcing my mouth to open in a huge "o" as your fingers dug deeper. "Tell me, whore, did you swallow their cum?"

"Stop it, Master...please stop." I leaned back, pulling from your hold, loosening the rope's hold had on my throat, shaking my head fiercely in denial. "I only let them touch me. Only ever touched them.

I just wanted to know what it felt like, Master. To know what those ladies felt when you touched them—when they touched you. I just wanted to know what it was like. I'm sorry. Please forgive me, Master. I won't be bad anymore, I won't."

I burst into tears unable to stand any more accusations, the events of the day taking their toll on me emotionally. I was desperate for you to believe me. To believe I wasn't lying otherwise you might discover the whole truth and then what would happen to me? How much pain and punishment would I have to endure?

It had felt good to have them touch me, but always when we'd gotten more excited, I stopped. I had been on the verge of stopping with Tommy as well when you walked in on us. It wasn't their touch I wanted. Not their touch I craved. But how could I say such to you? How could I make you believe me now? I opened my mouth to reveal all but it was too late, you'd already made up your mind.

You rammed your thick cock inside my mouth, thrusting it to the back of my throat, making me gag from its impact. Your hand sank into my hair when I pulled away, your fingers digging into my scalp yanking my head toward you, forcing me to swallow the full length of your erection. You forced my mouth wider as you rammed your thickness deeper still. I could feel your cock throb within the tight sheath my mouth provided as you held still for a moment, burying yourself to the base of your groin. You stepped closer, forcing my head to tilt back further that you might look into my eyes as you ravaged my delicate mouth.

Just as suddenly as you had thrust into my mouth, you pulled out of it and grabbed your cock with your free hand, rubbing it against my lips then slapping my face with it—my mouth. I could feel the wetness from my saliva on my lips and face and I wished the floor would swallow me and end my humiliation.

"I'm going to fuck your mouth like the whore you are, girl. There will be no mercy for you this night. You deserve none." Your hand grasped my hair forcefully as I pulled from you. You used your cock to slap my face and mouth repeatedly and I felt your cock harden from the sadistic pleasure you derived from flogging my face with it. Felt the hard warmth of your erection as you slapped me repeatedly across my cheeks then over my lips, pulling down on my chin. My face stinging.

"Open your mouth, whore. That's it. Now stick out your tongue. More. Now lick my dick. All of it—everywhere, girl. Show me what a good cocksucker you are." You ensured your words humiliated as they decreed your next command.

I whimpered as you stuffed your cock into my mouth. Tears of humiliation burning a path down my cheeks, leaving fire in my throat. My arms bound behind me as I knelt before you. The length of rope tied to my ankles and neck, ensuring I couldn't run away and hide as I wanted to. I opened my mouth, too afraid not to obey your instructions, and ran my tongue shyly, clumsily, over the tip of your cock. The warmth of your cock and its smooth texture surprised me as did the strange tingling at the juncture between my thighs. I was sure I'd go to hell for finding my situation slightly erotic despite my degradation and bondage—and in a strange way because of it.

At your command, I opened wider, brushing my lips over your cock tip then caressed the tip with my tongue again and again, closing my eyes, a soft moan escaping my lips. I opened my eyes, mortified, knowing you must have heard, that you must have noticed my reactions to touching you with my tongue. I was surprised to see you watching me curiously. For a brief moment, your hand was a soft caress against my hair, my cheek. "Someday, I'll teach you how a good girl sucks her Master; how she gets pleasure from tasting his cum."

Just as suddenly as it appeared, the tenderness was gone and your words were clipped and menacing once more, "But you don't deserve that yet. You're nothing but a dirty whore to me now. And I don't share my seed with worthless whores." With that you plunged your cock deep into my mouth once more—the *Beast* surfacing once again.

Your thrust slammed your cock into the back of my throat, forcing me to take your full length into my mouth. I gagged as the full force of your erection slammed into the back of my throat, effectively blocking my air passage. Your hand tightened in my hair, keeping me from pulling away when I struggled for breath. You fucked my face with the same wild intensity you used to fuck my virgin ass. Your balls added to the loss of my dignity as they slapped against my chin.

I felt your cock throbbing inside my mouth, heard your breathing become labored with each vigorous thrust as your hand tightened in my hair pulling my mouth back and forth. Suddenly you pulled your cock from my mouth, holding it with your free hand, pointing it directly in front of me as your cum exploded, spewing your seed all over my face...my nose...my mouth...my chin.

I cried out in humiliation and turned my face from you only to have your hand tighten painfully in my hair, once more holding me in place until every drop was released. Mortified, I could do no more than kneel before you. My tears mingling with the cum dripping from my face.

My sobs were all that broke the silence. It seemed an eternity before you spoke once more. Your tone left no doubt as to the consequences if I didn't immediately obey. I was quickly learning that you had shown me great restraint and patience over the time we'd been together, but my transgression with Tommy, having allowed him to touch me, fondle me, had changed all that. Gone was the loving affectionate Master I'd known and in his place was a strict demanding sadistic...*Beast*. I shivered uncontrollably at the thought.

"Look at me, girl."

It was hard meeting your eyes. How could I ever look at you again after this? How could I ever face you again? However, I was more terrified of bringing your wrath upon myself once more than the humiliation it caused me to meet your eyes and quickly did as you commanded.

"What did you learn today, girl?"

There was no hesitation in my voice, no thought necessary this time. I knew exactly what this lesson had been about and I would never forget it. Not ever. Not for a million years. And so I responded instantly, my eyes gazing into yours, my heart pounding, my chin lifting slightly. "I learned that I must never go against your rules, Master. I must never allow another man to touch me. And I won't, not ever again." I swore adamantly.

There was an evil glint in your eyes promising retribution as you ran your hand over my silky hair. "For your sake, baby girl, I hope you never do."

You took a step back and ran your hand over my face, rubbing your cum into it and causing me to turn a brighter shade of red from embarrassment as I realized you had no intention of wiping it off my face or allowing me to clean it off. You leaned over me, lifted me up in your arms and carried me to your bed.

You laid me down upon it, facing down before removing the rope from my throat and ankles. You didn't need to warn me not to try and kick you again or run away as you removed the rope. I wouldn't risk angering you again tonight not to mention my legs were stiff and cramped. The handcuffs you left on.

You walked to the dresser and removed a jar which contained medicinal cream and tenderly applied it to my bruised ass and thighs where the belt had cut into my flesh earlier. I winced as the nastier welts throbbed and burnt despite your gentle touch. Closing my eyes, I allowed myself to enjoy the feel of your hands upon me—so intimate. Strange how I didn't think anything of laying there before you naked or of your naked form beside me. I couldn't help but sneak a peek every so often at your gorgeous physique, at your cock, marveling how its length and thickness could possibly fit inside my mouth, let alone my tiny ass. I marveled at the fact that just moments before it had been buried deep in my mouth.

I blushed as I realized I had moaned out loud at the thoughts that entered my mind and the realization that it had never felt like this when Tommy or the others touched my ass or my thighs and yet your touch excited me, even now, despite your sadistic behavior.

I felt you rise suddenly and stalk to the closet removing a few items from it then returning to me. "Stand up, girl."

I immediately complied with your command, ignoring the ache in my body as my muscles protested the suddenness of my moves. You turned me so I was facing away from you. I felt you open the metal cuffs and remove them from my wrists only to replace them with fur covered cuffs, then locked the wrists together behind my back once more. My query, nothing more than a surprised gasp, was answered immediately. "You'll sleep better in these, girl."

Without hesitation, you lifted a collar to my throat and wrapped it around my neck than used a padlock to secure it in place. A two foot chain was immediately attached to the D-ring at the center of the collar and I stared up at you in bewilderment.

"I cannot trust you, girl, thus you'll sleep at the foot of my bed every night from now on until such time as you prove yourself worthy of joining me in it." You yanked on the chain, dragging me to the foot of your bed, and clipped the chain to a hook at the base of the bed.

"But I thought...." I blushed at the words I almost uttered which would have revealed my desire—my need. You chuckled having seen it on my face, smelled it rising from between my legs.

"You've a whore's heart, girl," you declared as if it were a known fact. "But I will never touch you in desire on the same day I touch you in punishment." You turned and walked out of the room leaving me kneeling at the foot of your bed. I felt the warmth of my cheeks as I blushed in embarrassment even more humiliated than before; my desire evident in my flushed cheeks, my hard nipples, and especially in the moist juncture between my thighs.

I felt the warm tears roll down my cheeks before I buried my face against the bed sheets. Mortified. Humiliated. Feeling every bit the whore you proclaimed me to be. I knelt at the foot of your bed—completely alone—utterly humiliated—and missing your presence.

Paris Light
By Leya Wolfgang

The view outside my window is stellar. Every night the Eiffel Tower becomes a flashing, dazzling beacon for five minutes every hour before it settles back to an all-over glow. Like it soaks up all the sensual energy of the humming city until it all floods out in a massive orgasm of racing light. Five minute orgasms! Five times a night! Every night! *Ohhh, the elusive O. It's not fair that an inert, metal erection get more satisfaction than I do.*

"Forget that jerk. Go to Paris, Alison," my sister urged. "Do it before you dry up like a prune." Lizzie had no idea how perceptive she was. My plummy juices haven't run since I walked in on my fiancé tapping his assistant nearly a year ago. What a cliché, but the act made an impact nonetheless. The sight of Jodi "with an 'i'" splayed out face down on his desk, her skirt hiked up around her waist and Gordon's dick buried in her ass, killed any interest I had in sex, relationships, or him. Not that he really did it for me anyway. If I'm honest, Jodi did me a favor when she decided to leave her morals at home that morning.

I've been enchanted by "this star called Paris" since seeing it through the eyes of Gene Kelly in *An American in Paris*. I was 7. I watched the screen in awe while my mom sang along with the actors. I fell in love with the blend of old world charm and cosmopolitan verve. Now that I'm here 25 years later and almost 65 years after the movie was made, the sense of romance and passion for life still pulses in the air.

A full moon rises in the indigo sky, another ball of light sitting atop The Iron Lady bathing the landscape in a silver sheen. As brilliant as the last three days and nights have been, I can't help but feel a dimming of the sensual splendor of the city without a man who loves me, someone to woo me and sweep me off my feet, kiss and caress me as we sit at a corner bistro sipping café au lait and feeding each other bites of flaky pain au chocolat.

While I nibbled on waffles with artichoke cream and jamon for lunch today, the young man standing beside me at the tapas bar wedged his knee between his girlfriend's thighs and bent her backward in a blazing kiss. I got singed by the blowback and drained my glass of dry Bordeaux blanc to douse the flames. Gordon never gave me so much as a peck on the cheek in public. He would have sneered at the open displays of affection, and naked hunger, and ruined the amorous ambiance. *Yeah, thanks Jodi.*

The memory of my delicious and arousing lunch stirs the hunger in my belly, and in more southerly parts of my anatomy. *Time to go.* My dinner reservation for 10:00 p.m. is at a restaurant that my friend Jasmine recommended. I smooth down my black, lace mini skirt before stepping into the great revolving door of my hotel lobby. The balmy air, redolent of perfumed cigarette smoke, envelopes me. I detest cigarettes, but this is Paris and the fragrance seems to be as natural as the scent of roses in an English garden.

A man spins out of the revolving door right behind me. He smiles at me and turns in the other direction. Something about his smile—it's more of a leer, really—rubs me the wrong way. I get to the end of the block and realize what set me off. His hair was a little too ragged, and his jacket was a little too shabby for someone who belonged in the hotel.

Waiting for the light to change, I look at the scenery. Six feet behind me is the same man ... staring at me. For the first time in this place, I don't feel safe alone. Seeing a break in traffic, I dart between a couple of cars, horns blaring, and power along the other side of the street. Within a couple of blocks, I have to slow down. My shins burn from pounding down the concrete, and I feel the sting of a blister bubbling up.

I catch my breath while I scan the area. "Just your imagination," I chide and resume my stroll.

A couple of blocks later, I'm drawn by a beautiful gown in a shop window. The slender sheath is adorned with sparkling sequins the color of a Mediterranean sea. "Oh, a mermaid dress. I wonder how it would look on me?"

"You would look très belle in that gown, Mademoiselle." *OMG!* He *is* stalking me. The way his feline eyes rake over my body is chilling.

I clutch my purse to my belly and stammer, "Merci. I'm very late." I take off at a run again. The cat is toying with me, I know, but I don't like his game. Then, I make a dangerous mistake. I turn a corner. In an unfamiliar city. Down a dimly lit street. That seems to be empty.

I'm a third of the way down the block before my body reacts to the recklessness my brain has already registered. In a panic, I spin to flee this mousetrap. *Wham!* I slam right into a wall. Of solid muscle. A piercing scream deafens me, and then I realize it's me. Strong hands grip my biceps.

"Vous êtes sûr. Calmez-vous, ma belle. Vous êtes sûr du mal." The voice is as thick and smooth as Bordier butter, not the grating whine of my predator. I look up into eyes as blue as a summer's day. Little balls of silver, reflections of that full moon, twinkle at me and ease my terror. Now I know why the name for Paris is *La Ville-Lumière*, the City of Light.

If only I knew more French so I could understand what he said. The concern on his face translates well, but his words mean little. When he speaks again, I almost don't care. He sounds so freaking sexy.

"I don't speak French," I blurt.

"Américaine?" he asks.

"Oui," I counter with one of maybe a couple dozen words I've learned since arriving. I wish I was better prepared because I feel completely idiotic, and this man is someone I don't want to be embarrassed around. Over six feet tall, solid, dark hair, black I think, curling gently at the crisp edge of a pristine, white shirt spanning broad shoulders. The cotton glows in the moonlight. I watch him form words, transfixed by the soft plumpness of his lips.

"You were running so fast, like you had the devil at your feet." Reality wrenches me out of my lust-filled haze.

"A man followed me from my hotel. I kind of freaked."

"Folle! Why did you not go into a café instead of letting him chase you?" The anger in his tone stuns me. The adrenalin surging in my veins pushes me to the brink of tears.

"I'm sorry. I panicked. At home I would have known what to do, but he caught me off guard. I was having such a lovely time here." I don't know what I'm apologizing to him for. I don't owe him any explanations ... yet, there is something about his presence that is strong and authoritative, commanding almost. And, of course, that face, and that body. He looks like that famous French underwear model. Heat rises up my throat and into my cheeks. I can't bear the disapproving look in those azure eyes. "I'm sorry," I mumble again.

"Ne vous inquiétez pas. Don't worry, ma belle. I will ensure that you arrive safely where you are going. And where would that be?"

"Oh, I have a reservation at Frappé at 10:00."

My pseudo-savior coughs in surprise and raises just his right eyebrow. I always wished I could do that. "Pardonnez-moi? Café Frappé or Club Frappé?"

"Oh, dear. I didn't realize there were two. It's very close to here. See?" I show him the text from Jasmine that has the address.

"You chose here? To go alone?" He uses his authoritative voice again and crowds closer to me, peering deep into my eyes. His very large hand lightly grasps my elbow. The heat wafting off him is incredible but oppressive.

I step back and say, "I told my friend how the waiter last night ignored me when I asked for a table for one. She promised me they would take good care of me at Frappé despite being a single in the City of Love."

"How well does your friend know you, and do you trust her?"

"She's my best friend, so, yes, I trust her." *What's his problem?*

"I see. You are not going to the club alone. Get in the car." I throw my hands on my hips and spread my feet in a power stance. I also jut out my chin in defiance. I don't care how hot he is, his bossy manner just got him uninvited to dinner—yes, I was toying with the idea.

"Do you know what frappé means, ma belle?"

"Of course. It means chilled. Jasmine knows how much I love iced cappuccino. I drink it all the time, even in winter." His laugh is more condescending than jovial.

"Get in the car, belle." He ushers me toward the vehicle we've been standing beside. I hadn't noticed how sexy it is. It's a sports car, red, of course, and has a yellow rectangle with a cute, prancing black horse on the hood. It looks expensive.

"As flashy as that car is, I'm not getting in. I don't know you. I just ran from one crazy man. You might be another." I tap my foot to let him know I'm not impressed.

"Je m'excuse. I apologize. My name is Alphonse Lemaire." He reaches into his inside breast pocket and extends a card pinched between his very thick forefinger and thumb. The motion of his thumb stroking along the corner, for some strange reason, makes my nipples tingle and my inner thighs flush. I take the card and hope he doesn't notice that my hand seems to have developed a slight tremble. I gulp because my throat seems to have gone dry. There is nothing on the card except for his name and a local phone number embossed in a black, bold script. When he asks for my name, I only tell him my first name.

"Alison, ma belle, please." He sounds impatient. "Your follower may be still waiting around the corner, and you will be late for your dinner." He gestures toward the car again. This time, he quirks up a gleaming smile that sends shivers sparkling up my spine. I can't resist, as foolhardy as it seems, and take his hand as he helps me lower myself into the soft, leather seat. The smell of leather always makes my heart beat a little faster. I ease back into the seat and look around while Alphonse jogs to the driver's side. There in the middle of the steering wheel is the yellow emblem again. I recognize it now. *Holy crap! He must have bags of money to afford this.*

I watch as first Alphonse's huge feet—oh my!—and then his long legs come through the open driver's door. He twists his perfect butt toward me, then sits in the seat as his tall body folds in. Illuminated by the interior light, I see the luxurious quality of his suit. I also notice fine details about the man that take my breath away, like crinkles at the corners of his eyes and a few flecks of silver at his temples. The lines bracketing his sexy mouth say that he smiles and laughs often, but the creases between his eyebrows say that he frowns just as much.

Alphonse smiles and starts the engine, which he guns before pulling away from the curb. The precision engine purrs. He doesn't speak while we drive, but I can't miss that he keeps looking at my bare knees. Every time he does, a fresh wave of heat ripples up my thighs as if he had skimmed his well-manicured hands over my skin. I'm disappointed that we only go five or six blocks before stopping. I would love to see how hard and fast he pushes this machine on the open road. Looking at the way he grips the steering wheel, I bet he handles it well. A quick flash of him gripping me and handling me startles me. *Mmm.*

A red-coated valet dashes toward the car, and I reach for the door handle. "Stay." I almost protest but pull back my hand. If he wants to treat me like a lady, I'll let him. Gordon certainly never showed me such respect. *Damn, I've got to get that creep out of my head.*

Lightning arcs between our fingers before Alphonse grasps my hand to help me out. He pulls me hard up against his left side, keeping his right hand in mine while his left hand reaches across my back and settles on my hip. This time I do protest.

"Hey, Mister. I know you French men are all touchy-feely, but there's a limit." That just makes him grip me tighter.

"Calmez-vous, ma belle," he croons in my ear. *Geez, he found my weak spot.* His steamy breath just melts me, and I fall into him. "Trust me, Alison. You need to stay very close to me. You will understand when we get inside." He leads us up the steps, locked together, but releases my hand to open the door. His other hand remains firmly planted as he ushers me in.

"Ah, Monsieur Alphonse. Bonsoir. We did not expect you tonight." He tells the host that I have a reservation, and they both look at me. *Shoot.* I made the mistake of leaving only my last name when I called earlier. Now Alphonse knows. The host looks at his list and says, "I will make adjustments." He then leads us through a set of red velvet curtains. The lighting is very low, really too low for a dining room, but I can tell the space is large. We follow him to a corner booth just to the left of the entrance.

Alphonse prods me toward the seat and slips in right beside me. He asks the host for menus. *I guess he's invited himself to dinner after all.* The man bows from the waist and retreats. I'm really getting annoyed by the way Alphonse is crowding me, mainly because his proximity is making my temperature rise and causing long-forgotten sensations in my girly parts. I slide to the wall to put some space between us, but Mr. Touchy-Feely just follows.

"Can you give me a little space, please?"

"Put your palms on the table, Alison." I stare at him open-mouthed because the command is so strange. And it definitely is a command. "Don't argue. Just do it." There's a ferocious intensity, almost a growl, in his tone. My hands fly up to comply. Alphonse places my left hand over my right. He circles his fingers around both of my wrists and clenches.

"Stop it." I start to struggle, but he crushes his fingers tighter and pushes my hands harder against the table.

"Look around, ma belle. See what kind of place your friend sent you to." Now accustomed to the dim light, the first thing I see is a stage in the center of the room.

"Oh, I didn't know there would be entertainment. Fabulous! What kind of music?"

"I doubt you will think the sounds to be music. Look around you, Alison, at the other patrons." At the next table is a blond man wearing all black leather. Sitting next to him is a blond woman wearing a red corset and what looks like tap pants. *What?!* She's not sitting; she's kneeling to his right, at his feet. My eyes jump to the next table. A red-headed woman in a shiny, black bodysuit is seated to the left of a man with black hair and no shirt. He has a black collar around his neck with a long chain linked to a ring in the floor at her feet. At the table beside them, a pale brunette has her head bent forward, and her wrists are shackled behind her in handcuffs.

My stomach churns, and my lungs all but stop working. I can feel the blood drain from my face as I see some variation on the theme everywhere I look. My shoulders crumple as my body shakes. I just want to disappear.

"The verb *frapper* has another meaning, ma belle. It also means to strike or hit, to beat or chastise. This is a BDSM club called *Struck*. Now, why would your friend, the one who knows you so well, send you here?" *Oh, good Lord. Dammit, Jasmine. What he must think!*

"I-I-I have no idea." His eyebrow arches in that sexy, annoying way. "Well, I've read *that* book." His smirk tells me he knows the one I mean. "But, it's just a fantasy."

"A fantasy, ma belle?" Alphonse leans even closer. He pulls my hands down and pushes them over my groin. The pressure eases the ache that I've been ignoring. He traces his nose from the tip of my chin, at a pace so slow that it's like torture, up the edge of my jaw and along the curve of my ear. "Tell me about your fantasies, Alison." *Holy shit!*

"N-n-no. I won't." He huffs a humid breath over my ear and pushes harder against my hands. Jesus, my panties are soaked. "I-I-I can't."

A thunk on the table makes me jump. The waiter sets a plate in front of me. I hadn't even ordered anything or been aware of Alphonse ordering. I push the man off me and straighten up. He chuckles and turns to the plate in front of him. "Eat your dinner. The show is about to start. I will pay attention, Alison, to what makes you blush and squirm. Your body will tell me your fantasies."

My eyes are glued to the center of the room. I have no idea what I'm eating, but I am always aware of Alphonse at my side. I'm mesmerized by the acts of bondage and torment that play out live before me. After our plates are cleared, Alphonse pulls us out of the booth to trade places with me and give me a better view.

At one point, the redhead across from us unhooks her boytoy and leads him to the stage. I'm fascinated by the way she controls him, right up until she reaches down and punches him in the nuts. I gasp and hide behind my hands. I can't believe that a woman can be so cruel, and that a man would just take it.

"Not a Domme, then. Good to know, ma belle." Alphonse strokes my slumped back and kisses the side of my head. He whispers, "Calmez-vous," every time the crack of a physical blow echoes through the room and the man groans in pain. Nausea turns my stomach; it just doesn't seem right that a woman should inflict such pain. Finally, Alphonse turns me toward him and pulls my hands from my face, telling me it's over, that most of his groans were ones of pleasure, and that they both had fun. He brushes my curls from my forehead and strokes my cheekbones with his thumbs. "Si gentille et tendre. Ma belle." I might be imagining it, but I think I can see flames flickering in his eyes. *Oh God, please kiss me.*

The clanking of chains pulls my attention back to the stage. The brunette with her hands cuffed walks past the departing couple—who are indeed radiant and walking hand-in-hand, go figure—and shuffles up the stairs, dragging the chain between the restraints on her ankles. Her spine is straight and she carries herself proudly. I wouldn't call the big black man who walks behind her handsome, but he is compelling. Two barely dressed men arrange what looks like a heavy duty sawhorse and then leap off the stage.

There must really be fire in Alphonse's eyes because I feel his gaze burning into me as I watch. The bald-headed man lays his hands on the young woman's shoulders and bends her forward, laying her upper body along the long edge of the padded top beam. He kicks her feet wide and quickly shoves her skirt up to her waist, baring her ass … that is facing right at me. For one sickening moment, I flash back to Gordon's office. *It's not him; it's not her.* I breathe rapidly to force the memory down.

"You think that is exciting, non?" Alphonse mistakes my reaction and strokes down my hip and rubs the exposed curve of my bottom as the man on stage circles his big, black hands on the brunette's tiny, white butt. *He shouldn't be touching me.* I don't know what the brute says, but his deep voice booms through the room. I swoon a bit and Alphonse pulls my back against his chest.

Crack! I jerk and gasp but don't turn away as a heavy hand strikes tender flesh. Three more blows come fast, and so again does my breath. *Okay, now maybe* this *is exciting.* The woman's moans call one from my own throat. "Oui, ma belle, c'est très excitant," Alphonse growls. The rhythmic slapping the man establishes entrances me. The woman's response is interesting, but it's the lust I see shimmering on the man's face when he turns the right way that makes my inner muscles clench and my clit vibrate. Of course, Alphonse sliding his hands under my butt and lifting me onto his lap might have some influence on that as well. *I can't wait for this to be over so I can regain some self-control,*

* * * * *

My plane will board in the next 20 minutes, so I have time for one last trip to the ladies' room. I gather my carry-ons. *Is that Alphonse talking to the gate agent? Nah, just wishful thinking.* The woman beside me looks up when I puff out a sigh of regret and walk away.

The show at Frappé and Alphonse's attentions had been so intense that I was completely overwhelmed. Heck, I've never even seen a porno, let alone watched other people doing such intimate things for real. Not every "scene" as Alphonse called them was sexual, but every one of them was erotic. And, shit, the way he touched me. I couldn't get enough and that scared me to death. Why? Because the host of a club called *Struck* knew his name.

I bolted, or tried to, once the spanking was over, but Alphonse insisted on taking me back to my hotel. I declined his offers to take me to dinner on any of my remaining nights. He didn't look happy when he finally admitted defeat. I made it back to my room just in time to see the Eiffel Tower climax for the final time of the night. I stuck my fingers in my soaked panties and stroked until I, too, exploded—only it lasted for five *seconds* and there was no dance of light. The whole exercise was empty and dull. I cried myself to sleep.

In the morning, I fled Paris, renting a car and planning my own sightseeing tour. I couldn't stay in the same city as Alphonse where the temptation to call him would be strong. I was already miserable without him and his kinky ways, but I wasn't brave enough to try out my fantasies with him.

I fix my makeup and look at my sweet, innocent face in the restroom mirror. "Maybe I'll try back at home. Jasmine clearly has been keeping secrets. There's gotta be safe places in New York to go to."

General boarding has already started as I approach the gate. When I hand my ticket and passport to the agent, she says, "Mademoiselle Granger. Un moment, s'il vous plaît. You have been upgraded to Business Class. Here is a new ticket and seat assignment. Please enjoy your flight." I don't understand what's happening, but she hurries me toward the jetway. The attendant at the other end gives me a fake smile when she looks at my ticket and shows me to 3A, a window seat. I grab what I want for the flight, and she stows the rest above me.

The aisle seat is currently vacant, but there's a briefcase on it. I hope my neighbor isn't a snob. I've never flown Business Class before, and I'm certainly not dressed appropriately. I'll probably sleep through the overnight flight anyway in this amazing seat that lies almost flat. The attendant offers beverages, and I take a glass of Bordeaux blanc to settle my nerves. I concentrate on the activity outside the window, and that helps as well to clear my thoughts of one incredible evening. I know I'll never find that kind of magic again. The shuffling of someone sitting beside me breaks through my gray funk.

"Bon jour, Alison." *Christ!* I slosh my wine on my pants and groan. I'd know that buttery voice anywhere. I take a breath before I turn and gaze into the bluest eyes I've ever seen.

"What are you doing here? Are you following me?"

"Non, ma belle. I'm going home ... to Manhattan." His mischievous grin blinds me. "Imagine my delight when I saw your pretty face in the terminal. I knew the Fates were smiling on us." *I had assumed ... Could I really have just gotten this lucky?* Alphonse loosens his tie, pulls it from his collar, and reaches for his buttons. *Could I get even luckier and catch a glimpse of his chest?*

I spy tufts of thick, black hair peeking through as he leans across me and slides my tray table in place. His eyes are luminous orbs of phosphorescence. "Palms." *Ohhh!* My pussy clenches and weeps, but my hands obey instantly. Alphonse strokes both hands before placing the left over the right. His fingers circle my wrists but release me. Then he wraps his tie around me and secures it tightly.

"It's going to be a long night, ma belle ..." he growls in my ear as the plane heads down the runway. "And I'm going to need both of my hands free for what I have planned for you, naughty girl. I will teach you not to run." Little rockets of joy burst and glitter in my brain. My stomach flip-flops as we lift off, or maybe it's because Alphonse presses my fists against my mound and circles them around provocatively.

I turn my head as we bank and am struck by the sight of the Eiffel Tower coming. I gasp and sigh when Alphonse whispers, "Calmez-vous, ma belle. Are you ready?"

"Yes," is all I need to say. I smile at the Iron Lady. *Tonight, I think I am going to outshine you.*

Retrograde
By Scarlet Hawthorne

Adam didn't recognize the number that appeared on his cellphone and let it roll to voicemail. The message left by the ER nurse told him nothing except it was urgent. Oddly, when he called her back, she asked who *he* was.

"You called and left a message for me! You don't even know who I am? How did you get this number?"

"Do you know a Madison Kirby?"

"No. Never heard that name in my life." He hadn't. "You're sure you have the right number?"

"We have a young woman here who had this number written on her hand."

He frowned and tried to put the pieces together, but too many were missing.

"We believe she is the victim of a sexual assault."

Fuck. They couldn't think *he* had done anything. He hadn't been with anyone since... "I'm telling you, I don't know anyone by that name."

"She has a head injury as well and appears...confused. Could I send you a photo?"

As long as he wasn't a suspect in a rape investigation. "Sure; go ahead." He clicked to receive the picture through his phone, and a vise coiled around his rib cage and squeezed. "I'll be right there."

He ended the call and focused on the image of the unconscious woman. Even bloodied and battered and covered in grime couldn't disguise Rachel Knight.

His search was over.

* * * * *

"You're certain she wasn't raped?" Adam hoped the ER doctor hadn't heard his disappointment, not that he was proud of himself.

"What is your relationship?"

"Family friend."

"Miss Kirby sustained a traumatic head injury and multiple contusions, and there are indications of attempted rape, but she put up quite the fight. Unfortunately, she doesn't remember the incident, and since she was in the mud and lake water, it's unlikely there'll be any physical evidence of her attacker."

"So she's being released?"

"We still need to do a CT scan for the head injury, and I'd like to keep her overnight for observation. Also, we're still waiting on the detectives to interview her."

"I thought she wasn't raped? Why do the police need to be involved?"

His voice terse, the doctor said, "We do have evidence of attempted rape, and Miss Kirby was almost killed."

He had to stifle his impulse to roll his eyes with a contemptuous snort at the name "Kirby." *Where the hell had the bitch come up with that one?*

"Can I see her?"

"She's in exam room B. I believe the nurses just assisted her with a shower. There's something else you should know. The concussion has caused a certain amount of retrograde amnesia; to what extent, we're not sure."

"You're telling me she claims to have amnesia?" Incredulity saturated his voice as he brought his hands to his hips.

"Not surprising considering her head injury. Honestly, I'm surprised she remembered her own name, but she couldn't give us an address, next of kin…"

What the fuck is she up to now? "But she had *my* number written on her hand."

"Yes, but there's still the chance she may not recognize you. You may notice some personality changes as well."

With eyes on the ceiling, Adam inhaled and exhaled fully. "How long does this retrograde amnesia typically last?"

"No way to say for sure. Days, weeks, months, forever. Sometimes it returns gradually. When we release her, assuming we see nothing in her CT or MRI, I would suggest that you slowly introduce her to things in her life, from her past, that might trigger something, help her regain her memory."

Such utter and complete bullshit.

The doctor ushered him into her exam room where she lay propped up on the hospital bed, clean now but her eyes still closed, and a purity emanating from her he doubted she had possessed in years.

"Miss Kirby, there's someone here to see you."

Her eyes fluttered open, landing on Adam, and that same electric tension that had tied him up in knots the first time he lay eyes on her a year before returned.

Her mouth fell open with her frown. "Do...I know you?"

Adam rushed to her bedside and took her hand. "*Madison*, it's me—Adam," he said in soft, saccharine tones.

The confusion stenciled on her face was damn near convincing.

"Someone will be in shortly," said the doctor before closing the door behind him.

"Wh-who are you? Why did you call me Madison?"

"Why'd you call yourself that?"

"It was the first name that came to me."

He yanked the sheet off of her without preamble, revealing the two hospital gowns she wore—one tied behind her and the other as a makeshift robe—and her shapely calves.

"Cut the crap, Rachel. We have to get out of here."

"Rachel?" She shook her head and closed scowling eyes, a hand rising to touch the protrusion on her skull. "Is that my name?"

"Come on. We've gotta leave before the cops get here."

She moved her legs to the side of the bed but would not stand. "Why? Are you my brother? My...boyfriend? Husband?"

He huffed out his frustration, aware that time was of the essence but struck by her innocent appeal, and gripped her arm to pull her to her feet. "None of the above, but if the cops take your prints, you're going to be handcuffed to that gurney."

Her cheeks bloomed scarlet, and he knew he had her. "Why? What have I done wrong?"

"We can chit chat about what you *haven't* done wrong later, but right now, you need to come with me."

Her wide, dark-chocolate eyes met his. "How do I know I can trust you?"

"There's a reason you had my number scrawled on your hand. Now let's go."

"They cut my clothes off me. I can't walk out like this."

The heat of her skin against Adam's palms combined with the confusion and naïveté painted on her face forced him to drop his hands and take a step back. "I'll figure something out."

He raced out of the room—more accurately, raced away from *her*. One weekend—just three days—over a year ago, and she could still get his heart racing and make his groin tingle. *Fuck her.* That's not why he was here.

Adam returned with a set of scrubs, complete with cap and shoe covers. She took the proffered garments and glowered at him.

"I don't have any shoes."

"That's the least of your problems. No one's going to notice your feet, Rachel."

"You seem to know my name, but I still don't know yours."

He let his head fall back with a frustrated growl before returning his gaze to that pale, chafed, beautiful face without a spot of make-up to conceal her true intentions. "I, for one, didn't lie. Adam. OK? Now get changed."

"N-not here...with you."

"Nothing I haven't seen before."

Blood rushed into her face, her eyes downcast. "So we're...lovers..."

"Don't worry, sweetheart, it was a long time ago in a galaxy far away. Now hurry up!" Still noting her hesitation, he sighed and turned his back to her.

Once she'd dressed, he gave her directions through the main hospital and told her he'd pick her up in front. He waited a few minutes—a good thing since a nurse appeared and had to be told *Madison* had gone to the ladies room—then he slipped out of the ER and into his car.

Rachel stood outside the hospital's main entrance fidgeting in those oversized scrubs. He pulled up with the passenger-side window down. "Get in."

She did, and not half a block away, she yanked off the cap, exchanging it for tear-filled eyes. He sniffed at how far the ice queen had melted.

"I...I'm sorry they pulled you into this, or I suppose I did."

He hardened his face and his tone. "I'm not. I've been looking for you for over a month."

She glanced up at him. "Why?"

"You tell me."

Leaning her head back against the car seat, she closed her eyes and brought her hand to her head. "I...can't think. If you were trying to find me, why would I have your phone number?"

"That's something I'd like to know."

A tear trickled down from the corner of her left eye, and Adam heaved out a reverberating breath.

"I swear to God, Rachel, if you're fucking with me, I will fucking kill you."

She covered her face with her hand and sobbed.

* * * * *

Rachel. The name somehow familiar but foreign. Her head throbbed and swirled with confusion.

"Where are you taking me?"

"Home. Stop crying. I'm not kidnapping you."

"I just wish I could remember...something. You know more about me than I do myself."

"Well, we're going to work on jogging your memory because I need answers."

"Why am I wanted by the police?"

His jaw tense, he gritted his teeth as they turned into the parking garage.

"Is this where you live?"

"This seriously doesn't look familiar to you? This is *your* home. Next door. Well, your car's not here." He pulled into the empty space and parked.

"Do you have a key to my...place? I don't have anything, not even shoes."

He escorted her out of the garage to the double-doors of the stone and metal building. "He'll let you in." Adam nodded toward the uniformed man opening the door and ushering them to the opulent lobby.

The doorman's eyes bulged in his shock-riddled face. "Miss Knight!" Rachel flinched at the name, someone else knowing her other than herself. "Thank goodness you're all right. So many people have been worried about you. You've been gone so long and didn't leave word."

"Miss Knight had an accident," Adam said. "As you can see, she's just been released from the hospital."

"I am so sorry to hear it. I'm glad you're recovering. Several people came here asking about you."

Gesturing toward Adam, she asked the doorman, "Do you know this man?"

"Er...I believe you came here looking for her as well, sir?"

"That's right. Name's Adam Fisher."

"I'm Bernard, sir."

"Bernard." Adam shook his hand, sliding a folded bill into his palm. "While Miss Knight is recuperating, please don't let anyone know she's back."

"You have my word, sir."

Flustered and dizzy, Rachel rubbed her eyes. "Bernard, my purse, everything, wallet was stolen. I don't have my key. Could you let me into my apartment?"

"Of course."

As Bernard stepped over to the reception area, Rachel peered around the richly furnished surroundings. "I actually live here?"

Bernard skipped back to them and handed her a keycard. "Here you are, miss. Please let me know if I can assist you in any other way."

"Th-thank you."

Adam grasped her arm and led her to the elevator. As the doors closed, she asked, "Do you know which floor I'm on?"

He took the keycard from her and slid it in and out of a slot before pressing the number ten. The elevator opened onto a luxurious, elegantly furnished full-floor apartment. "You're here, sweetheart. Home sweet home."

She shook her head. "I do not live here." With Adam's eyes on her, she walked across the open floor plan to the wall of windows then turned around, surveying the neat, new furniture and rich décor. "None of this looks familiar to me at all."

"It'll start coming back to you." Adam pulled back folding doors to reveal an alcove with a cluttered desk and a chair. "Your laptop's gone."

She walked over while he thumbed through the mail and papers on the desk. "What are you looking for?"

He shrugged. "Nothing here. All the mail is over a month old—mostly junk, postcard, a couple of letters from a church. I didn't know you were Catholic."

Her eyes widened, and she smiled. "Yes! I am! I remember that!"

"A shit lot of good it does me." He tossed the papers down and closed the alcove with a huff. He turned steely eyes on her, but they softened when they landed on her face. "You really have lost your memory. Haven't you?"

"Why on Earth would I be lying—especially since you're trying to help me?"

"Because that's the kind of person you are, Rachel."

She cringed and closed her eyes then pushed past him toward the open bedroom door. "Then why were you…with me?"

"It was only one weekend. I didn't know any better. You were beautiful and sexy, and I thought we both wanted the same thing. I was wrong."

"I'm sorry if Rachel hur—" She stopped in the doorway. Hangers, boxes, and discarded beauty supplies scattered around the floor and on the unmade bed, rendered the bedroom as chaotic as the rest of the apartment was tidy. "Good heavens!"

Adam squeezed by her, perusing the mess. "Looks like you left in a hurry."

"How do you know I did this? Maybe it was a burglar."

"Who steals your clothes and suitcase and leaves the rest of the apartment immaculate?"

She stepped away and opened the door to the other bedroom. "I must use this as a workout room. It's filled with some sort of exercise equipment."

Coming up behind her, Adam burst out laughing. "It's for a

workout, but that's not exercise equipment."

She wrinkled her brows as she walked in and touched one of the contraptions covered in black leather. "Then what is it?"

"Have you ever seen exercise equipment with straps before? Looks like you have your own mini-dungeon. That's BDSM furniture."

She yanked her hand back as if she'd been burned, nausea rising in her throat. "Why would I have this?"

He said nothing for a moment before taking a step forward to turn her to face him. He held onto her arms as he stared at her with fathomless dark eyes. "You're a slave, Rachel. A sexual submissive."

All the blood drained from her face then rushed up and set her cheeks on fire, the shock provoking an onslaught of silent tears. "A slave? I do this for money?"

He lifted a hand, gently wiping away her tears. "No, you're not a prostitute. This is just who you are. You enjoy it."

"The weekend you and I were together...did we use...?"

"No, none of this was here then. Your Master must have bought these."

Master? Trembling, she twisted away from his grasp. "I don't think I want to remember any more."

He followed her out of the *dungeon*, closing the door behind him. "I only tied you to the bed when I fucked you."

"*Please!* No more!" She strode into the bedroom and closed the door. "I've got to find something to wear."

The dresser drawers were open, and she spotted some clothes—a few nightgowns and other lingerie, plus a drawer full of socks. She gathered up some of the hangers and hung them on a rod before searching the closet. A few boxes remained on the top shelf, and she strained to reach them. The first one contained mementos and photographs. She studied one picture she found vaguely familiar and decided going through these things might help her remember.

In the second box, she found a wadded up shirt, but she couldn't pull it out easily. She knelt on the floor to unwrap whatever weighted it down.

Then she screamed and fell back, her hands flying up to cover her mouth. A knife had been rolled up in the shirt, stained with dry blood.

Adam bolted into the room and crouched next to the box. After a quick examination of the contents, he turned and glared at her.

"You fucking bitch!" He yanked her off the floor and out of the closet then slammed her against the wall, fury flaring in his eyes. "*You* did it! You killed my brother!"

"No!" She shook her head frantically. "No. I couldn't have."

"How do you know? I thought you couldn't remember."

For the first time, she feared him. Terror pumped through her veins, accelerating her pulse, and her aching lungs struggled for air. "Be-because I know I couldn't kill anyone."

He dug his fingers into her arm. "Then why do you have a bloody knife wrapped in *his* shirt?"

"You're hurting me! Someone must have put it there. It doesn't make sense that I would keep a murder weapon in my own apartment if I had done it."

"It would if you never planned to come back! Or only come back after the heat was off."

"Wh-when was he killed?"

"The night before you disappeared."

He released her and raised his hand. She shirked back, knowing he intended to hit her, but he struck the wall instead.

* * * * *

Adam turned around, afraid if he looked at her he truly would strangle her. He swept his hand across the bed with force, scattering a bunch of crap onto the floor. Rachel might not have put the knife into him, but she'd killed his brother just the same. She's the one who had sucked Seth into this fucking nightmare.

"How did I know your brother?" She still cowered against the wall. "Was he my…Master?"

He snorted and combed his fingers through his hair. "Not hardly. *You* turned *him* into a slave."

"I don't understand."

"A slave to cocaine—*and* to your Master."

Her quiet sobs behind him forced him to face her. Her beauty shined through even with red eyes and a runny nose, and wearing those ridiculous scrubs. That beauty had lured him in the first moment he saw her. Why did she have to be such an evil, conniving bitch?

"Shouldn't we call the police?" she asked with soft wide-eyed innocence.

"Are you ready to go to jail?" She hung her head, and he rolled his eyes. "The police can wait. Go splash some cold water on your face. Then we'll talk."

While she was in the bathroom, he looked at the knife again. No, she couldn't have rammed that blade into his back, but she had hidden it for someone. He had to get her to remember. He couldn't beat the truth out of her.

Then he grinned. Maybe he could *fuck* it out of her.

Rachel had been the star of his fantasies from the moment she'd dumped him until his brother died. If he had known that last night together would be their final fuck, he would have taken his time, relished it more. He had tortured himself wishing he could have her just one more time. Now he had the chance. Not only would he fulfill his wish, he could get revenge on her and her Master.

She came out of the bathroom, and he told her to sit down.

"Can we go in the living room?"

"No, just sit on the bed."

She cleared it off and sat down, averting her gaze. "How did we meet? Your brother and I...and you?"

"We first met at a munch."

"Munch? What's that?"

Jesus Christ. "Just a casual way for people in the, uh, lifestyle to meet. You and I hit it off. You said your Dom—"

"Dom?"

"Dominant. He'd left you, and you wanted to meet someone new."

"To take his place? Just like that? So that means...you're a Dom?"

"Yes."

"And your brother?"

"Not really. But I was single, looking for a sub—submissive—and you said you were going to be at this private party the next night. I wanted to see you again, and my brother knew the host and got us invited."

"If you liked me, I must have *some* redeeming qualities."

He couldn't think about those qualities right then. "What I didn't know at the time was that you gave Seth some coke as a thank you. Unfortunately, he kept coming back for more."

"Where would I get cocaine?"

"Your Dom, or Master, is a dealer."

"I really am a terrible person. What happened between you and me?"

He sat down on the bed next to her and touched her hair, causing her to start then meet his eyes. "We decided to see if we were…compatible, and we spent the weekend together. We were talking about writing a contract, but the next day, your former Dom came back, and you dumped me with a text—not even a call. Said that He was back and had promised to collar you."

"Collar?"

"Make you his slave. It's like a promotion."

"It doesn't sound like it."

"Until today, I never saw you or talked to you again. But my brother did. Once he knew you were back with this dealer, he kept coming to you for more. Eventually, he owed your Master so much money, he had to start dealing himself to support his habit."

"I…I'm so sorry."

"That's when I did try to reach you, help me get him out of it. You texted me three words: 'Not my problem.' Then a month ago, he gets stabbed to death, and you know who did it."

"But I don't."

"You do. You just can't remember. The doctor said if you went back to your regular life, something might trigger your memory."

"What are you thinking?" From the blush crawling up her face, she must have guessed.

"Rachel, you are a submissive. It's not something that you just do. It's who you are."

"You want me to submit to you."

"Yes."

"I'm not going back into that dungeon room!"

"No. Only what you and I did together that weekend."

She watched her shaking hands as she wrung them together. Rather than fading, the color continued to heighten in her face. "Are we going to have sex?"

Fucking hell! "So is that a yes?" That was easier than he had expected. He had anticipated some sort of argument from her.

"Sex?"

"Maybe. We'll just take it as far as we need to go. Agreed?"

She swallowed, then nodded. "I would do anything to get my memory back. But you're going to have to tell me what to do. I've never done this befo—I mean, I don't remember how to do it."

"That's all right. You will give me complete control, and I'll take care of you." He stood up and pointed at the dresser drawers. "Put on one of those nighties or something, and I'll see what I can dig up in the other room."

* * * * *

She stood in the bedroom in a black slip, and Adam—wearing only his jeans—hummed his approval as he caressed her breasts through the silk. His easy familiarity assured her they had, indeed, done this before. Pushing his fingers into her hair, he pulled her mouth to his and kissed her roughly while sliding the thin straps of the slip down to expose her breasts, catching her gasp of lost modesty in his mouth.

She had only a vague recollection of kissing, but she liked it. She savored his tongue and weakened under the force of his kiss. As he massaged her breasts, the tingling that had begun between her legs spread and tightened her nipples under his touch. He broke the kiss, leaving her panting.

"On your knees," he commanded.

I'm a submissive, she reminded herself, and obeyed, kneeling before him.

"Pull down the zipper." She could feel him, hard and thick beneath the denim and anxiously acquiesced. His erection sprang free, and she gaped at it. "You look like you've never seen a cock before."

A cock. "I...don't remember."

"Touch it. Go ahead. It won't bite."

She stared into his eyes, tracing her fingers over its velvety head and taking the silky shaft in her hands. She scoured her brain as an unfamiliar sensation that she thought must be desire pooled wet between her legs. Then a thought brought a smile to her face. "I remember! I *have* seen one before!"

"One?"

"Yes! David!"

"Here's something else you should remember. Don't mention one man when you're stroking the cock of another." He pulled her to her feet and turned her to face the bed. "I'd planned to have you suck it, but I'm afraid you *might* bite. Now bend over."

"Why?"

"I'm going to spank you."

Her hand flew back to cover her bottom, and she gawked at him over her shoulder. "Just because I said another man's name? I was excited to remember something. I think it's working!"

He chuckled. "No, this is not punishment. You like to be spanked before a scene."

A scene? She raised her eyebrows. "Spanking. I think you're making this up."

His smile reached his eyes—the first time she'd ever seen him smile—and he grazed his fingers down her cheek. "I swear it's true, but if you don't like it, I'll stop."

"You know, you're really quite handsome when you smile." She stretched her arms out and pressed her breasts against the cool sheet.

"Flattery will not lighten my touch." He slid the slip up, the cool air sweeping across her bare bottom, and immediately brought his hand down onto her right cheek.

"Ouch!"

"Hurts?" He smoothed his hand over where he'd slapped her.

"Um, well, no. Not really." She tried to decide if she enjoyed it or not but couldn't. "Get on with it."

He slapped her again, hard, then rubbed out the sting. "That was a good one!" she said and smiled.

"You see, you *do* like it."

"I feel kind of silly, actually."

He spanked her several times more, each time rubbing his hand over where he had struck. Then his hand traveled from her cheek to between her legs, and he thrust his fingers inside of her causing her to shudder and cry out.

"You see, you do like it," he said, his voice low and gravelly. "That's why you're so wet."

Her eyelashes fluttering and her heartbeat racing, she knew she liked that, what he did with his fingers, even as a flush of mortification rushed over her.

When he pulled his fingers from her, he slid the length of his cock along her soaking slit. "Do you remember this?"

"Not yet," she huffed out as her eyes rolled back in her head. "I think you better continue."

Instead, he withdrew and laughed as he rolled her onto her back, leaning over her and grasping her wrists. Despite her embarrassment, she couldn't help but smile up at him.

"Are you laughing at me?"

"Yes." He slammed his mouth onto hers, plunging his tongue in deep. She reciprocated, circling her tongue around his, and mewed. When he finally came up for air, he forced his words through his heavy breaths as he gazed into her eyes. "You remember that?"

"No, but I don't think I'll ever forget it again."

A crease formed between his brows, and he stood, helping her to sit up on the edge of the bed before turning toward the dresser. She glanced down at her bare breasts and pulled the slip up to cover them.

"I didn't say you could do that," he said when he turned back with a blindfold in his hand. She started to pull it down again, but he stopped her. "I'll take care of it later. I am going to cover your eyes now." She stared at the blindfold but said nothing. "We can stop at any time."

She nodded.

He smiled and placed the blindfold over her eyes, adjusting it into position. He swept his hands over her breasts and pulled on both nipples at once, and she couldn't suppress a moan. He curled his arm around to support her before pulling one of the beaded peaks into his mouth and sucking it through the silk. Something about being submerged in total darkness, not knowing what he might do next, heightened her arousal and made her less self-conscious.

"Lie back. Let's get you to the center of the bed." He helped to position her with a pillow under her head then took her left wrist and stretched it up at an angle. "Is that comfortable?" She nodded.

Some sort of silk cord glided across her arm, and he tied it around her wrist then to the headboard. As he tied her right wrist, her pulse quickened, the ropes triggering a surge of electricity from between her legs throughout her body. Then he tied her ankles to the footboard, spread-eagled, and she wondered what she looked like.

"Jesus, you look so beautiful like this." Had he read her mind? She inhaled deeply then released it. "Are you OK?"

"Yes, I just...well, I was going to say I don't remember ever feeling so relaxed before, but how would I? I can see now why I liked this, letting you have complete control."

The bed shifted under his weight as he moved between her legs. "That's right, I do. And do you know what I'm going to do?"

"You're going to f-f-fuck me?"

He didn't answer. Instead he licked up and down her slit, almost causing her to fly off the bed despite the restraints. He drove his fingers inside of her, forcing the air from her lungs. "God, you are so wet and tight." He pumped his fingers in and out until she thought she couldn't bear so much intense pleasure. "I cannot wait to fuck you. But you taste too good not to eat."

As he continued the rhythmic movement of his fingers, his breath hot between her thighs, the tip of his tongue touched a part of her that had to be the convergence of every nerve of her body. She writhed on the bed as his tongue continued to taunt her with overwhelming sensations.

"Oh, heavens," she managed to say through her rapid, shallow breaths. "What is that?"

He stopped just long enough to say, "Uh, my tongue."

"Yes, but...what are you doing with it. I...I feel like I might burst."

She squirmed under his attention as the tension within her rose to a fevered pitch. She couldn't breathe, she couldn't think of anything beyond getting *there*, but she had no idea what *there* meant. Then she did burst, her body overwhelmed with violent ecstasy; and even blindfolded she could see explosions. She knew she screamed but couldn't control it as tremors rumbled through her. When she thought she could bear no more, she reached it—the pinnacle—and the rapture released her to float down, down into cosmic bliss.

Spent and delirious from the experience, she didn't notice Adam had shifted up until he spoke. "How are you?"

"What just happened to me? Was that because of my concussion?"

* * * * *

Adam didn't want to laugh. He wanted to hate this woman, but he couldn't help it. He gazed down at her beauty in the afterglow, her chest still rising and falling with labored breaths, thinking that *this* had been caused by a bump on her head, and he started to laugh.

"Why are you laughing now?"

"Do you really have no memory of coming?"

"Coming here?"

He pulled off the blindfold, needing to see her eyes, a confused crease between them as she squinted in the dim light. He caressed her forehead then her temple near the lump before continuing down her cheek. "That was not because of your concussion. It was supposed to happen."

"Why?"

"Because that's what I was trying to do."

"*You* did that to me?"

"I did."

She smiled. "Can you do it again?"

He pressed his lips against hers to stifle his chuckles then leaned his forehead onto hers. "Definitely. But later. I guess I *am* going to have to fuck you since obviously your memory hasn't returned if you can't even remember an orgasm."

Comprehension lit in her eyes. "Oh, is *that* what that was?"

He shook his head and snickered as he kissed her neck, grazing it with his teeth. Pulling the slip apart, he ripped it, revealing her breasts. She arched her back and moaned as he nuzzled, kissed, and licked them, sucking her nipples. He snatched the condom off the nightstand, then ripped it open with his teeth. As he rolled it over his engorged cock, he glanced down at this gorgeous woman, tied and bound for his pleasure. He leaned over her, bracing himself on his forearms, and bored into her eyes.

"I have been thinking about this for over a year." He crushed his mouth onto hers with a ravenous kiss as, with measured restraint, he nudged the head of his cock into her tight sheath.

He thrust deeper the second time. As he met with resistance, she jerked her face away from his kiss, cringing and squeezing her eyes closed. "Wait!"

He stilled his body and raised his head, shock and awareness crinkling his brow, as he peered down at her. He stretched to reach the ends of the ropes to release her bonds from the headboard, but then she tried to push him off of her. He held her face in his hands and brushed his thumbs against her cheeks. "Shhhh…It's going to be OK." Her distress constricted her entire body, so he couldn't even pull out.

"Please stop! It hurts!" A tear trickled down onto the pillow.

"Relax. OK? Look at me." She opened her eyes, glistening with pain. "It's done now. Just relax and let your body get accustomed to mine. Take a deep breath and let it out." She did, and he could feel her release the tension as well. He moved within her with slow precision, laying a kiss on her cheek, her forehead, her lips with each stroke until she mellowed beneath him, her eyes closing, perhaps finding at least some modicum of pleasure from the experience.

Angst mitigated his own pleasure as he finished and kissed her, caressing the face of this lovely, gentle girl. Their eyes met and held.

"I don't understand." Her sweet voice carried on a ragged breath. "Why did it hurt so much?"

"Because you are not Rachel."

Caro's Fantasy
By Marie Tuhart

Caroline Montague sipped the crisp white wine wishing it would calm her nerves. She didn't want to be here at Allison's gallery. No, that wasn't quite true. She wanted to avoid the man across the room.

His lighthearted chuckle caused her to gaze at him once again. What made her so attracted to him? Yes, he was sexy. But also dangerous, sensual, confident. And from the way he stood, straight, tall, hips squared, hands at his side and with intense attention had her thinking he was a Dom through and through.

His gaze captured hers and she all but stopped breathing. His gaze bore into her like a living, breathing entity sending a clear message. *You are mine*. Her pussy moistened. She dropped her gaze.

Oh, this was so not fair. She didn't want or need a Dom in her life. She may be submissive in the bedroom, but outside of it, she was her own woman. She shifted and moved closer to the wall.

"Quit hiding." Her friend Allison strode up beside her, breaking the connection she had with the man.

"I'm not." Caro blew out a breath.

"Bull." The laughter in her friend's voice caused several heads to turn in their direction, including the man she wanted to avoid. "You promised to mingle. In return I wouldn't tell anyone who the talented artist is."

"Yeah." Hiding was a habit, but she had promised and she didn't break her promises. Her artwork was her domain and the last thing she wanted was someone connecting her art to the Montague family. Sometimes being a Montague could be a pain in the ass.

She glanced over Allison's shoulder and found *him* staring at her. Now, there was a man who wouldn't care about her family name or anything else. The other man nodded but the Dom didn't see it...he was striding toward her and Allison.

The woman in her admired the way the black tux hugged his wide shoulders, the way the jacket fit him at the waist and those long legs. The artist in her itched to paint him. Nude.

What the hell was she thinking? She closed her eyes and when she opened them, he was standing in front of her. His eyes were so dark they appeared black, but desire shimmered within their depths. She dropped her gaze.

"Good evening, Allison, Caroline," said Jacques appearing at their sides.

"Evening, Jacques," said Allison, her tone soft and seductive.

Caro hid a smile. She'd been telling Allison for years to go after Jacques, but her friend still held off. Maybe tonight she'd finally listen.

"This is my good friend Samir Merserna." Caro glanced up when Jacques began speaking only to see Samir staring at her. Samir. The name fitted his dark Mediterranean looks.

"Allison Martin, the gallery owner." Allison held her hand out. "It's a pleasure to meet you."

When Allison captured his attention, Caro breathed a sigh of relief. Her nipples were taut and her pussy pulsed from his intense gaze. This had to stop. He was a perfect stranger.

"You have a lovely gallery, Ms. Martin." His husky voice sent a shiver through Caro. Then his gaze was back on her. The wine glass in her hand wobbled. "And you are?" He took the glass from her nerveless fingers, set it on the small table by the wall before she spilled it all over herself.

"Caroline Montague." His hand captured hers. His rough skin caused every nerve in her arm to come alive.

"Ms. Montague, it is a great pleasure." His lips brushed her knuckles and heat flowed from there directly to her clit. Oh, this was so not good.

Jacques cleared his throat breaking the spell Samir had wrapped around her. "Allison, my dear, why don't you show me this new artist's work, while Caroline and Samir talk."

Allison glanced at her and then to Caro's hand still joined with Samir's. "Yes, let's." Before Caro could get a word out, her friend was striding across the room with Jacques. She'd get Allison for this later.

"What brings you to New York, Mr. Merserna?" He was still holding her hand. She tugged, but he tightened his grip.

"Samir." His husky voice sent shivers of awareness down her spine.

"Excuse me?" She tilted her head studying the lines of his face. He'd make a fantastic model for one of her nude sketches.

"My name is Samir." He invaded her private space.

"Samir, I don't think..." His fingers against her lips cut off her words.

"Don't think," he whispered, his palm cupping her cheek.

Her heart rate sped up. He was close, so close. "What are you doing?" The question came out soft instead of forceful.

"Touching you."

"Why?" Why wasn't she pulling away?

"Because I wanted to see if your skin is as soft as it looks."

"And is it?"

The desire in his eyes flared into a raging fire. "Yes." He shifted closer to her, causing her to take several steps until her back was pressed against the wall. He'd maneuvered her into the small alcove.

She swallowed. But didn't fight him. They were in a room full of people, the sound of voices filled the air. What could possibly happen? She tilted her head back to stare up into his rugged face. What was he? Six feet maybe a little over. It was rare she had to look up at a man and she liked it.

"I have to taste you." Before she could react to his words, he gripped the back of her neck and lowered his lips to hers.

His firm grip kept her from moving her head away, but when he traced the seam of her lips with his tongue she instinctively parted her mouth to him. His tongue swept in and tangled with hers. She stopped breathing.

The kiss deepened. Mint and coffee danced over her taste buds. Without thought, her hands rose to his shoulders. She should be pushing him away, but instead her fingers worked their way into his dark soft hair.

Samir's free hand slid around her waist, pulling her hard against him. Her breasts crushed against his chest. Desire and lust flared in the pit of her stomach and traveled through her veins faster than any drug. She wanted this man. Here and now.

Sanity returned. Breaking contact with his lips, she drew in a deep breath trying to control her breathing. His lips traveled over her cheek to her ear. His tongue caressed the lobe and she shivered.

"Samir." Her voice soft and almost pleading. So not like her.

"Shhhh." His palms swept over her back to her ass, pulling her against his hardening cock.

"We have to stop." This was madness. Complete and utter madness. She didn't allow men she didn't know to invade her personal space, let along hold her, kiss her, make her ache in all the right places.

He nipped her earlobe causing her clit to throb before he pulled back and stared down at her. "I will have you. Tonight."

Samir smiled as Caroline opened her mouth and then shut it. Good. She wasn't going to argue with him. Most submissives wouldn't. But her eyes were wide and while there was passion in her deep blue gaze, he didn't want to frighten her. Especially not in a gallery full of people.

"Have I scared you?" He ran a finger down her soft cheek, and his cock jumped. He wanted to hold her, kiss her, fuck her, have her scream his name when she climaxed, but scare her? No. He wanted to cherish her.

"No." The ring of truth was in that one word, and that pleased him.

"Good. Shall we leave for my place?" With his arm around her waist he started to guide her from the alcove to the front door.

"Release me." Her voice was low and her body stiff. But her face and neck was pink with arousal.

"And if I refuse?" So the little kitten had claws did she? His cock twitched. Oh, she made him ache to bury himself within her. What could she really do if he pinned her up against the wall? Or tied her over his favorite spanking bench? "Behave." His arm tightened around her waist when she began to pull away.

"Please." Her voice had gone low and pleading.

"Oh, I will please you, little one."

"We're in a public place."

"No one is looking." He glanced over his shoulder. They were safe, people were not paying attention to them. "Are you wearing panties?"

Her eyes went wide and he grinned.

"I have taken self-defense lessons. Now let me go."

"I don't take orders." His fingers tightened around her waist. "I give them. Disobey me and I will punish you."

Her head came up and she stared at him. Not a move a submissive would do without expecting punishment. Maybe she wanted him to punish her.

"I warned you."

Pain exploded in his groin. His mouth opened on a gasp and he released his hold on her. The little minx had kneed him. He hadn't expected that from her.

"Have a good evening, Mr. Merserna." She marched away. His gaze followed her as he got his breath back and waited for the throb in his groin to subside. She was going to be so much fun. And he couldn't wait to punish her with pleasure.

"Quite the little hell cat," said Jacques coming up next to him.

"Is it all set?"

"Yes, my friend. Allison has agreed to convince Caro to come back to the house for food and drinks."

"Good."

"Do you think you can tame her?"

"I don't want to tame her," said Samir. "I want to teach her. To pleasure her. To fuck her."

* * * * *

Three hours later, Caro sighed. Thank goodness this night was almost over. Her head ached and the reason was standing across the room from her.

Samir hadn't left as she expected. No, instead he'd taken up residence near the door and watched her all night long. And now Allison was telling her she'd promise Jacques they'd go to Samir's house for dinner.

"Allison, I'm tired and I have a headache."

"Food and company will clear that up in no time. Please Caro, I want to get to know Jacques, but I'd feel better if you were with me."

A sigh escaped her lips. "Dinner, then I'm going home."

How the hell had she gotten herself into this predicament? Her best friend was how. After dinner, Jacques and Allison had disappeared together leaving her alone with Samir, who was gazing at her like a hawk with a tasty meal in his grasp.

"I think it's time for me to go home." Caro stood. "Thanks for the meal."

"You aren't leaving." Samir stepped into her path, his hands grasped her arms.

"Samir, please." She'd been fighting against her desires all night. Samir had been a wonderful host, which made it harder for her to ignore him. God, she'd never wanted a man so much. Even though she'd kneed him in the groin earlier, her lust for him hadn't diminished.

"Please what?" His hand slipped around the back of her neck. "Please kiss you? Please fuck you?"

Her breath hitched in her throat. Did he really say fuck? Yes, he did. Her pussy clenched. "I..."

"Your safe word is Red."

This time her stomach did a little dance, and her brain to turned to mush. Oh, this was so not good.

"Do you understand what a safe word is?"

"Yes, sir," she whispered. Hadn't she been expecting this all night? Maybe that's why she let Allison talk her into coming. She wanted Samir, no, needed him. She needed his dominance to chase away the world.

"Good." He took her hand and led her through the house and into another room. He flipped the light on and guided her in. The door closed behind them.

Caro blinked. There was an enormous bed with a huge metal frame against one wall. Her gaze slid past it to the twin dressers, then on around the room finally coming to rest on what looked like a padded sawhorse.

With a huge intake of breath, she tilted her head back and looked at Samir. Lust and anticipation was etched on his face. A shiver of excitement went up her spine.

"You were a naughty girl earlier." His hand rose and brushed a lock of hair away from her face.

"Yes, sir." She let her eyes close, taking in the softness of his touch against her skin. She wanted to be here, in this room with him.

Earlier, she hadn't been so sure, but she was now. Her instincts told her he was a man she could trust.

"And you are aware that I am going to punish you?"

"Yes, sir." Why did the word punish make her pussy gush?

"But first." His fingers found the zipper on the back of her dress. Cool air caressed her back as he lowered it. "Your skin is so soft." The pads of his fingers traced her spine before he pushed the dress from her shoulders and off her body.

It pooled at her feet. "Nice." His palm covered her breast still encased by the lacy bra.

"Thank you, sir."

Samir grinned once again. She was so perfect, answered him with the 'yes, sir' he liked. Finding the fastening of her bra, he released it and her beautiful breasts spilled out of the lace.

Full, luscious breasts with dusky rosy nipples. His mouth watered. Soon. He let the fabric drop to the floor while his hands skimmed down the sides of her breasts, to her stomach where they were rewarded by her slight shiver and the flushing of her skin.

He kissed the valley between her breasts before trailing his lips down to the top of her mound. "No panties, my naughty one."

A giggle left her lips and he grinned against her skin, before reaching her feet. "Hold on to my shoulders."

He waited until she obeyed him, then he removed her shoes.

His cock strained against his slacks. First things first. Straightening up, he took her mouth. Without giving her time to adjust, he thrust his tongue between her lips.

Their tongues met and tangled together. Grasping her butt in his palms he lifted her and let out a groan into her mouth. Her legs wrapped around his waist and his cock jumped.

Once at the spanking horse, he broke the kiss. "Stand up, little one." Slowly she unwrapped her legs from his waist and lowered them to the floor. "You taste like a woman," he told her.

"And how is that, sir?"

"Fresh, feminine, and all mine." He nipped at her lips before setting her away from him. If he kept this up they'd never make it to bed. "Turn and bend over the horse."

When she hesitated, he swatted her on the ass. "Now, little one." She glared at him before lying over the horse on her stomach.

Good, it was at the right height. Striding over to her, he ran his palms over her ass before moving down to her ankles. Having her here like this made his palms itch. Stretched out in all her glory.

The stand was one of his favorites. Her body rested on the main part, supporting her, and left her body open for him to play with. And he was going to play with her, all night long.

Once finished restraining her, he strode over to the dresser and opened the drawer. He ran his hand over the selection of paddles until he found the one he wanted. Leather on one side, rabbit fur on the other.

Caroline was squirming, and he grinned. "Problems?"

"Umm, no sir."

He laughed. Her flushed body told its own tale. Arousal, excitement, and probably a little dose of apprehension. With long strides he reached her side and sat the paddle on her back.

A shiver went through her body. Samir made quick work of stripping out of his shirt, then removed his shoes and socks. He preferred to be in his bare feet.

His fingers skimmed over her butt and she jerked in her bonds. "Easy, little one." He'd be careful not to mark her skin only make it glow. He brought his hand back and smacked the fleshy part of her ass.

"Ouch."

"Do you know why I'm punishing you, little one?" He administered another. This time she didn't cry out.

"Because I wouldn't answer you at the gallery about my underwear, sir."

"Wrong." He spanked her several times, then paused. Her ass was already rosy and his blood thundered in his veins. Her hot ass would feel delicious against his skin when he fucked her.

He caressed her butt, and she let out a sigh. Then he slipped his fingers down to her pussy. The second he touched her, she stiffened and tried to wiggle her ass.

"Please sir."

"Do you trust me, little one?" He wanting to hear it, if she hadn't trusted him she wouldn't have let him tie her up.

"Yes, sir."

"And the spanking. Did it arose you?"

Caro let out a gasp as his fingers traced her pussy. "Yes, sir." She hadn't wanted to admit that to him. But what choice did she have? Outside of safe wording out and she didn't want to do that. She wanted this experience, the pleasure from his touch, from his punishment.

God, her body was on fire. Never had she been spanked so masterfully. Her clit pulsed with need. She wished he would take her to bed now, she wanted him.

"Good girl." He patted her hot butt, and removed his fingers from her pussy. "I'm punishing you because you kneed me."

"Oh that." She'd forgotten about that. It had been instinctive when he refused to let her go, and she did warn him.

"Yes, that." Whatever he'd set on her back was now taken away.

Oh hell, why hadn't she tried to figure out what it was? Instead she could only think about him and they way he was making her feel.

"Five swats with one side of this paddle, then ten with the other."

Fifteen. He was going to use a paddle on her 15 times? Instead of screaming her safe word, her pussy clenched.

The first hit had her sucking in a breath, but it wasn't too bad. By the fifth one, the heat from her ass had spread, and she was having trouble catching her breath. His cool hands caressed her ass, then up her back, soothing her until her breathing returned to normal.

He stopped touching her and she tensed. Nothing happened. Caro blew out a breath and..."Fuck." That stung.

Before she could think he began spanking her, never hitting her in the same spot twice and pausing to let the sting travel through her body. By the time the last one came, she let out a moan.

Her pussy was clenching with need, her clit pulsing and she could barely catch her breath. It had hurt, but it was arousing beyond belief.

Something cool hit her ass, and she jerked in the restraints. Hell, she'd totally forgotten he'd bound her.

"Easy, little one. It's lotion." He smoothed and caressed the lotion into her skin.

The lotion cooled her ass and helped her get her breathing under control. Then the restraints on her ankles were released, and Samir was in front of her releasing her arms.

"Okay, little one?"

"Yes, sir." And she was. Nothing had gone numb or hurt.

"Easy does it." He helped her up and onto her feet, keeping his arms around her.

"Thank you, sir."

"On the bed, hands and knees, ass facing the end of the bed."

Her breath hitched in her throat, yet she padded over to the bed. The mattress was firm as she climbed onto it, and positioned herself as he commanded. Arousal caressed her skin. It had been too long since she'd found this type of release in the bedroom.

The chance to let go of everything except the man commanding her, she needed this almost like she needed air. She turned her head to see where Samir was and let out a moan.

He'd stripped his pants off and was fully erect. Her pussy clenched with need.

"Eyes on the headboard." His harsh voice made her heart jump, but she turned her head and waited.

The mattress dipped behind her. The heat rolled off his body and she fought against wiggling her ass at him.

"How wet are you?" He thrust a finger into her pussy.

Caro sucked in a breath and let it out in a puff as he stroked his finger in and out of her moist pussy. With each pass, her muscles tightened trying to keep his finger inside.

When he added a second, her head dropped. "Please, sir," she whispered.

"Please what, little one?"

"Please, sir, fuck me. I need you so much."

"Your wish is my command." She cried out as he removed his fingers, but then his cock was there. "I can't be gentle, little one. I need you."

"Yes, sir." His fingers gripped her hips hard and..."Ahhhhh!" she cried out as he filled her on the first thrust.

Oh Lord, he was so big. So hard. And hers. Sliding out, he slid back in, then did it again and again building up momentum.

Her breasts swayed with each thrust, and Caro closed her eyes. Every nerve ending came alive. Her stomach tingled and her clit pulsed with need. And...she cried out as her climax hit her. She hadn't even expected it.

"You are so tight and so fucking sexy." Samir continued to

pound into her and she took every delicious inch of him. Yet she wanted more.

"Samir."

In an instant, he pulled out of her, flipped her over onto her back, flung her legs over his shoulders, and was fully seated inside her pussy.

"Mine." His lips took hers as he pounded into her, his hot tongue mimicking his cock.

Higher and higher he took her until she was shaking. Each time she got close to climax, he'd back down and then build her back up.

"Please, Samir," she whispered.

"Scream for me, little one. Let me hear your passion." He slid his fingers to her clit and pinched it.

Caro opened her mouth. Nothing came out. Her voice was gone. But Samir didn't let up. He kept pounding into her, his fingers playing and toying with her clit. She'd been denied for so long that her body didn't know what to do then...she screamed his name as her body clenched around his cock.

Three more strokes and he was pulsing deep within her pussy. His lips captured hers once again until she stopped shaking.

"You are so beautiful when you orgasm."

She brushed her fingers over his sweaty chest and smiled. "I think we both need a shower."

"Yes, then on to round two."

* * * * *

Samir rolled over and found nothing but empty mattress. He frowned. Where was Caroline? He sat up and listened. No shower running. Slipping out of bed, he padded to the bathroom before pulling on a robe and going down stairs.

His muscles ached, but it was a pleasant hurt. Last night was fantastic and he wanted to repeat it. But first he had to find Caroline. With quiet movements, he checked the kitchen. Empty. Maybe she was in the sun room.

When he saw her he breathed out a sigh of relief. She was curled up in one of the oversized chairs, sketchpad in her lap, pencil flying over the page. He didn't think she'd leave him, but last night was intense.

"Good morning, darling." He bent from behind her kissing her cheek, she smelled like strawberries.

"Morning." She kept sketching, but her soft neck arched for his touch.

"Interesting sketch." He nuzzled her neck. The sketch was of him lying sprawled out on the bed.

"Yep." She put her initials in the corner before tossing the book and pencil onto the table. He rounded the sofa and pulled her into his arms.

"Did you enjoy last night?" Thank goodness she'd put a robe on. His cock was already begging for more action. If she were naked he'd be inside her without hesitation.

"You know I did." Her arms entwined around his neck. "Thank you for making my fantasy come true." Her lips brushed his.

"I'll have to admit I was a little skeptical when you first told me." Three weeks ago, Caro had approached him with the fantasy of meeting a stranger and having him take control. He hadn't expected it to be such a turn on.

"And you enjoyed yourself, didn't you?" She gazed up at him with those deep blue eyes.

"I think more than you did." He cupped her ass and was rewarded with a soft moan. "So what is next on the fantasy list, wife?"

"I was thinking." Her fingers trailed down between the vee of his robe. "Maybe we could do a harem kidnap fantasy, husband."

"Right up my alley." He pulled her to him and captured her mouth, while silently thanking whatever god sent this beautiful, adventurous, bedroom submissive wife to him.

Point of No Return
By Kestra Gravier

Pu'uala knocked on the cockpit door. "Morning tea, officers?"

"Sure, come on in. We're just setting in the final adjustments to the flight plan after the laser fueling," the Captain said.

Pu'uala pushed through the doorway and balanced the tray on one velcro'ed arm as she clipped her tether into the wall slide.

"...log one, four, zero, twotwenty sixteen. Thirteen souls accounted for." The Lieutenant spoke to the ship's computer.

"Ouch!" Lieutenant Wolfsnare flinched as she sloshed the tea while working to release the china cup from its restraints.

"Oh, I'm sorry Lieutenant," Domestique Pu'uala said as she wiped away the offending spots. "After four weeks, I'm still not quite accustomed to serving in these tight quarters."

"Can you join us, Domestique?" the Captain said.

"Yes, I brought an extra cup," Pu'uala said as she fitted the tray into a wall anchor and set about fixing her drink.

The cockpit had the obligatory windshield, provided at the insistence of the program's original pilots and mission psychologists. The starfield stretched limitlessly, a background of featureless black, without the color notes painters included in depictions of *noir*. It made the view surprisingly technical, instead of artistic. On this side of the windshield, digital panels and analog dials provided an endless supply of information on the state of the ship.

The Captain gestured with his cup towards Pu'uala's upraised arm. "I never heard how in the world you were able to sneak that aboard."

A narrow snake was wrapped around her forearm, lazily tasting the air with its forked tongue. She pointed to her generous breasts and said, "He was quite content and warm during the boarding process."

"Lt. Wolfsnare and Doc advised me to let it be, but now I would like to hear *why* you brought a snake onboard the Mayflower."

"Captain," Pu'uala leaned forward and the tip of her braid floated in front of her face. She flicked it aside. "SpacAdmin gave me the designation of Domestique, and you and I both understand all the implications of the post."

Lt. Wolfsnare looked away.

"In my culture, I am a respected wisewoman. My role is, ultimately, sustaining and fortifying the spirit, and I do that with all the techniques and talents available to me. At times, in your Western culture, I would have been called a witch. So the best analogy I can make is that Resta is my familiar."

"And you thought it appropriate to smuggle a snake onto my ship?"

"My advanced western degrees are going to be much less value in establishing a foothold on Mars, compared to my wisewoman responsibilities. And Resta is part of being a wisewoman. Of course, he is non-venomous."

"Well, I'm afraid to imagine what else you might have brought aboard…Speaking of your responsibilities, we hit PNR tonight and I'd like to have a celebration for the crew. Can you pull something together?"

"Certainly. What did you have in mind?"

"Party details left to you. I want to move us off the current military footing and more towards a community setting. Use name cards, and leave off the military designations. Once past PNR, I'd like to drop titles."

"Sir," Lt. Wolfsnare broke in, "do you think that's a good idea? I mean, we'll have rationing on the surface, potentially dangerous situations, and personnel conflicts. Wouldn't an intact chain of command help keep order and keep us on schedule?"

"Perhaps in the short term. We're establishing a foothold, yes, but it's also the foundation for the long-term community to follow. And I want the basics of democracy and cooperation to already be well established."

"But it may be years before the next transport comes."

"Yes, and that is why…"

"Excuse me Captain, Lieutenant; it's time for me to be in the Agro station."

"Dismissed, Domestique."

Pu'uala secured the tea tray, untethered, and pushed back out the door, latching it behind her. She dropped off the dishes in the mess, and then made her way to the Agro module, where she spent the necessary time feeding the goats, refreshing the mulberry leaves for the silk worms and fertilizing the small garden patch. She also went through the checklist for maintenance of the flora and fauna embryo stores, the real source of the biodiversity that would help sustain the group over the coming years. That, and the 3-D printers. But the printers, in her opinion, lacked soul.

She latched the entryway to the Agro station and keyed in the code. Like all critical functions on the ship, the Agro had a primary resource person and a back-up who knew key information necessary for the survival of the ship and crew. Pu'uala had primary responsibility for all domestic and agricultural services.

Pu'uala considered the arrangement as she loped down the corridor, long ago having perfected the push-off and glide that propelled her quickly but provided enough control that she didn't constantly bang her head or limbs on the unforgiving ship surfaces. The first week's crop of bruises had provided the necessary feedback for a quick learning cycle.

The living plants and animals were not considered critical, but the embryo stores were, and Doc served as the back-up for those. If both Pu'uala and Doc were lost, well, the mission would be in a world of hurt, Pu'uala knew, but it could possibly survive. Other functional knowledge, divided among the crewmembers, was even more critical.

* * * * *

Doc pulled herself along the corridor railing, heading towards the Evac slots. "Why they can't just call them toilets, I'll never know."

Pu'uala smiled. "'Toilet' would set up an expectation of something like home."

"Yeah, I guess our fittings and hoses aren't much like home."

"No, not at all. Captain wants a PNR celebration tonight, I've got to get prep underway. By the way, thanks for the serum. I don't expect to need it, but glad you were able to concoct it."

Doc released and floated up close. "I'm really not happy about that. You owe me."

Pu'uala planted a kiss on her cheek. "I know, doll. And I expect you to collect."

Doc headed toward Brody's chamber. As the mission leader, he had overall responsibility for all aspects of the project and kept in close contact with Base Command. He was also her lover.

She glanced along the passageway, and saw Eli Trask, one of the mission specialists, turning the corner and moving out of view. Not one of her favorite crewmembers, Trask most resembled Napoleon Bonaparte in appearance and psychology. Objectively, she knew it was almost impossible that the rest of the crew did not know her liaison with Brody, but she chose to try and observe some propriety.

They had been a clandestine couple before the flight, Brody not wanting to leave his well-heeled wife before departure. Now, without an expectation of return to Earth, Brody considered himself single. Almost Talmudic reasoning. She knocked, then pushed into his area.

"Katrina, this is a pleasant surprise." Brody eased back from his console, and slid the hood shut.

"I had some time…"

"And we should put it to good use." Brody pulled Katrina to him and slid his hand behind her head, gripping her short hair. He lifted her away from the chamber boundaries, removing her leverage. He kissed her, gently at first, then with more force, until she sighed and brought her arms up and around him. His hand moved to cup her breast.

"These coveralls are practical for many things, but not this. Remove them." He kept hold of her hair, twisting it, suspending her. Katrina gasped from the pain in her scalp as she squirmed her way out of the one-piece uniform. Functional, command-issued bra and panties were all that covered her. She has long ago lost any sense of embarrassment with Brody. He would not allow it.

Brody extended his arm, and Katrina watched as his gaze swept up and down her body. His expression left no doubt as to his opinion of her underclothes. "Those go, too."

Before she began to further undress, she snuck a peak at his crotch, rewarded by the sight of his erection pressing through his equally uninspiring coveralls. Desire surged, and she was glad her panties were there to absorb the sudden excess of moisture. His grip tightened, prompting her to shed her undergarments.

"So nice of you to stay shaven, even with our limited amenities. Very pretty."

"Thank you."

"I don't have much time, Katrina, but I didn't want to let today pass without you."

"I wanted to see you, too, Brody."

"Very well, then. Move to the end of the bed."

Katrina toed off and hung just off the floor at the foot of the bed. Her body hummed and she was giddy at finally having Brody all to herself. Except for the crew and the mission, of course. His hands ran over her body, following the contours of her breasts, waist, then hips, finishing with a smack to her ass cheek, which sent her flying into the bedframe.

"Perfect. Hold still a moment." Brody reached under the bed and pulled out tethers with cuffs on them. He fixed one around each of her ankles.

"Lovely. And you won't float away." Another set of tethered cuffs appeared from the mid-bed frame and Brody captured her wrists with those. Now secured, Katrina was bent forward slightly at the hips, presenting Brody with a pleasing view of ass cheeks curving down to long legs, with a hint of her nether lips peeping out between her legs.

He smacked her again, and she bounced slightly, letting out a yelp. Brody tightened the tethers, pulling her forward more. He walloped her again, catching the underside of her ass and lifting it with the blow. Buttock flesh wobbled nicely, but Katrina was held fast by the tethers.

"That looks very nice, love." Brody stroked his fingers along her pussy lips, catching moisture and spreading it along her slit. Katrina moaned and pushed back, seeking more. He pulled his hand away and swatted her once again, raising a faint red mark on her skin.

"In my time, Katrina. But since you want more stimulation, let's try this." Brody moved to her side and began to stroke her nipple. As she writhed with increasing arousal, Brody increased the pressure and twist until she was moaning.

At that point, he fastened a clamp to the distended nipple bud, eliciting a shriek from Katrina, followed by "No, no, no."

"Katrina, look at me, focus on me." She dragged her head up and panted, working to lock in on his gaze. "What is your word?"

A beat. "Persimmon."

"Very good. And do you wish to use your word?"

Katrina panted, holding his gaze, twisting, trying to get away from the bite of the clamp.

"Your word?"

Katrina shook her head.

"Tell me."

"N-n-no."

He brushed the clamp and she yelled again, an incoherent sound.

"Can you keep silent?" He stroked her wet sex.

Katrina swirled in the sensation, unable to process the question. He pulled on the clamp and she yelped.

"I'll take that as a 'No'. In that case, I'll need to gag you so you don't disturb the rest of the ship." He placed a small soft ball in her mouth a latched the straps at the base of her skull.

"Now, let's try this." He gave the clamp a tug and Katrina screeched behind the gag. He stroked her back and said, "Breathe through it, love. I'm very pleased."

He began to spank her, varying the rhythm, intensity and target, preventing Katrina from anticipating the next blow. The clamp jumped with each hit, evoking paroxysms of groans and muffled shrieks. Katrina tried to turn away, thwarted by her bonds.

"Warm and red. Just perfect." Brody moved to the side, into Katrina's line of sight. He stripped away his coveralls and underwear, freeing his erection. Katrina gazed avidly as he stroked himself, increasing the stiffness of his cock.

She moaned and wiggled her ass. Brody reached out and flicked the clamp, causing it undulate in the zero gravity. Katrina bucked and shouted behind the gag.

Now he was behind her again, pressing his cock into the hot wheals on her ass. She tried to push back, but had no leverage, and moaned in frustration. Brody nestled his erection in the crease between her ass cheeks and reached around to knead her breasts. They swelled, her nipple distending further against the clamp and streaks of pain darting from her nipple to her clit.

It wasn't long before Brody's other hand snaked down to stroke her, rubbing along the sides of her prominent nerve bundle, never bringing his touch directly over the most sensitive tissues. By now Katrina was moaning continuously, straining towards an orgasm. She couldn't hold herself still, and the combined milking and swelling of her breast and the increasing pressure of the clamp was sheer torture. Sweat popped out on her skin.

"Do you want to come, love?"

Katrina nodded her head, twisting around to try and catch his eye, silently pleading for relief.

"Very well, and after you come, I'm going to take you. Do you understand?"

Katrina nodded again and tried to push back. She earned a swat. He shifted his fingers from the sides of her clit to directly over the extended bud.

"You're drenching my hand. I love your wetness." Katrina was panting, beyond comprehending his words. Her muscles were tense, her breast a heavy, hot mass of dull ache with sharp, bright stabs of pain shooting from her nipple. Her orgasm coiled deep in her pelvis, pulsing and growing. Her moans shifted to growls as her body demanded release.

Brody's breath stroked her ear. "Come for me." Her orgasm unfurled, sweeping over her, shaking her body, smoothing away any jagged sensations and then pulsing with calming power.

Brody's hands were between her legs, a cloth absorbing excess moisture. cool air hit as his fingers split her labia apart. Heat emanated from his cock as he probed, rubbing along her slit, then bumping her asshole. Chills swept along her back as Brody's cock moved to the soft tissues around her vaginal opening. Then he was pushing, entering her. His fingers gripped her hipbones, pulling her back onto his cock, slamming into her pelvis.

She felt him stiffen further, deep inside her body. His fingers dug in deeper, and his thrusts became faster, harder and less rhythmic. His body tightened and he seated her fully on his cock and arched into the hot moistness. He groaned out his orgasm, jerking as hot semen spewed forth.

Brody slumped over her back, sweat sticking their skin together.

After several moments, he drew a deep breath and pushed off.

"I'm going to leave the gag on, love, until the clamp is off. Hang in there." The pressure eased, then she shrieked as the blood came rushing back into the compressed tissue. Brody suckled on her nipple until the pain eased, holding her close. Finally, her breathing slowed and he removed the gag, wiping excess saliva away. Gently, he kissed her.

"Now, let's get you cleaned up."

Katrina hung limply in the tethers, accepting his sure touch, appreciative that Brody's chamber had its own water spout. Once washed, he patted her dry, being especially gentle around her tender breast.

Brody left Katrina tethered to the bed by an ankle as he collected her clothing then helped her dress, zipping her coveralls closed and exchanging a final kiss.

"I'll see you at the PNR party, Brody."

Katrina floated out the door, shifting in the air to ease her cramped muscles. She smiled as she passed Jernigan, another mission specialist. His coveralls were undone to the waist, exposing a blue and gold Embry-Riddle T-shirt. The eagle mascot peered cross-eyed off his chest. She heard him greet Brody before the door shut.

* * * * *

Pots clanging and the rapid sound of chopping reached Grant Adair, the mission safety specialist (better described as an adventurer) before he arrived at the mess prep. It still surprised him that no aromas wafted through the corridors.

He entered the kitchen, catching a countertop to halt his forward momentum. Domestique Pu'uala was working with Bitton and others, multiple microwaves whirring away. Pu'uala's blonde hair was messily pulled up and her blue eyes were obscured by glasses that had partially slipped down her nose. Adair paused for a moment to acknowledge the attraction, but knew he would not avail himself of the sexual services included in the Domestique area of responsibility. She had done things to the coveralls with duct tape that made her all the more alluring. Still, he knew he could resist, a five fingered date notwithstanding.

"Why all the activity?" Adair found himself turning up his Texas twang, knowing ladies responded favorably to his accent.

"Oh, Major Adair, hi. Party tonight, Captain's orders. Everyone in the RecPod for dinner," one of the cooks said.

"What're we celebrating?"

Pu'uala answered. "PNR. Captain wants to mark the passing and change the interactions between the crew."

Adair picked up a chef's knife and made short work of some root vegetables while he talked.

"I'm looking for Trask."

"I haven't seen him all day. Guys?" Pu'uala asked.

"No ma'am, we haven't seen him." The two erstwhile cooks didn't look up from their prepping.

"What's up, Adair?" Pu'uala asked.

"Just post-landing stuff. I need to review with Trask some of the pod extension protocols for when we land. The sooner we can expand from the core ship, the happier we will all be. Oxygen will be key and I need Trask to review my plans."

"Oh, more space. That'll be wonderful." She ran her hands over her torso. "Privacy. Heaven."

Adair launched a pile of evenly diced vegetables over to Pu'uala.

"Nice knife work," she observed, while rounding the pieces up in a bag

He grinned at the cooks and casually flung the knife. It hit, quivering, in the center of a "Danger! High Pressure" sign.

Adair sketched a salute. "Ma'am, it'll be a pure pleasure to accommodate you."

* * * * *

Doc looked around the RecPod, noting the paper streamers decorating the upper corners of the room. Electronic candles lit the central table, a focus in the low ambient lighting. Trask was near the head of the table. It appeared to Doc that he would have been pacing, had circumstances allowed. Instead, he twisted back and forth on his wall tether. Trask's minions were scattered about the room and Adair slouched at the other end of the room.

Pu'uala loped in and out of the room, securing serving dishes to the table. Bitton, the computer expert, was inserting wine servings into the covered glasses. Jernigan entered and joined Trask.

The Captain arrived and pulled himself over to Adair. Other crew members filed in. Doc glanced at the clock, surprised Brody was not here, front and center, for the celebration. This mission was the crowning achievement in his amazing career as a space entrepreneur.

"Shall we begin?" Trask held onto the head of the table.

Pu'uala looked up in surprise. "The Commander and Lt. Wolfsnare aren't here yet."

"Let's proceed anyway."

Doc pushed forward. "Major, that's not your place. Brody should be here."

Trask scowled, his knuckles whitening around the table edge. He glanced over at a minion, who nodded and moved in front of the door. Doc saw Adair straighten and drift back to the wall, partially merging with the shadows.

The Captain pulled upright at the table and faced Trask. "Major, please stand down. This is a celebration and we should all be here. We are transitioning--"

Jernigan had moved undetected behind the Captain and pushed him into a chair.

"What the—"

"Captain, I am relieving you of command," Trask said. The room grew silent, looks shooting between crewmembers.

The Captain attempted to push upright but was shoved back down by Jernigan. "By what right…"

"You can't," Doc interjected.

"This makes no sense. No sense at all," Bitton said.

"Quiet," Trask said. "Here's what's going to happen. I assume leadership, Jernigan will assist me. Our control will be switched from SpacAdmin to BlackRio Command immediately."

"No," Doc said. "Brody won't allow it."

Trask looked to Jernigan, who nodded. "Brody no longer has command. In fact, I personally ensured Brody would no longer be able to join us at all."

Doc looked over at Jernigan. "What have you done?"

Jernigan shrugged, his cool Teutonic gaze passing over her and moving on. "What I was told to do."

The room spun and Doc couldn't gain control of her orientation to the floor and walls. Pu'uala moved over and got Doc upright and secured.

"Wait, don't say anything more," Pu'uala whispered to Doc.

Bitton asked, "What's this about BlackRio? How can Cheney's organization take over from our command center?"

The Captain asked, "Where is Lt. Wolfsnare?"

Jernigan smiled. Trask responded to the Captain as he pulled himself along the table. "Lt. Wolfsnare is now with Brody in the freezer. Neither will be joining us again. Moving on."

Trask continued, "As I said, I am now in charge. SpacAdmin Huntsville is no longer providing oversight to this mission. We are now under BlackRio direction and our station will serve BlackRio interests."

Bitton spoke up. "You need all of us to run the ship and the station. All of us who are left. What if we don't want to…to work with you?"

"Ah, very good question. I do need co-operation from the remaining team, or at least most of you. And you, well, you all need oxygen."

Silence hung heavy in room as they individually processed the information. Doc worked through it first. She wiped the tears from her face. "Oxygen synthesis and control, responsibility of Brody, Lt. Wolfsnare and Trask. And SpacAdmin."

"Exactly Doctor. Now only I, and my contact at the BlackRio Command and Control, have that information. If you want oxygen, you work with me. If you want continued oxygen, I stay alive."

"This is completely unacceptable, Trask." the Captain struggled to rise. "Get your damn hands off me, Jernigan."

"On the contrary Captain, it is *all* that is acceptable to me." Trask flicked his hand and Jernigan placed a compressed air tool against the Captain's temple and pulled the trigger.

The Captain's body swung away from Jernigan, head leading, and smashed into the wall. The body rebounded and was snagged by Adair before it could carom further around the room. Doc slid her tether along the wall track to the Captain.

She reached out for him, but Adair showed her the Captain's misshapen cranium and shook his head. "Nothing to do for him."

Trask continued, "Your attention please. A couple of other items before we adjourn. Assume you are continuing in your present assignments until you hear otherwise. I will have sole access to Domestique Pu'uala's carnal duties. Doc, you will be available to Jernigan--"

"Are you out of your mind? I will not…"

Jernigan jerked Doc away from Adair and brought the air tool into the vicinity of her head.

Trask said, "You will. And the rest of you can sort things out among yourselves. Now please go to your respective primary stations. Pu'uala will bring food around if you want dinner. Adair, Bitton, take the body to the freezer."

"Hope there'll be enough room," Adair remarked.

"What was that, Adair? Do you have something to add?" Trask asked.

Adair moved out of the shadows to the table. "There's been enough said and done here, to my mind." He stared evenly at Trask.

Trask was the first to break away. "Fine. Everyone, dismissed."

* * * * *

Adair put down his fork. "Thanks Pu'uala. Despite everything, this really hit the spot. Shall we begin?"

Bitton, Adair and Pu'uala gathered around the end of the counter to analyze the situation. A plan began to formulate. Forty minutes passed, and then the signal light came on, summoning Pu'uala to the Commander's chamber.

"What the hell?" Bitton said.

"I imagine Trask has taken over Brody's chambers," Adair said.

"And now he wants to celebrate his success."

Adair said, "You don't have to go down there Pu'uala. There'll be another opportunity, another way." He looked furious. Bitton put a hand on his arm.

"You know this is the best time, before new patterns settle in, before Trask consolidates his hold on the ship and the people." Pu'uala moved closer, ran her hand along Adair's cheek. "You go do your part, and I'll do mine. Please be careful Adair. And you too Bitton."

"Grant. My first name is Grant, Pu'uala."

She leaned forward and placed a kiss on Adair's cheek. "Good luck, Grant."

* * * * *

"Enter."

Pu'uala balanced herself just inside the doorway, looking at Trask. "You called?"

"Yes, I'd like you to spend the evening here." He prepared two glasses of wine and passed one to Pu'uala. "Can you adjust to the new order of things?"

She dropped her gaze to the floor. "Yes, Trask. I work for the Commander, now that's you."

"Good. Come here." Pu'uala toed over to him and raised her face for a kiss. Trask claimed her lips and moved his hand to her breast. A moment passed, then Pu'uala moaned in apparent pleasure and she wrapped her arms around his neck.

"What's that?" Trask pulled her arms down and the sudden movement caused the couple to bounce ceilingward.

Pu'uala's eyes widened momentarily and she took calming breath. "You've seen Resta before, I wear him all the time." They both watched as the snake sluggishly undulated its grip on Pu'uala's forearm, and then quieted back down. Pu'uala relaxed.

"That sucker must like outer space. He's certainly grown."

"Yes. Can we get down from the ceiling?"

Trask wrapped his arm around Pu'uala and pushed off the ceiling, propelling them down onto the bed. He proceeded to strip her out of the duct-taped coveralls, uncovering non-regulation lingerie. He ran a finger under the lace edge of the overflowing bra cup. She shivered and bucked, causing Trask to fly off her.

"This is going to be more difficult than I realized," Trask said.

"Let's get you out of these awful coveralls, and I'll show you some tricks to make it easier." Pu'uala ran her hands over his chest and the snake raised his head.

"What's your hurry?"

"What's your reluctance, Trask?"

"None." He reached out and overbalanced again.

"Here, let me help you." Pu'uala eased him out of his clothes until he was clad only in a smattering of body hair on his chest, belly and groin. His erection sprang thickly out of its nest of curls, precum already glistening at the tip.

"Lie back. This will work better if we use a tether, okay?"

Pu'uala stroked his cock, stoking his arousal, waiting for his answer.

"Oh, yes." He groaned, straining toward her.

Pu'uala helped him position himself on the edge of the bed and found Brody's cuffs. She strapped one around his ankle. Then she leaned forward and licked at his cock and used her breath to ruffle the hairs covering his scrotal sac. His cock strained upward, angry and full.

She pulled herself up his body, rubbing her breasts as she went. She brought a side cuff up and captured his wrist, securing it to the bed. He pulled at it.

"What're you doing?"

"This way you'll be balanced, and there will be no unexpected floating away." She gave a twisting pull along the length of his shaft, eliciting a moan, and he relaxed.

"But no more."

"No more needed."

Pu'uala reversed herself and straddled Trask, the lace of her panties pulling taut over her plump sex. She rocked back so he could reach her with his tongue. After a swipe, she rocked forward out of his reach and pumped on his cock shaft. More precum pearled and trickled down the crown. Pu'uala rested her forearm along his belly, absorbing his warmth.

"Mmm, what's that?" Trask shifted his hips, lifting his cock higher in her hand.

Trask stilled. "I said, what is that? Hey, is it that damned snake? Get it off me!" He tried to buck.

"Keep still Trask." Pu'uala sat up and moved aside, showing Trask the tail of the snake slipping off her forearm as it stretched along his body, heading for his cock. "You were right, this is a bigger snake. And not my Resta. This is Nuoc. Not a benign species."

"What's going on?" Both watched the snake ripple on his torso as his erection shrank away. A line of glistening precum stretched from cocktip to belly."

"I want the code to unlock the OX files on the central computer."

"No."

"Let me explain. I am giving you a chance to tell me now. No, don't struggle, Nuoc will warm up that much faster. He's going to be attracted to the fluid coming out of your dick."

Trask stilled and watched the snake progress a bit further towards the warmth of his groin.

"If you don't share, I'll let Nuoc bite you."

"If I die, you don't get the codes."

"Oh, you won't die right away. There is about a four-hour window, a painful window, where anti-venom will still be effective. Once we pass that window, it will take another six hours to die, an agonizing time for your nerves to necrose and your organs to liquefy."

Pu'uala paused and they both looked at his cock shrinking away from the snake, ball sac shriveling.

"That's a good story, but I don't believe it. You couldn't do that to me, to anyone. And everyone will die if I take the OX codes and you can't reach SpacAdmin. Jernigan and Simon will prevent that."

"Will you give me the code?"

"No."

"Last time." She stroked the tail of the snake. "What's the code?"

"Fuck off."

Pu'uala got off the bed and grabbed a rod leaning against the wall. She pushed back to the bed and stood there. Then she used the rod to tug on his ball sac, flicking the head of his penis with its luring serum away from Nuoc. The snake lunged, capturing its prey with sharp, hollow fangs.

Trask screamed, a long sharp ululation, which even the high tech soundproofing couldn't absorb. Sweat broke out all over his body, drenching the sheets.

Pu'uala scooped up the expended snake and confined it in one of the containers on the desk. She turned back to the bed where his penis was already blackening and swelling.

"I'm going to be right back."

Blood was seeping from cracks in the penile skin when Pu'uala returned with Doc.

"Oh, my god. Pu'uala. What have you done?" Doc pushed to the bedside, surveying the bloated mass in Trask's groin. "The second snake?"

"Yes." She pulled a syringe from her pocket. "And this, Trask, is the anti-venom. Doc made it for me when we first got on the ship."

She dropped it in a box and locked it with her fingerprint. "Doc will administer this when we have the OX codes. If you give them to us in the next four hours. If you give them to us after that, well, we can still end your suffering quickly."

"Fuck you."

Pu'uala poked his scrotum and another scream rolled around the room. Doc pushed out the door, hand to her mouth.

"Watch your language. Doc will check on you every fifteen minutes. When you give her the code, I'll come unlock the syringe." She paused on her way out. "Oh and your guys think you are tucked up for the night with me. So don't expect rescue."

Out in the hallway, Doc bumped gently against the wall, waiting. She could still hear Trask in pain, even after Pu'uala pulled the door shut.

"Why didn't you tell me?"

"Because you wouldn't have gone along with the plan. You know Brody would have, he was ruthless. Now, to make you feel better, you can minister to Trask. Pain meds won't work very well because the nerves themselves are dying, but you can do what you need to."

"Oh, thanks for that."

"If you knock him out, he won't be able to give the OX codes and I *will* let him die. Come get me if he gives you the codes."

Pu'uala met Adair and Bitton back in the mess. Adair's left eye was swelling closed and blood seeped through a rent over his left shoulder. Bitton cradled his left wrist.

Adair leaned over to kiss Pu'uala. She said, "Welcome back Grant. And you Bitton."

Adair said, "Okay, status report."

Pu'uala explained the situation with Trask. Both looked a little pale when she had finished.

"You next Bitton," Adair ordered.

"Okay. We knew the Captain, Brody and Wolfsnare were down. Doc, Trask and the three of us are accounted for. Our other crew members are in their quarters."

Adair continued the report. "On our end, we locked Jernigan in a storage bin. Trask's contingent had anticipated we would make a try for the annex computers and were guarding the access." He gestured to his injuries. "However, they weren't successful. And their number has been significantly reduced."

Pu'uala moved closer to Grant. "Doc should be able to fix you both up right away."

Bitton picked up the story. "Once we reached the annex, I was able to fire up the computers and access my backdoor. After that is was just a matter of circumventing firewalls and whatnot to seize control of the OX."

Grant laughed. "He's being too modest. He was in a race with BlackRio command to gain control of the info. It was touch and go. Once we had the codes, we were able to patch back through to SpacAdmin and get them coordinates on BlackRio's command center. I don't think they will be heard from again."

He turned back to Pu'uala. "I hope things weren't too difficult for you with Trask."

Pu'uala hid her face, but said, "Oh no, I never even had to take my panties off."

"Good." He hugged her. "What's next?"

Pu'uala said, "I guess we administer the antidote to Trask." Just then the light came on, a summons to the Commander's chamber.

Doc met the group in the corridor, notepaper in hand. "Over two hours, I'm impressed. I wouldn't have thought he'd last fifteen minutes," Pu'uala said. "Let's get him fixed up."

At bedside, Doc administered the anti-venom through the IV line she had already established. Then she knocked Trask out.

"Will he make a full recovery?" Pu'uala asked, a note of hope in her voice.

"I don't know that I can save the penis and scrotum. But I can probably hook up an ureterostomy so the kidneys can drain. With the proper support, I think everything else will recover."

Bitton and Grant waited out in the corridor to receive the report on Trask's condition.

"Okay, everyone is accounted for. Let's gather at 23:00 hours to reassess," Grant said. "Right now, I'm going to take a wash and a nap. God, a lot has changed quickly. He offered an arm to Pu'uala. "Care to join me?"

"Of course, Grant."

Doc stared after the couple in amazement.

"Love, I just don't get it," Bitton commented as he turned away, heading back to his computers.

* * * * *

The survivors collected in the RecPod at the appointed time. They all looked to Grant.

"Good evening. This past day has been one of great change and loss, and, ultimately, triumph. We started as a party of 13 and now we are eight. We have passed the point of no return, so we must continue on. While we take stock and reorganize, I am assuming leadership of the mission. If anyone has objections, let's discuss them now."

The group looked around at each other. No one spoke.

Grant grinned. "It feels like that part in a wedding where you speak or forever hold your peace."

Doc raised her hand. "What about Trask? He's going to require a lot of care and resources for the next few months."

Grant sighed and looked around the table. All fidgeting and side conversations stopped. "Trask will not be a concern to us."

"But…" Doc said.

"I made my first unilateral decision as the ranking military onboard. Ill, Trask is a liability. Recovered, he is a danger. I eliminated that danger. For better or worse, I did not want any of you to have to make that choice. However, the disposition of Jernigan, we will discuss."

Pu'uala pushed over to stand next to Grant, silently offering him support. Doc looked away, but did not leave the table. The others offered various indications of support or kept silent.

Major Grant Adair addressed the group one final time on this transition night. "We were sent to establish a foothold on Mars. The remaining members of the Mayflower will have to do just that. To survive, we will have no room for sentimentality, only honor. We will pave the way for the waves of settlers who will bring with them luxuries, complexities and love."

He paused. "Happy Valentine's Day. Now go get some sleep. Tomorrow starts our adventure."

A Virgin Again
By Helena Stone

She waited, naked, in the middle of the room. Standing straight, with her shoulders pushed back and her gaze fixed on a spot a short distance in front of her feet. It felt as natural as breathing after all these months. Tanya's skin seemed to have come alive, while excitement and fear battled for dominance in her stomach.

"Today we're moving on to something new."

His voice took her by surprise. Even after all their time together he still managed to sneak up on her. How did this powerful man manage to move without making a sound?

Tanya glanced up at Caleb. "What, Sir?"

"That's for me to know and for you to find out and accept. Trust me. Follow my orders like a good girl and you'll discover soon enough".

Before she lowered her gaze again, Tanya got a glimpse of a heated grin spreading across Caleb's usually composed face.

"Touch yourself. Make yourself nice and wet for me."

This, at least, wasn't new. Over the four months they'd been together, Caleb had taught Tanya exactly what he expected from her.

Tanya's movements were almost automatic as she turned around and walked to the bed before climbing on top of it. Making sure to keep her ass in the air, she slowly crawled to the wooden headboard. She turned around and sat down with her legs spread in front of her. She loved this part of their sessions. The idea of his eyes on her as she explored her body with her hands was enough to kick-start the heat in her belly.

"Good girl. Beautiful." His voice seemed to flow over her skin, leaving goose bumps in its trail.

As he'd taught her, she started with her breasts. Tanya touched herself lightly. Fingers skimmed across her skin, trailed underneath her breasts and traced the outline. Her nipples tightened in anticipation of what she would be doing next. The urge to play with the hard tips burned through her, but Tanya knew better.

"Look at you." Caleb's voice had grown deeper, the first signs of lust betraying themselves. "Your body is like a finely tuned instrument, anticipating my every command. Move on."

It felt like a reward. Pleasure built as she moved her fingertips across her breasts to her now very sensitive nipples and rolled and pinched them. The harder they became, the more heat moved from her breasts to her vagina. The throbbing between her legs intensified, begging her to pay attention to it.

She'd tried to figure it out. Tanya had spent hours thinking about her body's reaction to his voice, the automatic urge to follow his orders and the instant need she felt whenever he was close. It always drove her crazy and tonight was no different. She wanted more, yearned for the sensations to intensify and squeezed her nipples hard.

The moan escaping her lips seemed to amplify the flash of desire rushing through her body. The pulsing sensation increased, begging her to touch herself, to move her hand to the heat steadily building in her center. She resisted the urge although she couldn't stop herself from squirming on the bed.

"Getting needy, girl? I know what you want. And you'll get it. You'll even get what you don't know you want yet."

She took a sneaky glance at his face. The heat smoldering in his eyes was gratifying and only served to make her more desperate for whatever it was he had in mind for her. She yearned to give herself more sensations, couldn't wait to bring herself to what she knew would be a powerful release. The desire to please Him was stronger however, an aphrodisiac in its own right.

"Beautiful." His voice soothed her, as it always did. "All mine to do with as I please. I can smell your need, girl. I know what you want."

"Please, Sir." Her juices were slowly coating her thighs and would soon leave a damp patch on the covers. Tension grew steadily in her core. She knew it wouldn't take more than a few touches to her clit to give her the release she so desperately needed.

"You beg so beautifully." Satisfaction sounded in his voice. "Touch your cunt. Get your fingers wet but keep away from your clit. Your orgasm is mine."

Months of training had taught her not to rush things. He wanted her to tease herself and she'd learned to enjoy the slow torture even while it continued to frustrate her. Her skin came alive as she slid a hand down. Her muscles quivered at the light touch flitting across her stomach. For a moment she considered ignoring his order. The memory of what had happened the last time she'd pretended to accidently touch her clit and made herself come, held her back. A week without orgasms was not an experience she wanted to repeat.

She was wetter than she'd expected and lost herself in the pleasure. She played with her lips, coating her fingers with her juices in the process.

"Get those fingers nice and wet and lick them. Taste yourself."

This was new. She'd licked her juices off his fingers, but never from her own. She glanced at him again, careful not to raise her gaze enough to catch his eyes. She saw his hand on top of the bulge in his tight black pants. The realization took her by surprise, as it always did. She had as much power over him as he had over her. He needed her submission as much as she desired to obey him.

She pushed two fingers between the lips of her pussy and coated them in her juices. The movement made her palm rub against her clit and the contact sent shudders through her body.

"Do not come. Lick those fingers."

Reluctantly she moved her hand to her mouth and, parting her lips, allowed her fingers entrance. She liked the taste of herself, always had. She would have preferred his fingers in her mouth. The taste and smell of his skin combined with her saltiness always brought her to a special kind of high. The idea of him watching her as she sucked her juices off her own fingers made up for the loss of that special treat.

"Good girl." The heat in his voice was unmistakable. "Keep your fingers in your mouth." He walked around the bed with his hand still on the pronounced bulge in his trousers before sitting down and reaching for her.

"Let's see how wet you are, my little slut." His fingers played with her juices, spreading them around before he touched her swollen clit.

The response was automatic. Desire took over and she pushed against his hand. He chuckled softly as he flicked, rubbed and stroked her sensitive bundle of nerves, making her squirm in front of him.

Just when she thought she couldn't take anymore, her Master moved his hand down and pushed. Tanya arched her back, searching for more penetration. She was so close. The pressure was almost unbearable and all the more exquisite for it. Tanya couldn't help herself. Her body had a mind of its own as it started moving against his fingers, searching for the touch that would take her over the edge.

"Not yet." It was a groan more than a voice and Tanya rejoiced. Caleb was as hot as she was. He'd explained it to her several times and still the moment took her by surprise. This was indeed an exchange. The power flowed between them. He demanded her submission and she gave it. In the process they both found exactly what they craved.

He withdrew his fingers from deep inside her and stood up. She watched as he opened his trousers and stepped out of them. The sight of his erect cock took her breath away, as it always did.

When he sat down and stroked between her pussy lips again, she anticipated an attack on her clit. Instead he moved his slickened digits lower. She could feel a trail of her own wetness going from her vagina to her ass. When she felt her own juices being rubbed against her asshole she stilled.

"Can you guess what we're going to be doing, Tanya?"

He gathered more wetness before he massaged her tight back passage again. She felt pressure against the hole. His finger forced her to open up to him and rubbed the moisture inside her. She tried to relax into the sensations but couldn't stop her body from fighting the intrusion.

"I know this scares you." His voice had gone soft and comforting. "I want you to trust me. I know this will be good for both of us. Relax. Surrender. Give this last innocent part of you to me. I want to have all of you."

The finger hurt while his voice soothed her. She wasn't sure what she felt. Her body seemed to want this intrusion as much as it worked to reject it. The pain was there and gone, leaving a new and exciting afterglow in its wake. When he pulled his finger back she sighed, but it wasn't relief.

"Do you trust me?" His voice brought comfort to her confused mind.

"I do, Sir. Always."

"Will you give yourself to me? Do you offer me your virginity?"

Virginity. She hadn't thought about it like that but it sounded right. This was like the first time all over again, both exciting and scary. Just as she had years ago, she found herself shifting between overwhelming want and fear of the unknown. But there was no doubt in her mind. If Caleb thought she was ready for this, if it was what he wanted, she'd trust him and give him what he asked for.

"You have all of me. Take what you want." Even as she spoke the words, Tanya knew they were true. She was his and didn't want to be anything else. Caleb had made sense of her confusion, had recognized all her hidden desires and answered them. He hadn't been wrong yet. Every new experience had been a revelation. She trusted him with her body, her mind, her heart and her soul.

When his wet finger found her hole again she pushed against the pressure, searching for a repeat of the painful pleasure she'd experienced a moment earlier. She groaned as he forced the tip of his finger past her muscle and deeper.

He didn't stop until the flat of his hand rested against her ass cheeks. He circled the finger inside her and Tanya felt a rush of heat running through her, making her pussy contract.

"I'm going to fuck you there. I'm going to push my big, fat cock all the way up your ass until you think you're going to tear in two." His voice got softer until it was barely a whisper in her ear. "And you will love it. I know you will." The combination of heat, dominance and desire in her Master's voice intoxicated her.

Tanya's ass clenched around Caleb's finger in a combination of fear and excitement. She wanted Caleb to take this virgin part of her. But she was afraid it would hurt too much. She didn't want to disappoint him but couldn't imagine anything other than pain would follow, once he entered her.

He slowly withdrew his finger from inside her and moved away. Grabbing her hips he turned her around until she was on her hands and knees, facing the headboard.

"Soon we'll do this face to face." She heard the package tearing and had no problem visualizing Caleb pushing the condom over his big cock. "I can't wait to see what you look like when I fuck your ass. Until then, this will be easier for you."

He placed a pile of pillows underneath her pussy before pushing her bum down, leaving her on her belly with her middle and ass raised. He spread her legs and grabbed a bottle from the bedside table. He squirted lube on his hand and she could hear him rubbing it all over his hard and sheathed penis. Another squirt and lube was massaged into her hole. Two slippery fingers pushed against her muscles, past them and into her ass. It hurt and Tanya tensed up.

"Easy baby, it's so much nicer when you go with it."

Tanya trusted Caleb and allowed his voice to relax her. He'd been right. The hurt turned into deep pleasure. She felt full. When he moved his fingers inside the rigid constraints, Tanya groaned. With every movement, his fingers were wider apart, stretching her further, giving her the combination of pleasure and pain that made her vagina clench.

Fear and discomfort retreated into the background as excitement grew. She wanted more and moved her body against the scissoring fingers inside her. She was shocked to discover she was on the verge of coming.

She nearly cried in frustration when Caleb withdrew his fingers.

"Remember the rules, girl. You don't come unless I tell you to. All of you is mine, including your orgasm."

"Please." She whimpered. "Please don't stop. Please, Sir."

He wasn't done with her. With one hand he spread her ass cheeks apart and she felt the tip of his throbbing cock against her hole. Fear tried to make its presence felt again. The fingers had been wonderful but his cock was much bigger. As the tip pushed into her, a burning sensation made Tanya scream and she tried to scramble away from Caleb and the intrusion.

"Stay still." His voice was soft yet didn't allow for disobedience.

Without removing his cock, Caleb placed a firm hand on her lower back and forced her to stay in place. Very slowly he started pushing. Inch by inch Tanya could feel his big, swollen cock entering her ass, stretching her beyond comfort, through pain to something she couldn't describe.

"Remember losing your first virginity, girl?"

"I do, Sir."

"Tell me about it." His voice forced her to focus on something other than the invasion.

"I was scared but he knew what he was doing." Memories flooded back. "He was like you. Older than me and in command, although he wasn't a Dom."

Caleb was the first man she'd fully submitted to. She'd played kinky games before but until she'd met her Master she'd never even considered surrendering to a man.

"Was he careful with you? Did it hurt?"

The ache in her ass combined with the pleasure it triggered made her stomach and leg muscles clench and relax. Her pussy soaked the pillows beneath her with her juices while her clit pulsed against the soft material. For a moment she forgot she'd been asked a question and was supposed to answer it.

"Tell me, girl. Did it hurt?"

"It did. But not for long. I remember the sharp pain shocking and scaring me, but disappearing again almost before I could process all the feelings." Tanya sighed. "I'd forgotten about that. The pleasure that followed is a much stronger memory now."

"Just as it will be tonight. A few moments from now, all you will feel is ecstasy beyond your wildest imagination."

* * * * *

He rested for a moment when he was all the way inside her. She was aware of every inch of his cock as her body tried to adjust. He'd never seemed this big and hard before.

"Are you okay?" The concern in his voice took care of her last reservations.

"Yes. I'm..." Tanya didn't know what she was. She was pain and pleasure, need and fear. She was... "I'm yours."

"Yes." His voice sounded gruffer as he pulled back until all but the tip of his cock had withdrawn again. "You are mine. All of you belongs to me."

He started slowly. Pushing in and pulling back in a steady but calm rhythm. Tanya lay still, too absorbed in the feelings he sent through her body to react.

As his movements became more forceful,l she discovered it was exactly what she needed. She moved with him, meeting him stroke for powerful stroke, actively searching the discomfort at the root of her pleasure. Every push created friction between her clit and the pillows, building the tension in her body. She was so close. Moving harder, she chased an orgasm she knew would be like none she'd ever had before.

"Do. Not. Come."

Tears of frustration escaped her eyes. She didn't think she'd be able to hold back but fought her body with everything she had. The need to not disappoint him stayed stronger than the urge to come, but only by an ever decreasing margin.

"Yes my, beauty. God, you feel so good."

Somewhere in the back of her mind a triumphant voice told her his control was as fragile as hers, but she couldn't think about it. She needed all her concentration to keep her body under control and still it wasn't enough. She knew she would reach the point of no return with or without his permission, despite her best efforts.

"Please. Sir, please. I can't. Too much. Please."

"Yes. Come for me. Now."

Her whole body tensed. The orgasm started all the way down in her toes. Fulfillment shuddered its way up her body, through her center where she clenched around his cock, until it came out of her mouth in a loud scream. But it didn't stop. As he kept on pounding in and out of her ass, her body continued to convulse until at last a loud groan told Tanya he was there as well. He pulled her close, her back against his chest, as his cock seemed to expand inside her before she felt the condom fill with his hot cum. His ragged breaths were almost as satisfying as her own orgasm had been.

Her body appeared boneless as she collapsed to the bed. When he withdrew from her she missed his filling presence. Her mind floated. She couldn't think. He moved away and she mourned his absence until he returned and pulled her close.

"My girl." Her foggy mind recognized the pride in his voice. "All mine. For always."

She snuggled closer before whispering, "Yours. All of me, for always, Sir."

You're Mine
By Gray Dixon

Lucien returned.

Not in a dream, and not even as a nightmare. No, he stood outside my apartment on West 22nd Street waiting for me to come to him, the whacked son of a bitch. That wasn't kind, but damn, didn't he get the message to leave me alone? This was the third time in a week he'd shown up on my doorstep, and the man really pissed me off. I should've called the police, but Lucien wasn't exactly a stalker, not really, not in the legal sense. An ex-lover? A lovesick psycho? I didn't know anymore. I was so damned confused about who I was after what I did and wondered where my life took a wrong turn.

How did I get this way? I was fucked up and unable to leave my studio flat without the fear he'd convince me I belonged to him. Belonged to him! Now there's some screwed up shit. My best friends would've told me to put a restraining order on his ass. After all, I was an attorney and knew the drill. Yeah, right? Tell my insatiable libido to forget him…or my heart.

Everything in my life changed a month ago. I'd dared to deny Lucien the one thing he wanted most. My body, mind, and heart I freely gave to him. Except…he wanted all of me, including that which I couldn't part with.

I'm not sure how I got out of his clutches, but I bear the scars to prove the pain I endured for the seven days before I made my way safely back home, the one sanctuary he dared not enter without permission. I may have to rethink my safety since he showed up again to test those boundaries. No doubt his intentions were to drag me back to his place. The thought of how he'd punish me for running away caused shivers to ripple up and down my spine.

The seven days and nights I spent in his dungeon were filled with pain, and dare I admit now—pleasure beyond anything I'd ever experienced in my life. I thought he was whacked at first. Ha! I was no different and tipped the scales as outlandishly whacked too. I still can't get a grip around the fact I succumbed to the man's power and persuasion without an ounce of resistance. I missed him, craved him, and had to find a way to deal with the almost uncontrollable need to be with him again. I question my sanity now, peering through the blinds, vacillating back and forth about my feelings for the man.

Pulling my attention from the window, I shifted the cord to close the outside world from my sight. I plopped down on the futon, leaning back on the down pillows.

"Think. How can I get out of this?"

Speaking aloud to no one, I began to believe I was losing control. Only the four walls of the small apartment on the third floor of a hundred year old home in the Chelsea area of New York City answered back with the creaks associated with older than dirt houses. I shook my head hoping to make the image of the man standing outside my building go away.

Hell! If that was only possible, I'd have done it ten times over the second I ran. Wasn't happening. If I hadn't surrendered to lust that night, maybe I wouldn't be debating with myself. Over *him*.

Lucien had the ability to melt ice with only his gaze, or turn me to a blubbering idiot with his soft baritone which was an aphrodisiac to my ears. A goner the second I saw him, I have to admit I was just as much to blame for my current predicament as he was.

The first time I saw him at the Clover Leaf Grill and Bar, he smiled at me as he closed the space between us. I nearly lost what little control I had remaining from staring at his beautiful body. Ten feet separated us, and I stood—paralyzed, physically and vocally. His lips turned up in a way that had my brain stumbling all over itself. For a second, I felt like a complete fool.

Knowing now what I didn't then, I think it was his aura of power that snared me. The bar went silent. I didn't see anyone or anything but him, and my body reacted with an uncontrollable desire to have him fuck me right there.

Yes, I was horny. I'll admit it now and even then I knew my weakness and inability to escape him. I couldn't help myself. Okay, so I'm weak, and a pitiful excuse of human flesh. Flog me.

Lucien stood inches away when he finally stopped stalking toward me. "Hello." Simple, direct and no embellishments of lousy pick-up lines was his way. His voice was deep and sensual, with a slight hint of a rasp. Blood rushed from my brain leaving me fumbling for some semblance of intelligent and coherent words in response.

Swallowing convulsively, I tilted my head back to stare up at my soon to be lover and master. My knees trembled and nearly buckled.

The words on the tip of my tongue finally stumbled out, but I couldn't stop gawking at his mouth with the way they pursed together with the last vowel sound he made. God, I was a hopeless case and it didn't help he was close enough that his cock pressed against me.

Thinking about his heat against my body that first time brings back the same kind of shivers I felt then. I thought I'd lose all decorum right there in the bar, much like now. *Run to him* my irrepressible lust said. Deal with his sadistic nature, no matter how psychotic. My friends would've disowned me. If they knew what I'd done with Lucien, the gossip could get me booted out of the firm. Not that it was much, other than the kinky way we got off with one another, and yeah I may be complaining at the present, but at the time I didn't care. In hindsight, my friends probably didn't notice how crazy I acted around a perfect stranger. I remembered scanning the room to see where they were, and quickly discovered they were fully engrossed in conversation with other patrons.

Somewhere in between checking out my friends and returning attention to Lucien, he whispered in my ear. "You're beautiful, so sweet and innocent." He traced my mouth with the pad of his finger, outlining my lips and gooseflesh blossomed on my skin under his touch. I knew then I was in deep kimchee.

I couldn't remember experiencing that kind of response to a man. I fell hopelessly in lust with every six foot plus inch of male specimen. He smelled so incredibly masculine with the musky cologne invading my space that I was instantly swept away in the moment, falling deeper under his spell. The masterful man reeled me in with little effort. I didn't know at the time how or why I let someone I'd barely met tease me and take advantage of my general awkwardness when it came to meeting guys.

Lucien moved closer, if that was possible, touching my arms, stroking his palms over my thighs and ass as I backed up to the bar. If anyone saw how he pawed at me, they didn't let on. He continued to talk with his deep, yet soft voice laying out all the pleasures he could deliver.

I can't remember much about the remainder of the evening at the Clover after the first tender brush of his lips against mine. He said he wanted to give me a private tour of his special place. Yeah, heard that line before, too many times, but whether it was the couple of drinks I'd consumed or his intoxicating presence, or that sensual kiss that made my toes curl, my mind said follow him to the ends of the earth if he asked.

"Come with me, little one. I'll protect you, care and nurture you. No harm will ever happen to you. You're mine to cherish forever." His breathy voice whispered against my ear as he fisted his hand in my hair. "You're mine, and I'm not letting you go." His words resonated in the room, taking me captive with his seduction.

Every red flag and alarm went off in my head when he said that. What the hell was I thinking? Obviously, I wasn't. With my fingers interlaced with his strong grip, he practically dragged me from the bar and down the street. I didn't even get an opportunity to tell my friends I was leaving. Another stupid thing I did that night.

What seemed like a good thirty minutes later, we walked up one street and turned onto another. My memory is hazy about the little details. We passed many people on the uneven paved sidewalks, and a number of cars traveling along the narrow streets honked horns along with the red of brake lights lighting up the path. We finally came to a row house on East 41st Street, but I couldn't remember the address today if I tried.

Upon entering the dark residence, he led me to a door and down an unlit hallway. The dim light from wall sconces hung on the walls cast odd shadows over the surface that seemed like stone. I began to feel as if I'd fallen back in time and walked within the corridors of a medieval castle. For the first time, my stomach roiled with fear. How stupid could've I have been to go off with a stranger I'd just met at a bar and follow blindly to a dark house in a part of the city known for weird-ass stuff? All the ghosts and voodoo and other scary things—murders, fights, or muggings were enough to keep anyone off the streets after certain hours of the night. There always was the chance of running into a serial killer, right? Well, I just knew I was about to become a statistic and had to quickly figure out how the heck I'd get out of the mess.

Despite my fuzzy, paranoid thinking, I decided he was a little on the kinky side and taking me to his dungeon as we walked down a staircase. A basement? Really? The idea made me laugh inwardly, but hey, I was into that and it might be fun and a nice way to spend a couple of hours of mind-blowing, destressing sex. A spanking or two with some bondage thrown in for extra spice always made for a fun night. I've attended a number of BDSM clubs over the years, not many, but enough to know people were varied in their kinks. I've also dabbled privately with a few guys but nothing on a long-term basis. The fact that I brushed aside the possible serial killer scenario in favor of submitting to Lucien stuns me.

The world of dominance and submission is a very personal one. Trust is essential and the objective for both partners must be respective growth and joy. I didn't know if I normally would consider diving into the deep end of the lifestyle, but every now and then playing made me feel good and complete somehow. At the time, having a nice intense flogging followed by a good fucking by Lucien sounded exactly what I needed. For Lucien, I decided in a split second to go along with staying and playing. Did I mention I'd been acting stupid all night?

One big problem with that crazy plan was that it was a bad one at the start and I knew it. I couldn't fight my way out of a wet paper bag in the condition I was in—one too many cocktails and celibate for six months, a volatile situation. I skimmed my free hand along the walls. They were concrete, cold and sweaty. I began to feel like we were entering a 1950's bomb shelter.

Finally, the end of the claustrophobic corridor came to an open doorway. Lucien stopped and turned to face me. "Close your eyes."

Yeah, I was certifiable at this point if I did as he asked. I must have been on drugs or something because I obeyed without reservation. I was in the dark and dank chambers of a possible maniac killer and blindly following his orders. *Please, someone help me* I screamed inwardly, but a lot of good that would've done for my situation. I was so far down the rabbit hole I couldn't turn back if I wanted to. Lucien was what I wanted and I'd decided I'd do what he commanded just to be with him. Yeah, I closed my eyes and that was the second stupid thing I did that night. Or, was it the third? Did it really matter anymore? If I were the judge, I'd have declared me legally insane.

"Very good," he'd said. "Now, hold my hand and walk forward."

I shuffled my feet, feeling uneasy but kept my eyes shut. I was so aroused, my heart raced, and adrenaline ramped up inside, at such a high rate I swore I'd come out of my skin because of the anticipation. After about ten steps, we stopped and he released my hand.

"Don't move and keep your eyes closed."

What seemed like minutes, he finally said, "Open."

I did, allowing my eyes to adjust to the dim interior. My eyes widened at the sight slowly coming into view. We were alone and Lucien sat upon a throne, actually more like an oversized tufted leather chair with ornate gilding. He had a generous length of rope coiled around his arm. I didn't want to think about what he planned to do with it, or with me. I nonchalantly glanced around the room to show I wasn't worried.

The room was small, but not cramped. Black walls, ceilings, and floors darkened the atmosphere. The place was in fact decorated like a no-shit dungeon, a sadist's pleasure house, a scary-ass torture chamber I found exciting as much as frightening. A padded bench was situated to my left, the ideal height for bending over to take a good spanking. My insides did anticipatory flip-flops at the thought. Across the room a St. Andrew's cross stood tall and ominous. The black paint shined to a high polish and the metal rings and chains gleamed in the low light. The thought of being restrained and at the mercy of Lucien's whims made my breath catch.

Gothic clothing, most of it black or white adorned a wall, almost as if it were art. In the opposite corner, various leather objects were piled on top of a long wooden table. On closer inspection, I made out a bullwhip, a leather-covered wooden paddle, velvet-padded handcuffs, and other various sex toys.

I closed my eyes for a moment, took a deep, measured breath and then opened my lids to see him staring back. He assessed me, gauging whether or not I showed fear, anxiety, boredom or excitement. To be honest, I don't know how I looked but I sure as hell felt everything at once.

When I came to my senses, I should have yelled at him to let me go and promise not to say anything to anyone. Or, I could have taken another approach and called him nasty names along with a few choice expletives just to see how far I could intimidate him into not hurting me. Those hair-brained ideas went right out of my head when the wicked grin formed on his lips. My body wasn't buying any of the bullshit my brain put out, anyway.

"Don't be frightened, little one. Come here." His tauntingly masculine voice echoed off the stone walls, demanding obedience from the soft yet harsh tone. The tall, dark and scary man stood, tossing the rope onto the seat of the overly garish chair.

I obeyed his command, without reservation, and stepped forward the five feet or so between us. I was completely screwed and had to play along until I figured out how to get away or find myself the victim of one psycho serial killer.

"Very good." He grabbed my jacket, and for one brief moment, I thought he'd kiss me, but he didn't.

No, instead he began to strip me. First, the jacket in one smooth motion, followed by unfastening the buttons of my silk shirt and I just stood there letting him. After he removed my shirt, he retrieved the rope. He motioned with his finger, indicating he wanted me to turn around, which I did without hesitation. He pulled on both my arms, yanking them behind my back. I tried to fight back knowing instinctively he had plans to restrain me, eliminating any chance to get away. The grip around my arms only tightened with my feeble, futile struggle.

"Don't," he murmured close to my ear. "If you fight me, I promise you'll soon come to regret your actions."

I relaxed as best I could and the hemp was wrapped around my wrists, binding them together. The knots and wrapping worked their way up to my elbows. I couldn't move. The last vestige of dignity and chance for escape was gone.

When Lucien finished with his handiwork, he turned me around. "You look very pretty, little one," he said, cupping my face in his palms. "I knew you were the one the moment I saw you. I should've been more careful bringing you here. I normally test my targets before—"

"Target? You *are* a serial killer," I shouted, struggling with every ounce of strength I had left.

"Shhh," he whispered, holding firm on his grip of my face. "I promise you, I'm not."

I wasn't sure to believe him or not and opened my mouth to give him a few choice words. Before I got one syllable out, he moved quickly, crushing his lips to mine, making all those four-letter words catch in my throat. The power of the kiss caused our teeth to collide, and the sting produced from slicing my lower lip made me grimace in pain.

Lucien freed our embrace long enough to mumble an apology, but then gently brushed another kiss against mine. His lips were so cool, but they were soft too. He applied more pressure and then slid his tongue along my lower lip. I jerked when he hit the nick from our clash of teeth. His hand lowered to the front of my neck, grasping firmly and holding me still. His other hand slid around the back of my neck. He drew me closer as his grip pulled the short hairs at the base of my skull. "I'll be gentle with you. For now."

I laughed. In hindsight, I should've controlled my nervousness and kept my mouth shut. But, would I have listened? Probably not. "Do you think you'll get away with this?"

"Oh, little one." My captor clicked his tongue in admonishment. "Do you think I care if I do or not?"

Before I knew what to say, his tongue eagerly tangled in my mouth. The hand around my neck slid further down and over the side of my torso, slipping around to the back and pressed against the small curve above my ass. Lucien's assault on my mouth continued, kissing me to the point I thought I became one with him. I could taste the lingering coppery traces of blood from the nick on my lip. I should have known then something was up with him because he didn't seem bothered in the slightest about sharing blood. Despite the fact I'd been out of practice for a good six months, the evidence pressing into my lower abdomen proved he was very excited, enjoying our interlude.

Lucien eased his mouth away from mine and trailed more kisses across my cheek and began nuzzling my neck. His hands tightened at the back of my head and buttocks. My skin prickled with goose bumps skittering up and down my spine.

"What are you doing to me?" I murmured.

He nipped at me. "What I wish. Are you in pain?"

No, I wasn't, but I was confused, conflicted with my feelings.

"Do you want me to stop?" he whispered against my skin.

I couldn't do anything except shake my head, slowly, stunned into silence.

He traced the center of my back with his fingernails, the sharpness mixed with sensuality sending me further into the rabbit hole. "And what of this? Shall I stop?"

I was so light headed with arousal, my breathing changed to panting. "No" The word hissed out in a whisper.

He trailed his hands from my ass, to my hips, to my abdomen, and then he reached between my legs, he rubbed the crotch of my pants. The contact turned to kneading of the flesh under the material and brought on a sweet, deep throbbing. The pangs of desire spread out to every nerve ending in my body.

"And you're enjoying this," he whispered. "Right?"

Did he have any idea how right it was? He was the incarnation of all my major masturbatory fantasies, but I just never had a face to those dreams. He'd take me naked, half-dressed, in the open, or a dungeon, covered in heated sweat with him fucking me in an alley or my bed. I didn't care how, perverted or vanilla.

Lucien let out a low groan to match mine as he slid his fingers past the waistband of my pants. When his lips grazed the side of my nape, I felt a nick on my flesh which became more painful. He sucked and licked on the skin of my neck, drawing it into his mouth. The strange sensation was startling and yet so right in an erotic way.

Unfortunately for me, I couldn't even pretend that I wasn't aroused having him so close. I swear I heard his heart beat along with mine. His fingers inched deeper into my pants. He held me so tight against him, I begged him to release my hands and loosen the zipper to bare myself to him. I'd shivered so hard I thought I'd fly apart if he didn't take me then and there.

To no avail, I took several deep breaths to calm my racing heart. The adrenaline surging through my veins spiked. Blood pounded in my ears. A wave of dizziness swept over me. My nipples hardened, and the arousal growing caused a moan to escape my lips from the intense sensations building. I squirmed as my body continued to fill with heat and desire.

Again, I should've known something seemed amiss because of my overwhelming need to have him thrust inside me with everything he had. I ached deep inside. Maybe that's what kept me frozen in place instead of pushing Lucien away and running out of there as fast as I could. Curiosity, insanity, or something else?

At the time, I shirked the arguments for getting the hell out of his clutches. For another reason, I struggled against the ropes binding my arms. God, I wanted to run my palms over his skin.

"Shit," Lucien growled.

It was the only warning I got before what happened next. To this day, I don't remember how Lucien moved so fast and was at my neck again, burying his fangs into my throat. At first, I let out a loud yell, but the shock faded and the pain turned to pleasure. Sweet and delicious pleasure, the kind that instinctively had me humping Lucien's thigh wedged between my thighs. The sensation was amazing. Logic screamed run away, but my body ignored the pleas. Instead, I could only struggle to free my arms to escape his embrace. Lucien groaned against me.

Then something had changed in the caress. The power of his sucking didn't seem right, and my mind comprehended the pain. For a few precious seconds I was confused, with my brain trying to put together the pain and pleasure from whatever the hell Lucien did. I let out a long breath, groaned, and opened one eye. Biting! The freaking weirdo bit me hard.

I summoned every ounce of strength I had and rammed my knee into his groin and he released his hold. "You fucking bit me, you psycho killer!"

Lucien smirked as if he didn't care. "You loved it," he'd pointed out, crossing his massive arms across his broad chest.

"What the fuck?" I managed to scream aloud when I saw the blood. "No I didn't." The demand was weak to my ears.

Lucien stepped closer, blood dripped from the elongated fangs protruding from his mouth. "Did I hurt you?" Lucien asked as if everything was cool between us.

"What the fuck just happened?" My gaze shifted from his mouth to his eyes. Fuck, I'll never forget the first time I saw the red glow. I wanted the green ones I fell for back at the bar. "What did you do psycho?"

"What do you think? Please stop calling me a psycho. I don't have a mental illness." He stepped even closer. "Let me fix your wound."

I stared in confusion and horror. The nauseating panic filling my stomach churned to a pitch fire in my gut. I felt weak and my legs became like rubber, almost giving out from under me. "Who are you?" I managed to ask.

Lucien's bright green eyes returned but there still was an eerie glow to them, and then he offered up the most evil grin I've ever seen on anyone. "You know who I am. I'm Lucien Kushnir. What I am has been lost in translation over the millennia. I've been given enumerable names in every culture around the globe, but the names were insignificant and didn't truly describe me. I despised the term demon, or devil. But the more recent kind of description of vampire—the sparkly kind, makes me cringe. Today, I prefer my birth name of Lucien. Welcome to my realm, little one."

I shuddered so hard, my teeth rattled. "What? You are a whack job? Are you one of those Goth types who think they're vampires? What do you want with me?"

"No, another one of those weird human beliefs I'm afraid. Do not be afraid of me. I told you I won't harm you. I'm sworn to protect. You're mine."

A drop of blood splattered on the floor, a sting rose on my neck. I struggled to free my hands, but to no avail. "What do you call that? You tried to have me for a midnight snack. Let me out of these ropes."

"No. I want to give you more pleasure than you ever could imagine. Just name it and your wish is my command."

"Okay, I'll bite. What does it cost me, my soul?" I snorted the last part, knowing deep down my predicament wasn't funny. I then laughed harder, not because what he said was funny. I usually break into hysterical laughter when I'm scared. Believe me, the tingling my body felt wasn't from arousal anymore. I hoped I only imagined what he said about being some kind of demon. They didn't exist. Hell, vampires didn't either, which meant Lucien had to be some demented dude on the prowl for his next kill, crazy as the Mad Hatter. I obviously fit the bill. The target he stated earlier.

Lucien's brow pinched, but he remained silent.

As much as I tried to ignore it, and hoped I was wrong, and went so far as wish for it to not be true, deep down I knew what he admitted was true. "How about you let me go and I'll forget everything you just told me." I didn't know how I'd get away considering I was half naked and my arms were tightly bound behind me. I was defenseless. "I won't tell anyone. I swear."

He glared at me like I pissed him off. "You came to me willingly. I've not lied to you. I'm an immortal warrior who enjoys blood, sex and not necessarily in that order. When I say I will not harm you, I mean it. If warranted, however, a bit of punishment might happen."

That scared the shit out of me. Punishment could mean something different to me than him. The difference between a hard spanking to edgy knife play. "Mmm, yeah, sure. What I believe is you think you're some creature who likes blood and I'm pretty sure I'm standing in the company of a deranged person in need of serious help." In hindsight, I probably shouldn't have called him that because, based on his expression, I quickly realized I was in deeper shit.

"Oh, I picked well. You will be such a pleasure to play with and do my bidding." That damned wicked sexy grin combined with his husky voice got to me, again.

"What do you mean?" I managed to squeak out.

"What do you think? I want you to submit to me, freely and completely. I'm also what you might call a vampire but I don't want your soul, only your blood and body. I'm not interested in killing you either. I like you."

He liked me? Really? I'd taken a few more steadying breaths and swallowed the lump in the back of my throat. The unrelenting and overwhelming magnetism exuding from every pore of his exquisite body sucked me back into his vortex. I couldn't resist the pull, no matter how hard I tried. I needed him. I couldn't speak at first and nodded.

He kept staring at me, making me even more confused.

Torn between being scared shitless and more aroused than I'd been with anyone before, I managed to speak. "Don't you think we should negotiate before we get down to business. Maybe a safeword?" I tried to stall for time, but my argument was kind of pathetic.

"Submit to me, little one. You can use whatever word you want, but you can't fool me or yourself because I know you want this."

Lucien's muscular frame pressed against me. He was right. I couldn't deny my arousal and need for him any longer. The man towered above me, the top of my head tucking comfortably under his chin which seemed so weird at the time. I'm not short by any means, but anyone would be when compared to this giant of a man. His body touched all the right spots on me and I squirmed in a half-hearted attempt to get free from the ropes in order to touch him. I longed to run my hands over the man's chest, and more.

The smell of incense burning mixed with leather, all with the promise of primal and addictive sex wafted around us. Beneath those scents, Lucien's distinct maleness loomed. I couldn't resist the dominant control.

The leisurely trace of his fingertips down my naked chest, along the hard muscles of my stomach, grabbed my total attention. He stopped at the waist of my jeans as before. I thrust my hips forward into the touch. I was desperate for him to go lower. The move only resulted in Lucien chuckling, and instead of going where I wanted him to go, he went higher. He lightly caressed my cheek and jawline, brushing his thumb over my bottom lip. I shuddered. He knew exactly how to use those hands. All thoughts of running away, psycho or not, deserted my head. No matter how hard I fought against succumbing to him, I couldn't help but tilt my neck into his soft touch and possibly feel the tug on my body with his blood kiss again.

Lucien's gaze captured my blurry-eyed one and gave me a sensual smile. He trailed his hand lower, the way I wanted and yearned for. I arched into his caress. The man did his best to destroy my last bit of control.

"Submit to me, little one, and I'll give you everything you desire."

I did give in to the promise, but I didn't realize what those seven days would do to me. I reassured myself I'd survive. Shaking the memories off, I rose from the futon and wandered back to the window. Carefully, I raised one of the narrow slats of the blinds to peek out.

Lucien wasn't there, not on the sidewalk across the street or anywhere else from what I could see. The last time I saw him, an hour ago, the vampire stared up at the window. There were a few parked cars along the sidewalk. Maybe he hid behind them. Either this was a good thing, or maybe not. I didn't know whether to be afraid or relieved.

Sadness wrapped around me the moment I turned from the street scene.

The week I spent under Lucien's command had been seven days of exquisite pain and pleasure. What I couldn't deal with was giving my life for him. He pushed me to my limits each day, demanding I join his world of existence. I couldn't submit to that one thing. As much as I was smart enough to know this couldn't work, and tried to deny my feelings for the man's control over me, I had to find a way to break his hold. He'd become my drug of choice, my addiction to blissful wholeness.

Yeah, I've had some kinky sexual escapades over the years, but turning into a vampire didn't exactly ring my bell as something I wanted to do. What I definitely knew was submission to another was a gift. I wanted the man, no denying that. If not for the fact he wanted me to be a blood-sucking creature of the night or his meal ticket, I could see myself with him for a long time. I have to wonder now if the reason that I had an uncontrollable desire to be with him was because he used some kind of vampire power to persuade me.

I had to suck it up and confront him, but the meeting had to be in public. I wouldn't have the fortitude to fend off his advances if we were alone. He needed to earn my respect and trust, not demand it, and I know that's what he would do. Demand and control the situation. No, I had to agree to see him in public.

The phone rang, ripping me from my thoughts.

The shrill ring sounded again and I decided to let the answering machine take the call.

By the fourth ring, the click followed with my recorded voice greeting the caller. Then the message played.

"You're mine, Adam."

A Hart for Talia
(An excerpt)
By Roz Lee

Nick splashed cold water on his face, then braced his palms on the granite countertop. *Damn.* Bringing Talia here was a mistake. But what choice did he have? She couldn't stay in Hart's single fleabag motel. Not that it was an option anyway. It was Valentine's Day. Every farm hand for 50 miles around would be in town looking for a good time. The motel would be booked up, and he doubted anyone staying there would be getting much sleep. The walls were paper thin, and the headboards were the old-fashioned kind—not bolted to the wall.

    He'd noticed her two weeks ago when she'd first shown up at the gym. There weren't many new people in Hart, and none of them looked like Talia Summers. Classy. Hot. He wanted desperately to order her to her knees, to see her look up at him with those blue eyes of hers. He wanted to hear, "Yes, Sir," from her heart shaped lips. He wanted to own her body. There was something about her that called to him. That haughty air she put on hid something. *Passion.* When she submitted, she'd do it completely, beautifully. He was sure of it.

    He willed his body to cooperate then went in search of food. Living so far from town, cooking was a life skill he grew up knowing.

    He pulled a tray of leftover lasagna from the refrigerator and popped it in the microwave. When the house became his, one of the first things he'd done was modernize the kitchen.

    Leaning against the counter while the casserole dish spun around in the microwave, Nick glanced at the gleaming countertops and appliances. His mother would like the new look, if he could ever pry her away from sunny Florida to see it. She would like Talia Summers, too. She probably wouldn't approve of the things he was thinking about doing to Ms. Summers, but he couldn't worry about that. He'd come to terms with his sexual inclinations years ago. In college, he'd discovered his natural instinct was to dominate, and there wasn't anything sexier than a woman who trusted him to see to her pleasure.

The microwave dinged, snapping him back to reality. He removed the dish, put a few bakery rolls on a plate. While the rolls warmed, he pulled two water bottles from the refrigerator and set them and the lasagna on the table he'd eaten at all his life. Then he went in search of his houseguest.

"Any luck?" he asked from the doorway.

"Some." She looked up from the notes she was making on the pad he kept next to his computer. "Tomorrow is going to be a busy day. I don't know what I'm going to do."

"About?"

"Well, my laptop for one. All my research is on it."

"It's backed up somewhere, isn't it?"

"Yes, of course it is, and its password protected, but still. It's sensitive material, and my company isn't going to be pleased to know it's out there somewhere."

Nick straightened. "Could the thief have been after your research?"

She stood and paced away from the desk. Nick went hard just watching her body move in the tight workout gear. "I don't know. Maybe. But they took everything. If they wanted the research, all they needed to take was the laptop."

"That would be obvious then, don't you think?"

"I guess you're right." She stopped her pacing in front of the desk and bent, placing her palms flat on the desktop. She hung her head between her shoulders, but all Nick could see was her ass in those tight spandex pants. "I'm screwed."

If only. Maybe she needed something to take her mind off her troubles. He had to admire her strength. She hadn't crumbled and shrieked like most women would when she saw what had been done to her car. She hadn't shed a tear for the lost items. So far, she'd been in complete control. Maybe it was time to relinquish some of that control to someone else.

Nick closed the distance between them. He stopped short of

pressing her over the desk and grinding himself against her. "That could be arranged," he said as his hands settled on her hips.

She froze. Electricity crackled between them.

"Two options here," he said into the silence. "You say, 'No, Sir,' and we go eat leftover lasagna and forget this ever happened, or you say, 'Yes, Sir', and I take you, right here and now." He stroked her hips, admired the firm muscles there. "The choice is entirely yours."

A tremor shook her body from nape to toe, but she remained where she was. He took that as a good sign. "Take your time, Talia. Let me tell you what I'm going to do to you if you say yes. Do you want to know?"

Her head bobbed. Not a good enough response for what he was asking. "Say yes if you want me to tell you how I'm going to fuck you."

A moment of silence. "Yes."

"Ahh, that's a good girl." He stroked his hands over her hips, once, twice, admiring the feel of her curves, imagining the firm skin beneath the fabric. "First I'm going to peel these pants off you, right here where you stand. Then I'm going to take my time examining all the possible places I could stick my dick in you. When I'm through, I'm going to pick one, and fill it with my cock. I'm going to take you, standing here, bent over the desk my ancestors have been fucking on for generations." His fingers trailed over her hip, then down the sharp cleft of her ass, all the way to the damp spot between her legs.

Shit. She was wet all ready. "Yes, Sir or no, Sir, Talia."

Talia shivered as his fingers found the wet spot she knew was between her legs. *Damn.* There was no point in trying to deny her attraction for the man now. She considered her options. Lasagna, or sex with the hottest man she'd seen in forever. And it had been even longer since any man had wanted her in such a blatantly dominant manner.

Over a desk, from behind.

He wanted an answer, not just a yes or no, but a submissive one. *Yes, Sir.* The response played through her head, formed on the tip of her tongue. She opened her mouth.

"No, Sir."

His hands slipped from her, and cool air replaced the heat from his body as he stepped back. Talia pushed up from the desk and spun around, dropping to sit where her hands had been. A muscle ticked in Nick's jaw, but his hands hung loose. You could learn a lot about a man by the way he took sexual rejection. Nick, though not totally unaffected, took it well. He was in complete control. Good to know.

"The lasagna is getting cold." He turned and disappeared down the hall. Talia followed him to a giant eat-in kitchen, typical of old farmhouses. This one, while still retaining the rustic feel, was thoroughly modern. Nick was setting plates on a table big enough to seat a family of twelve.

She pulled out a chair and sat. "I'm sorry, Nick."

He placed silverware in front of her, then took his seat across from her. "No problem. I misread the situation." He scooped lasagna onto a plate and handed it to her. "I should apologize."

"No need." She waited until he'd filled his own plate before she took a bite. Someone knew how to make lasagna. "Wow. This is good."

"Thank you."

She looked up in surprise. "You made this?"

He shrugged. "It's my mother's recipe."

"You cook, you're the Sheriff, your family has been here for generations, you like dogs, you live alone. You're sexually dominant. What else do I need to know about you?"

"That about covers it," he said between bites. "I also don't force women, and I'm rarely wrong about one's submissive nature."

Talia brought her napkin to her lips and dabbed. "You weren't wrong tonight, Nick." He raised his eyes to hers. "I thought we needed to get to know each other a bit more, establish some ground rules before we get down to what we both want." His gaze had turned from curious to ravenous. "And I was hungry," she added.

"Ground rules," he said. "You're right. Let's discuss them."

"I only submit sexually. I won't be your slave, except to your sexual needs. I insist on monogamy as long as we're together. If that's a problem, then we won't be together. Safe sex, always. I have a safe word, and if I use it, all play stops. No questions asked."

"Bondage?"

"Within reason."

"Pain?"

"I'm particularly fond of spanking. I haven't experienced

anything else. I'm open to it, but I insist we discuss it beforehand."

"Discretion? I don't think the good citizens of this county have any right or need to know about what goes on inside my home."

"Granted." She nodded in agreement.

"You'll wear my collar."

"Only during play…for now. If things work out between us, then I'll consider wearing it full-time."

"Agreed. Anything else?"

"No. I don't think so. You?"

"I'm done. Take your clothes off."

His voice brooked no argument. Talia pushed her chair back and moved away from the table where Nick could see her. Excitement coursed through her blood as she began to peel away the layers of her clothing. It had been a long time since she'd submitted, but she remembered to cast her eyes to the floor. She wished she could see Nick's face when he saw her for the first time. Would she please him? She already knew he desired her, she'd felt his erection pressing against her backside when he had her over the desk. Her shirt hit the floor first, followed by her pants.

"Look at me, Talia."

Her breath caught in her lungs when she saw the raw need in his eyes.

"Now the bra. Keep your eyes on me." She did as instructed and was rewarded by the hunger she saw there. "Take off the panties and spread your legs for me."

When she stood naked before him, he asked, "What's your safe word?"

"Petunia." He smiled and repeated the word.

"Okay, then." He turned his chair to face her. Her eyes drifted to his lap, and his tented workout shorts. She'd never seen him in anything but workout gear, but she knew she'd melt at his feet when she saw him in uniform. "Eyes down now, Talia."

"Yes, Sir." She studied his sneakers. Clean, but well worn.

"Come kneel between my legs."

Talia did as he said, desperate now to touch him, to have him touch her. She remembered the way he'd described taking her in the office, and almost wished she hadn't said no. If she'd let him fuck her then, she wouldn't be aching now.

"This is the way I want to see you every day—naked, on your knees, waiting for me to give you pleasure." He stroked her hair gently. "You're a beautiful woman, Talia, and I promise to see to your pleasure often. This is my pledge to you. In return, you will allow me to take my pleasure with your body. Do you make this pledge to me?"

"Yes, Sir. My body is yours."

"Very well. Return to my office and wait for me there—on your knees."

Time passed slowly, and even on the plush rug, Talia's knees began to hurt as she waited for Nick to come to her. He hadn't specified where she should kneel, so she'd chosen the center of the room, facing his desk with her back to the door. Warm air came from the floor vent across the room, but a draft from the window on the other side had her nipples painfully erect. Anticipation of what Nick would do when he arrived had her pussy aching and wet. Her skin was cold, but her insides were ablaze. She kept her hands to her sides, palms open and forward, her eyes focused on a Texas star carved into the bottom edge of the desk.

It seemed like forever before she felt Nick's presence behind her. He crossed the room and stood behind her. "I like seeing you there, waiting for me," he said. "Have you changed your mind?"

"No, Sir. I haven't changed my mind. My body is yours to command."

His bare feet and legs came into her line of vision. "Good. Earlier, I promised to examine every possible place I might fill with my cock, but before I do that, I think it's only fair you see what you have agreed to accept into your body." Her heart pounded. She'd fantasized more than she wanted to admit about what Nick looked like naked, and now she was going to find out. "Look at me, Talia."

Her gaze traveled up the length of his legs, liberally dusted with dark hairs, to his cock that stood at attention from a well-groomed groin. He was big. As big as any man she'd ever seen, and bigger than any she'd ever had inside her. Her mouth went dry, imagining how he would stretch her, fill her.

"Higher, Talia."

She forced her reluctant eyes to take in the whole man before her. He was more magnificent than she'd imagined – all bronze skin and toned muscles. He wasn't hairy, but he wasn't smooth either.

"Use your safe word now, or submit to my examination of your body. I will be thorough, you can be sure." God, she hoped so. She needed his touch.

"Please, Sir. My body is yours."

"Stand, and resume your position over the desk, like before."

Talia pressed her palms flat on the desk and spread her legs. Goose bumps rose on her skin waiting for Nick to touch her. When he did, her knees almost buckled from the sheer pleasure of it. His hands covered every inch of her back and ass, then he spread her cheeks and cupped her pussy in his palm. His fingers found her clit, stayed to play until she was breathless and near to begging, then they swiped through her juices, entering her hard. She groaned at the invasion of one, then two fingers. He twisted his hand, dragging his rough fingers against the sensitive tissue inside. She gasped and wiggled her ass.

"Still, Talia. You're permitted to tell me if I hurt you. Am I hurting you now?" he asked.

"No, Sir. It feels good."

He dragged his fingers from her and before she caught her breath, he plunged one wet digit past the tight barrier of her ass. The sudden invasion weakened every muscle in her body and sent a clear message of submission to her brain.

"You're tight here. Am I the first?"

"Yes, Sir." Mortification and heart pounding excitement warmed her face.

He wiggled his finger and her arms gave out. She pressed her hot face against the cool blotter on the desktop.

"I won't use this one tonight then. Soon though, unless you tell me otherwise. Think about it, Talia." He pushed another finger in beside the first. She'd never felt anything so wicked. She was aroused and embarrassed at the same time. Weak with desire and need. "Think about me fucking you here. I'll be gentle at first, then when you're used to me, I'll ride you hard. Your pussy will ache for attention while I'm in your ass." His fingers retreated, then pushed back in. "Maybe I'll give you something to fill your pussy, too."

She groaned at the mental image of him filling both holes at the same time. Nothing had ever made her want the way that image did.

With his free hand, Nick flicked open a carved wood box on the corner of the desk. It took only a moment for him to sheath himself.

His fingers stretched her ass as the head of his cock stretched her inner lips. She held her breath waiting for him to take her completely.

"Exhale, Talia."

She let the breath out and he filled her in one slow, firm stroke. She sucked in another breath and held it as his balls bounced against her clit.

"Breathe, sweetheart." Heat spread through her where his hand stroked her spine. "Relax. Give the control to me, darlin'. I'll make you feel good."

Talia let the breath out and willed the tension in her body to go with it. He was right, she was trying to hold onto control. Nick's hand roamed her body while his cock and fingers filled her. He bent over her, measuring her breasts, tweaking the nipples to hard points before sliding his hand lower. He toyed with her navel, finger fucking it until she wanted to scream with frustration. He hadn't moved since he'd seated himself inside her.

She sagged against the desk, ceding control to Nick. He seized it with both hands, literally and figuratively. "That's it," he said, as he pulled to the brink, then filled her again. "Let me take you there, sweetheart."

He took her there—one slow, incredible stroke at a time, until she was desperate for release. "

"Please," formed on her lips, only to be swallowed on a moan.

He crooned instructions to her, which she obeyed without question. "Breathe. Touch your breast. Say my name. Beg me to let you come." His voice stroked as surely as his hand and cock.

"Please," she begged, aloud this time.

He reached around and pressed his thumb against her clit. Circled. "Now, Talia. Come for me now."

The orgasm broke over her like a summer storm across the prairie—sudden, violent, yet a welcome relief from the heat. His fingers left her ass, and with both hands on her hips, he lifted her feet off the floor. Talia gripped the edge of the desk to steady herself. He pounded into her, seeking his own release. It came with the same force as hers, invading her body with its force. Feminine power flowed through her veins. For one spectacular moment, Nick had lost control, and she'd been the one to bring him to it.

Psychology and Misconceptions of Roles in BDSM
By Dr. Charley Ferrer

There is a common misconception that individuals who participate in BDSM activities, whether as Dominant or submissive, have a few screws loose. All too often, from a psychological perspective, they are immediately diagnosed as having some sort of pathology and perhaps sociopathic tendencies. This is far from the truth! And yet, in some ways—in some individuals—perhaps there is a little truth to it, especially since the line between pathology and eroticism is so thinly veiled. In fact, in several states, BDSM activities are considered unlawful even when performed by consenting adults and some couples have been arrested because of it.

Prior to 2012, the *Diagnostic and Statistical Manual (DSM)*—the psychologist's reference guide to psychological disorders—considered sadomasochistic desires and behaviors pathological and in need of treatment. (Just as they had deemed homosexual desires and activities a pathological disorder in need of treatment prior to the DSM-4.)

In the DSM-5, which debuted in 2012, BDSM was de-pathologized as was cross-dressing, fetishes, and trasvestic fetishes. The DSM-5 now considers these behaviors and desires "non-disordered paraphilias" and "atypical sexual desires not in need of treatment". That is so long as there is no undue emotional discomfort or distress to the individual, and the activity is consensual in nature.

I have to chuckle at that clause "emotional discomfort and undue stress" since many men and women who find themselves drawn to Dominance and submission often struggle with their desires; especially submissive men and Dominant women who are in direct opposition to societal norms and the prejudices they've been taught.

BDSM Anthology

We have the National Coalition for Sexual Freedom (NCSF) to thank for their efforts in this regard and working to safeguard our sexual freedom as well as the many professional and non-professional advocates who put themselves and their careers on the line to help bring about this change.

Legally, the acceptance of consensual sadomasochism is different in every state. In some states, even consensual BDSM is a crime. Thus, every person should learn what's legal for their state as ignorance of the law is not an excuse, and it can get you thrown in jail.

Have you ever wondered what these people look like?

Well, let me tell you. They look just like the men and women you see walking down the street or sitting on the bus or train beside you every day. He or she is your neighbor, your co-worker; dare I say, even the person sitting next to you at church. They are men and women like you who have families and jobs, perhaps even children. They come from every economic and social background as well as religious, ethnic and sexual orientation. They have the same hopes and dreams you have of someday having a home, a loved one and basically having a happy fulfilling life.

They might even be you!

I want to point out that an individual doesn't just wake up one morning with these desires. These desires have been with him or her since childhood. As John Money asserts, Dominance and submission is their Love Map.

These mentally healthy men and women do not participate in BDSM activities because they wish to be abused nor do they desire to perpetuate malicious acts on another human being for a sexual thrill. Nor do they desire to hurt or injure someone who's put their faith, trust and even their very life in their hands. They participate in these activities because it is what they've learned and find comfort and sexual satisfaction in. It is their Love Map, and yes, they are normal!

Hollywood, and some pop authors who do not understand the dynamics of this intensely erotic and diverse lifestyle have perverted (no pun intended) the fundamental truths of the BDSM lifestyle out of ignorance or for their own gains, perpetuating misconceptions and myths that have led to discrimination and bigotry toward participants; much as in decades past the same was perpetuated against gays and lesbians. And just as with the LGBT community, many BDSM lifestylers who are discriminated against have been fired from their jobs, become ostracized from their families and some have even lost custody of their children.

Yes, there are criminals in our society who dominate their victims and do horrible sadistic things. Yes, there are individuals in relationships who manipulate their partners and abuse them. However, these abusive behaviors are not the foundation of *Dominance and submission*. Though these negative behaviors can be found in the BDSM community, they are more prevalent in the population at large.

It may surprise you to learn that the majority of the men and women who participate in BDSM activities and embrace Dominance and submission as well as Master/slave relationships are honorable people who communicate their boundaries and learn how to engage in healthy relationships through various workshops and interactions. Unfortunately, as with any other community, we tend to notice the bad apples first and this taints the way for the rest: Though I would love to paint a wonderful picture of honorable men and women and portray individuals who just want to be free to love and express their inner libertarianism, the truth is there are individuals—both men and women—who enter the BDSM community for the wrong reasons. Some use it as a way to exorcize their childhood and adult demons; to feel powerful because in their everyday life they don't; and sadly, to be "abused" because they're so broken from their past life experiences that they try to find a way to recreate those past traumatic experiences. Regrettably, instead of going to therapy where they belong and can begin the healing process, these individuals turn to BDSM. The reasons vary greatly from individual to individual.

As for those who use BDSM as a spiritual or self-actualization path, they too find their own delicate balance within service and the vast array of power exchange activities.

It's paramount to understand that BDSM is not merely about sexual conquests or interactions. It is about so much more! Some relationships do not incorporate sexual activities at all and merely focus on various aspects of service or Dominance and submission. At times the relationships involve a spiritual connection, at others an emotional or physical one. Sometimes the connection is in the form of mentorship and acceptance, not only from the Dominant but from the slave as well. These roles are forever intertwining, blurring and readjusting as each individual receives what they need from the relationship and grows in a positive way from it—if it is a healthy relationship.

A slave boy I know shared with me the following passage with, which I believe puts into perspective the essence of BDSM.

"When the purpose of the interaction is not just orgasm but another kind of release as well, one moves to a deeper level of relationship that is more sophisticated and requires more thought and communication

I'd like to introduce you to the primary types of mentalities that comprise the community. These unique individuals who carry themselves with dignity and honor and respect the rights of those around them and those they interact with.

Dominant

He or She desires to establish a connection with an individual who is willing to give and share of themselves completely. The Dominant seeks someone who is willing to follow directions and be guided even when the submissive/slave doesn't always concur with the decisions made. The Dominant seeks a man or woman who will be there to share their essence and embrace the life the Dominant is trying to build. At their core, Dominants crave to share the true essence of themselves, their desires and their eroticism with someone who will cherish these gifts and offer their surrender in return. As with any other relationship, the Dominant may desire to merely brush along the surface and delve into basic levels of BDSM going no further.

The Dominant is the giver. This individual is in charge of the relationship. He or She sets the rules, safeguards their partner, administers training and correction as S/He deems appropriate and desirable in their personal relationship. The Dominant also dictates and administers punishment for any violations of the rules and/or transgressions the submissive may be guilty of. S/He is entrusted with the emotional and physical safety of the individual S/He interacts with. The Dominant is responsible for establishing and reinforcing the protocols of the relationship. Dominants have an alpha personality and are used to being in charge. However, you don't need to be in a management position at work to qualify as a Dominant.

Ironically, most dominant males at work are actually submissive at their cores and more service-oriented women—at work—are dominant at their cores. I think this dichotomy shows the irony of our societal norms.

A female Dominant is often called Mistress unless she chooses another title for herself such as Ma'am, Lady So-and-so, Owner, Master, Goddess, etc. Some Dominants merely use their first names. It is a personal choice. When interacting with his or her Dominant, the slave/submissive will use Ma'am or Sir as honorifics.

There is a small percentage of women who use the title Master instead of Mistress. Personally, I do not like the name Mistress, as there is a negative connotation to the word. For some men, there is the expectation that sexual favors are owed to them or that the female Dominant has less value than the male Dominant. There is also the subconscious belief by some men and women entering the BDSM community that a Dominant woman is nothing more than a pseudo-professional Dominatrix and should be considered little more than a prostitute as "She is there to serve the submissive"—in essence giving him a "free" BDSM session.

Most romance novels, if not practically all, designate the woman as Mistress or have her slave call her by her given name such as Mistress Stephanie. It's your choice what you wish to have Her called and by whom.

Proper etiquette dictates that the Dominant is always shown respect, even in written form, by capitalizing their title (Master/Mistress) and their pronouns. For example: using a capital "M" for Master/Mistress anywhere it appears in the sentence and capitalizing any pronouns which relate to the Dominant such as the "Y" in You when the submissive is referring to them, such as, "The chores You requested were performed, Mistress."

The abbreviated version of Dominant is Dom for men and Domme for women.

Master/Mistress:

Though they embody the characteristics of the Dominant, this individual will take the relationship one step further into an emotionally and physically intense level of connection, which is not merely about playing and satisfying desires. This individual, whether male or female, will explore the full spectrum of possibilities, opening the door to growth, not only for the submissive/slave, but for themselves as well. The Master has a willingness to teach, share and experience *Eros* and *Thanatos* (the dark shadow of desire) with another and balance the two halves of their soul. The Master's intention is not to harm but to enlighten; to accept another's vulnerabilities and teach the submissive/slave the power he/she holds within, since a slave who has poor self-esteem doesn't serve the Master nor themselves to their full potential.

Imagine a relationship based on trust and acceptance that is continuously affirmed; this is what the Master/Mistress strives to achieve. The level of control and commitment required from their partner is the key in these relationships. Masters tend to be more disciplined and structured than Dominants. There is a higher level of intensity and mastery associated with these relationships. Also, there are standard and individualized protocols and etiquettes that dictate the interactions of a Master and His/Her slave.

It is more common for a Master to have several slaves dedicated to various tasks in the Master's home or life than it is for a Dominant to have multiple submissives. Also a Dominant/submissive relationship tends to be more couples oriented; however there are many polyamorous households that practice Dominance/submission principles.

There are also separate community and educational functions specifically geared toward the dynamics of Master/slave relationships, which are focused on the development of the Master and of the slave, as opposed to the typical BDSM events and community play parties. There is also a belief within that community that as you grow in maturity and desire for higher levels of interactions with your submissive, you move from the introduction of BDSM and mere play phase into a Dominant/submissive relationship, and ultimately to a Master/slave relationships. Not all D/s relationships move into the more restrictive aspects of Master/slave dynamic even after years of cohesive and positive loving interactions; however, if they do, they still may not consider themselves in a Master/slave relationship. The beauty of BDSM is its ambiguous definition, thus leaving it to the specific individual couple to create and define the relationship that works best for them.

Mommy/Daddy Dominants

Another specific type of Dominant the role of the Daddy and Mommy. Note that though they may refer to their submissives as "little boys and girls," their partners *are in fact adults*.

Daddy and Mommy Dominants bring their own unique behaviors and psychological connections to the BDSM table. Though they may be Sadistic and sexual with their *little girls* and *boys*, depending on the role-playing age, their approach to dominance is often based on guidance and mentorship. Daddy and Mommy Dominants can be more affectionate or stricter depending on the behavior of the "child."

Please remember that when I mentioned *little girls* and *boys*, I am specifically referring to those men and women who are of **legal age** and enjoy roleplaying NOT chronological minors. These adult age-playing individuals open their imaginations and hearts and fulfill that essence of themselves that they didn't get to interact with during their childhood or that they just want to share and explore more of with someone they trust to guide them and keep them safe.

Sadist

Unlike Dominants and Masters, Sadists are not necessarily interested in the D/s dynamics of the relationship and may have a more egalitarian interaction and relationship with their slaves or submissives. Then again, they may be even stricter in their rules, protocols and requirements. Regardless, the Sadist is nonetheless in charge of the relationship and the Master of it!

A major psychological difference between a Sadist and a Dominant is the fact that Sadists are turned on by inflicting physical pain and mental stressors, much more so than a Dominant, and thus taking interactions to a higher emotional and physical level of torment. And though most Dominants enjoy inflicting some levels of pain on their submissives or slaves, whether through use of a flogger, a spanking, a whip or hundreds of various toys, Sadists create a painful and/or psychological intensity that would make your typical Dominant cautious. It is the sadism itself that creates a sense of *rightness* and *peace* within the Sadist's mind and body. The Sadist enjoys pushing limits and taking the submissive/slave on a journey of physical, emotional, psychological and/or sexual exploration. They will often engage in more advanced levels of emotional and physical interactions, such as edge play. Where a typical Sadist will push against physical limits and endurances, an Emotional Sadist will push against the slave's fears and emotional issues, thriving on fear play and mind fucks, which are the basis of psychological play.

It should be clearly understood that the Sadist is *not* attempting to injure the submissive/slave in any way; S/He is merely interacting at a level others may fear to tread. Also the Sadist, at times, will push His/Her own limits when interacting with a slave at various levels and may be emotionally affected by the same. (Think advance statistical evasive Ranger training and/or Special Force psychological training for a somewhat vanilla comparison.)

The Sadist in these interactions is **NOT** interacting in a pathological manner! There is never an intention to **injure** the submissive, merely to share a part of themselves—what they may consider a sacred part of themselves.

Sadists are typically very discerning and selective in their choice of individuals with whom they will interact, and to what level. Sadists are extremely committed to the safety and well being of those they interact with. Yes, there are some who aren't; however, there are idiots and dishonorable individuals in all walks of life. As I mentioned before, in these interactions, there is no pathological behavior as there is no malice intended!

I find Sadists to be more loving and attentive to their slaves, especially after an intense scene, ensuring the slave's physical and emotional well being.

The best analogy I can use to help you distinguish between a Sadist and a Dominant is that Dominants sometimes needs a "reason" to discipline and punish His or Her submissive/slave; a Sadist merely needs a place. (Smiles, okay, maybe that was a bit cavalier, but you get the gist).

submissive

The submissive desires to be of use to the Dominant, trusting his or her gift of submission will not be abused. He or she longs to share that part of themselves they've hidden from the rest of the world. Their need to be of service, to take care of another, to surrender themselves completely sexually, physically, emotionally, to make their Master's/Mistress' life easier as that brings the submissive joy and actually fortifies them and gives them the strength to battle life's challenges.

Though the submissive tends to have a beta personality, he or she can be very domineering in their own way and often chooses to surrender to only one other individual—their Master. This individual is the other half of the D/s relationship. He or she follows the rules and is of service to the Dominant. The submissive role is not always sexual in nature. The submissive may be merely providing service to the Dominant in some manner, for example: house cleaner, computer expert services, preparing meals, etc.

It is the submissive's duty to obey and adhere to the dictates of his/her Master/Mistress. The underlying premise is to be of service. As a submissive, he/she typically has more liberties than a slave. One of the major differences between a slave and a submissive is that the submissive may be a free agent and can interact with whomever he or she chooses to until they become the property of another.

In written form it is common practice for a submissive to use a lower case "i" when referring to themselves as they consciously reinforce the decision to see themselves as belonging to another and taking a more submissive/subservient role. Also his/her name is never capitalized, such as, "Dear Master, i have completed all the tasks You asked of me. Respectfully, joshua."

Please note, this submissive subservient role does not imply less value, but merely a difference in the equality and roles within the relationship. a different one.

Sub is the abbreviation of submissive.

Sexual submissive

Though not all submissives or slaves are used sexually, the sexual submissive's primary purpose is sexual use by his/her Mistress/Master. However, whereas a submissive will defer the leadership role to their Dominant or be subservient to his/her Master/Mistress in all areas of the relationship, this rule/dynamic is not true of the sexual submissive.

The sexual submissive is typically very dominant in his/her own right and often has an alpha personality in all other areas of his/her life and only relinquishes control in sexual matters. Outside amorous interactions, this individual is very opinionated and focused on what they want in life, what they want to share with their partner, as well as the type of everyday egalitarian relationship structure they desire to engage in with their partner.

The sexual submissive may also have very intense masochistic tendencies. However, outside of the sexual arena, their submission is not really present or is minimal. The best example I can provide of this dynamic is the general who goes out and leads his men into battle, then gladly surrenders to his lover only to once again take control of his life after that particular interaction is over. He can allow his lover/partner to take the lead in the relationship; however theirs will be more of an egalitarian union than the typical D/s relationship.

slave

As these men and women make the transition from submissive to slave, they relinquish their ego and societal norms to surrender themselves unconditionally to their Master/Mistress, allowing the Dominant to take the lead and rebuild or redesign their lives in a more positive direction, knowing that surrendering completely to their vulnerability and handing it over to their Master/Mistress will bring with it affection and acceptance unlike in many vanilla interactions where such behavior would be seen as a weakness.

There is an old saying in the community that it takes more strength and courage to kneel than it does to stand—and the slave embraces this concept. It is through their complete surrender that they find the essence of themselves and can then share it with another and the world at large in a multitude of ways. It may surprise you to know that often very powerful men, like doctors, Wall Street executives, even Special Forces soldiers are among the most submissive and/or sexually submissive men there are.

Slaves can be either male or female. Their entire purpose is to "be of service" to his/her Master/Mistress and make his/her Dominant's life simpler and happier. The slave gives up many of his/her "rights" (by choice) to allow the Master/Mistress to dictate the slave's interactions and responsibilities within the relationship.

Typically, slaves will have set protocols that they are required to maintain in public as well as in private. Transgressions are met with physical and/or emotional consequences.

The major difference between a slave and a submissive is the ability to deny a Master's dictates. Whereas a submissive may have some say and veto privileges within the relationship and/or activity being performed (in the form of limits), a slave does not. Also, when interacting in physical and/or sexual activities, the slave has no rights to deny what is done or required of him or her. The slave lives within the limits their Master/Mistress has established for them.

Within the relationship, the slave has consciously given his/her agreement to participate in current and future "consensual nonconsensual" activities and interactions with his/her Master and others designated by the Master/Mistress in either a physical or sexual nature, thus becoming a slave in the true sense of the word.

It should be understood that, though the slave is objectified at times, he/she is very well cared for and held in high esteem and deep affection, even loyalty, from the Master/Mistress. The Master takes his or her responsibility to the slave's physical and emotional well-being very seriously and will guard the slave against any harm.

The slave belongs to his or her Master/Mistress!

It should be understood that an individual might consider themselves a "slave" but have no Master/Mistress at the moment. The emotional and psychological makeup of a slave is vastly different from that of a submissive. The bottom line is that the fundamental psychological aspect of a slave is to give themselves without reservation because it is in their nature—their very core—to do so, to become enmeshed with their Master/Mistress completely, taking their relationship to a deeper more spiritual level.

Proper etiquette for a slave to use when addressing himself is the third person. For example: "Master, is it acceptable for Your slave to prepare Your bath?" Or it can follow the submissive's format: "After i go to the grocery store, i will clean Your home."

Regrettably over the years, I've noticed that many submissive women who seek a Dominant man outside the BDSM community actually find an abuser instead. It's a shame that these women don't realize that it is the above description of the Master that they seek, and perhaps if society weren't so biased against sexual freedom, these women would know where to look. Unfortunately, women aren't the only ones who find an abuser when searching for a dominant partner; male submissives experience this as well.

Masochist

A masochist is an individual who enjoys the more physical aspects of BDSM. He or she will engage in more physically demanding interactions and edge play activities. Masochists enjoy riding the waves of pleasure that pain produces in their body. For them, the pain they experience at the hand of their Master/Mistress is an intensely emotional connection as well as a higher level of surrender. Most masochists will not use a safeword, as they will allow their Mistress/Master to choose for them when the experience will be over. This level of surrender reinforces their connection and is often their way of overcoming their fears of the activity or reaching a higher level of consciousness through the acceptance of pain. (This concept of achieving a spiritual connection with the self or another is evident in many of our religious beliefs and is a major component of Christianity; remember the common practice of priests reaching divinity through self-flagellation? Or the belief that to "suffer" is a way to reach God?)

A rare subgroup of men and women sometimes fall into the category of emotional masochists. These individuals thrive on emotional pain and fear. Not all masochists are able to explore this realm.

Though most masochists are submissives or slaves, it would be erroneous to classify them all as such. Some masochists have alpha personalities and are very dominant in their own rights, much like sexual submissives. Thus, these masochists enjoy pitting themselves against their own fears, using the Dominant as their catalyst for this purpose; others merely enjoy the endorphin rush they can experience through pain. There is also the ability, as mentioned before, of working through an emotion—guilt, shame, etc., and using pain as the cleanser. In this instance, the masochist is *using* the Dominant as a gateway to overcoming or achieving his goal.

A masochist is considered either a submissive or a slave and is treated accordingly. In writing they often use the lower case "i".

Sadomasochist

Some Dominants have masochistic tendencies but not submissive ones. This is what's called a Sadomasochistic personality. This individual enjoys the edgier/darker aspects of physical and/or sexual interactions with his or her slave. Like a switch, they will enjoy giving and receiving pain. However, the major difference between these two personalities is that this Dominant would never surrender their will to their submissive or slave.

For example: the Sadomasochistic Dominant may enjoy giving **and receiving** pain, however he/she would never kneel before her slave nor beg. This Dominant would also never be in servitude to the submissive. These Sadomasochistic individuals may also enjoy allowing their submissive to feel empowered by engaging in rough sex and force; however, at the end of the day, it is the Dominant who will say how much the submissive is allowed to do and when this type of play is over. Plus, a deviously wicked Sadomasochist may even lovingly make His/Her submissive pay for his rough treatment of their Master/Mistress at a later date and time, thereby reinforcing the power dynamics and their control.

Property/ Objectification

This individual is regarded as lower in status than a slave or submissive and is thought of as the Master/Mistress' property. "It" has no rights to object to anything asked of it. It is often objectified and given a number (for example: 4663) rather than a name or nickname. Its given name is not used when referring to him/her. It can be used sexually or physically in whatever manner the Dominant decrees. This individual has an internal desire to surrender all and have no opinions, options or responsibilities aside from those dictated by its Master. This individual is typically found in the most intense levels of BDSM interactions.

Objectification occurs when a submissive/slave is reduced to the sole dictates of his Master/Mistress. In this role, the slave has no rights. They are literally an object for the Dominant's use. H/she (the slave/submissive) is there solely for the purpose assigned, whether that is to serve as sexual stud/whore, to withstand the restraints of a particular role or to act as particular object (such as furniture or living art—think of the Roman slaves used for this purpose) or for whatever activity the Dominant dictates. Some individuals are objectified in sexual service, others by being designated as furniture, an animal or something else.

Others forms of objectification can be implemented through the clothing the individual is allowed/required to wear, which strips away his or her identity and provides the slave with another. This may include wearing a full facial hood or taking away his or her name—their identity—and giving them another (typically a number or a "derogatory" name such as *dog* or *whore*). The submissive/slave would then only be referred to as "it" and when referring to "itself" would do so in the third person.

Force can be used at times, as well as corporal punishment. Though this interaction may seem derogatory or demeaning, it should be understood that the individual being objectified did voluntarily surrender to begin with and provided his or her consent to the interaction. In essence, they are repeatedly providing their consent to such treatment every time they show up to interact with their Master/Mistress.

This objectification often provides the individual with a sense of well being and feeling of belonging. Some slaves will objectify themselves in their desire to be of service and to surrender all sense of identity and control to their Master/Mistress. By doing this, they have achieved complete surrender, which is their ultimate goal, what turns them on and/or completes them.

It's essential to keep in mind that what you may judge to be immoral or distasteful, the parties interacting in it find it erotic and freeing. Also, this objectification is not in any way abusive or an example of domestic violence, as the individual was not coerced or forced into accepting this role in the relationship. For the slave/submissive it is what's right for them and is an integral part of who they are. As I mentioned previously, BDSM is *not* domestic violence. In a domestic violence situation, the individual would have never chosen to participate in these types of activities; and in BDSM the property/object consciously and willingly does so.

Before you pass judgment, it may surprise you to realize that this training and objectification is very similar to how the military trains its new recruits, turning them from civilians into soldiers who obey orders on command—regardless of what that order is.

Please note this is not a derogatory position. Property/objects are actually highly valued and guarded by their Masters, as they are so vulnerable and openly surrender all they are to their Master/Mistress. Such individuals are rare gifts and highly prized by their Owners. There are, of course, exceptions: those who belong to disreputable or severely sadistic owners can be sorely misused in many ways.

One of the things to keep uppermost in your mind when engaging in BDSM activities is that each individual is different. What feels good and erotic to you may not be perceived in the same manner to another. You are the ultimate judge of how you interact with others and what you desire in your relationships.

The object is referred to in written form as "it" (always in lowercase form) and will refer to him/her self in the third person. For example: "Master, *it* will go to the store and *it* will return with all Your required items."

Switch

This individual incorporates various aspects of both a Dominant and submissive personality. They enjoy both aspects of the power exchange, though their personality typically falls more onto one side of the power exchange spectrum than the other. Within the community, Switches aren't always seen in a positive light, as some believe them to be merely submissives wanting to dabble in domination, or merely someone who wants to casually play at the lifestyle. However, others believe that a Switch is able to experience both aspects of the lifestyle, though not as intensely as those who identify as one role or the other.

It's not uncommon for someone new to the lifestyle to identify as a Switch, as they are unsure where they feel most comfortable. Many Switches start out/are considered Service Tops as they are performing a service for another individual, and their relationship with or dominance over that individual ends when the scene is over. A Switch would never be considered a Master.

Some submissive men new to the BDSM lifestyle will identify as Switches, since they feel guilt or shame about being a submissive man. Submissive men often have to combat their own prejudices and those of their counterparts—Dominant men—who may look down upon them for their submission and not consider them "macho" enough. Also, it should be understood that some straight men will accept control and offer service to Dominant men, limiting their interactions to physical interactions but not sexual ones.

Switches can follow either the Dominant or submissive rules for capitalization—they get to choose which protocol to follow. I've often seen them use the lower case "i" when referring to themselves, thus, internally identifying as a submissive.

This is an excerpt from **BDSM The Naked Truth** by Dr. Charley Ferrer. I invite you to read the rest of the book to discover more interesting facts about the truths of Dominance and submission. Authors will gain great insight from my book, **BDSM for Writers**, written specifically for writers in the BDSM genre. Feel free to visit my website www.BDSMTheNakedTruth.com or www.BDSMwriterscon.com which provides valuable information and articles on the BDSM lifestyle. Also sign-up for your FREE BDSM Checklist.

...How I Feel?
By Cara Downey

I listen to them talk about their relationships… They discuss the highs and lows. Oh my man did this or my man did that. God, I am so tired of hearing this. I have become accustomed to just nodding my head, and once in a while, adding my two cents to the discussion. I don't really have that much experience in the love department. I have yet to find the man who will unleash my desires, and push my limits and take me to new heights.

I am pulled into the same daydream I had at work.

I am tied the bed, he is having his wicked way with me. I feel the flogger come down on my body; my breathing is rough, hard, coming in pants. I try to rein myself in; I do not want it to end so soon. I ask him if he can bring the flogger down on my sex. I am not sure where that came from, but he doesn't deny me. On the contrary he obliges me. I scream out in desire when the first lash hit my sex, leaving me wanting more.

I feel the flogger, as he pauses and glides it across my body. I bit my lower lip, because if I don't I will explode, and he isn't even inside me yet. I cannot believe how turned on I am. I know that this is only the beginning and he can keep me on the edge for hours before allowing me to orgasm. In this, he is in control. I gladly give him my submission, because I trust him. My desire is to please him, which in turn gives me pleasure.

With a flip of his wrist, he brings the flogger down again, but stops before hitting my sex. I am tied to the bed. Arms and legs and middle, and it limit me from lifting up my lower body to try and meet him halfway. I grunt in frustration, and he smiles his deliciously evil smile. Knowing that he has me right where he wants me, begging for his touch, begging for the flogger, he is the Master of my mind, body and soul.

He knows that I am not ashamed to beg for his touch for all that he is willing to give me. Because I know that we he is giving me, is equal to or paramount to what I freely give to him and more. I love how he compliments me, encourages me, and knows me inside out. How can a person know another person, inside out, to their depths? I never thought that I would find him, but here I am. I relish our connection and commitment to each other.

Oh God, my panties are wet! One of my girlfriends asks me if I was listening. I totally zoned out there. I need to figure out who I am and what I want. I am so tired of just settling. I take a deep breath and ask if they are happy? They look at me as if I have two heads. I chuckle because I know that they do not understand me, or how I feel. I tell them that I am tired of settling, and I am no longer going to do it. I am about to explain when I turn my head, and I see my future starring right at me. The connection is that instant. I literally feel the pull of his dominance. It is what I desire, what I need…how I feel!

Submissive

God I love this man, I didn't realize it until now how much I love him. I was so afraid at first; I didn't think I had the strength to be what he needs. It was there all along, but I continued to deny the truth, worried about the views and perceptions of the outside world. He was so patient with me, soothing me, but also stern with me, if the situation warranted. His words of encouragement are everything.

I studied as much as possible the life of a submissive, I wanted to know and learn as much as I could. His pleasure and I being able to serve and deliver that pleasure was paramount. I wanted to be more than what I was; I wanted him to be proud of me. I knew that I had the strength within me, to deliver. I wanted him to look at me with reverence.

Some question why a woman would want such a title? Why would a woman with intelligence willingly submit to a man? Why would a woman subject herself willingly to answer his every desire? The answer is simple; it takes a strong woman to submit. It not only gives pleasure to him, but it gives pleasure to her as well. The knowledge and power to know, that you are the one, who puts that gleam and look of hunger in his eyes.

My training was intense. I wanted him to push my limits, and bring me to new heights. There were times when I made mistakes, and I felt unworthy of his love or even his touch. But he was ever so patient. He explained the process, and understood, when it came to my growth. I did not mind being pushed to my limits. The pleasure I gave him, he returned tenfold.

All I've learned has now led me here. Content, strong in my service to him, I am now, kneeling waiting his return. His playroom, our sanctuary, I await his arrival. I hear the car pull up to the driveway, and I know he will be here soon. I can hardly wait; I am jumping out of my skin. I am in the respective position, with my head and eyes cast down. It is as if he is here now, trailing the back of his hand across my left cheek in admiration.

I hear the alarm, letting me know that he has entered the house. He will make me wait, because he is the master when it comes to anticipation. I wiggle, because my excitement is at the brink, about to take over. I am stronger now; I dial it back, maintaining the control he has taught me. I do not want this to end even before it has started. My training has ended. This is it. This is the beginning of pleasure and passions abound.

I hear him on the stairs now. I know that he has changed beforehand, it is our routine. I will do anything to please him. He will be topless, showing off his wonderful upper body. He will be in a pair of faded Levi's blue jeans, barefoot. The door opens, he is admiring me from afar, and I can feel it. He is making his way over to me slowly. Oh God, how I love this man, I will do anything to please him.

Dominant

Damn I love this woman. I never thought this day would come, that I would find her. I would sit and stare off into space, wondering when my time would come. I am not going to settle for less, I refuse. I am demanding, but that is who I am. I realize now, how much I love this woman after finding her, I'll be damned if I give her up.

I have been with a lot of submissives; I have trained a lot of submissives. I can honestly say, that none of those women can compare to her. I knew that she was a submissive from the moment I laid eyes on her in the bar at the restaurant. She was sitting with some of her friends, talking and laughing. The moment she turned and I saw her smile, the innocence in her eyes, I knew she was mine. I had to have her, it was instantaneous.

Our first encounter was nerve-wracking for me. I had to rein in my control and play it cool. I could tell that she was nervous, the way she would worry her bottom lip with her teeth. I had to take things slow. This woman was going to be my one and only submissive, there was going to be no one after her. The connection I felt between us was that strong. I knew without a doubt that she felt it too.

The training was hard. This was new to her, even though she was a natural submissive. She would research as much information as possible, with the purpose and dedication of pleasing me. The night she safe worded out, put everything into perspective for me. She cried the entire night. Worried that I would end the relationship, I had no intention of letting her go.

It was my fault. I was caught up and didn't acknowledge her needs. I damaged the trust of her submission, because of my lack of attention. The tears she shed and her statements of failure tore at my heart, because it was I who failed her. I made it a mission, right then and there, that she would be put first.

Together we overcame, and are stronger than ever before. I exited my office, thinking about her. I cannot wait to get home to her, enjoy my time with her, in our playroom. I cannot wait to explore her, to love her, and feast on every part of her delectable body. I eagerly navigate through traffic, so I can make my way home and closer to her my sub.

The anticipation is killing me. My beautiful sub, always so willing to please me, I find myself questioning how I was blessed to have found her. I know that she hears the alarm, letting her know that I am home. I will not keep her waiting. I will change into my faded Levi's jeans, I will be barefoot, and topless.

I enter, and I know that she can feel me admiring her from afar. Damn, I love this woman. All of her training and patience has led to this moment. She is so strong. I love how she assumes the position, eyes cast down. I never had to discipline her on that. Damn, I love this woman, and I am going to relish in her service, and enjoy every part of her.

Shibari

The look of trepidation was to be expected. I have used methods to bind her with before, but I have yet to use rope on her. I explained to her during the beginning of our relationship, that there would come a time when I would bind her hand and foot. I would use any manner of binding that I see fit in time of play. As I look at her now, and see, worry with a mixture of wanting. I rein myself in, because I know that for some people, not just submissives, binding by rope, is a totally different experience than being bound with the use of handcuffs or even a silk scarf.

I explain that I will be binding her arms, legs, and her upper body. Once I have explained in detail how I will be binding her, I see only heat and the anticipation of wanting in her eyes. I tell her to assume the position on the bed. I run the back of my left hand on her skin. She is soft and smooth to the touch. I find myself thanking Lush for that. I start with her left ankle. I start winding the rope around her left ankle, slowly making my way up her left leg. I stop when I am at the top of her left thigh. Taking the rope looping it between her thighs, with the knot over her clitoris, then wrap it once around her left thigh, and wrapping it around her stomach, and her right thigh.

Then I start to slowly wind her right leg, making my way down her right leg, until I stop at her right ankle. I take the next set of rope and work on her upper body. I start with her left wrist winding it slowly up. Once I reach her left shoulder, I wrap the rope around her stomach all the way up to her breast. I loop around her left shoulder and her right shoulder, leaving her breast open for my view and pleasure. I slowly wind the rope around her right arm all the way down to her right wrist. I look at the finished product. I am amazed at how beautiful she is. I tell her that she is so beautiful, and I wish that she could see herself.

I start to massage her body, and I hear her soft moan. I place soft kisses to her left breast, giving attention to the puckered nub that has come out to play. I give the same attention to the right. I help her up and tell her to assume the position on the bed as she would on the floor. I can see that she is eager to please me. I pull out my erect penis, which has jumped to attention, and seems to have gotten harder at the beautiful site. I tell her to open her mouth and get ready to please me. She doesn't hesitate; she licks her lips in preparation of taking me into her mouth. I stroke myself up and down, I can hardly contain myself. I remain in control. I do not want to scare her in anyway. I tell her to open, and to take as much of me as she can.

The head of my sex enters her mouth, and she runs her tongue on the underside, making me shudder. She hallows out her cheeks to take more of my girth. As she begins to take me deeper and suck in earnest, she is moving her hips. Now she understands the reason for the knot of the rope that is over her clitoris. She has found a steady rhythm, between pleasuring me and moving her hips. I tell her that I give her permission to move in whichever way or manner she feels, in order to bring herself to orgasm. Tonight is about her serving me, and bringing me to orgasm. But I am not going to ignore or deny her the benefits of what the rope is doing to her.

I feel myself about ready to release. I feel the pull of the orgasm, as it is pulling at the base of my spine. I fist my hand in her hair, as my body comes to release. I feel her body release her orgasm right in tune with mine. She swallows all that I have to give, and she licks and laps up my shaft to clean me of my release. I am in awe of her, and her selflessness. When I look into her eyes, all I see is contentment, and peace. I am sure that what I see in her eyes is nothing more than a reflection in my own eyes. I couldn't help myself; I had to show her what it meant for her to trust me. I picked her up and placed her in my lap with her thighs still bound and opened.

I kiss her. I am vengeful with the kiss. I can feel myself getting hard underneath her. I assist her, by lower her onto my erection, and slowly enter her inch by inch. Once I am sated to the hilt. I hold still to give her a moment to adjust to me. I take her left breast into my mouth, giving it attention. She lowers her head and moans as she grinds her pelvis over my erection. I give the same attention to her left breast. She pulls at her restraints, the sensation is too much. I begin to move, and she counter thrusts me. I let her take control, I hold onto her hips, and she is riding me with all that she has. I fell another orgasm building at the base of my spine.

I feel her vagina walls, flutter around me. She is pulling me in deeper, and I can feel her about to release her passion all over me. I pump into her a few more times, and as her orgasm, washes over me. I release mine after one final thrust. I place a soft kiss to her lips, and then I make work of unbinding her. Once I have released her, I see to her aftercare. I carry her to the bathroom, and I start to run a bath. The feelings I have for this woman, is all new to me. So naturally submissive, and all mine. I am still amazed today at how lucky I am.

Playroom

I never thought the day would come. Day in and day out, I would walk pass this room, stand in front of the door and wonder when I would share this part of myself with someone. Thinking that this day would never come, and then she came along and changed everything. I knew from the moment that I saw her, sitting at the bar with her friends.

Laughing and talking, then when she turned her head, and our eyes met. I knew without a doubt that she was the one. Now here I am a bundle of nerves. I am about to put the key into the lock that will open the door to my heart's desires. No longer will this door remain locked; not with her here. I relish in the joy that I am feeling. I am amazed at how fast it happened.

Our first time together at play will be here, the playroom. I am pleased with the progress that she has made in her training. The pride that she exhibits in wanting to please me. We have not played in the playroom. I did that not just for her benefit, but also for mine. She is a natural submissive, so it was well worth the wait.

The excitement is building, and I want her in here so bad. I have to remain cool, and under control. I am her Dom. I look at the setup, loving how everything is in its place. The spanking bench in the left corner, oh how I image her lying on her stomach, ass presented to me. I have the riding crop ready. Before the night is out, I will have her spread out on primed and ready.

I am glad that I took the time to ensure that all toys and gadgets are cleaned and ready for use. Due to her lack of experience, I have been running a skeleton crew from the master bedroom. I did not want to overwhelm her, so I decided that taking it one day at a time- and slowly-was the best option. Rushing can only lead to mistakes. A great Dom is one that knows his sub, her needs catapult his. Taking my time with her has only enhanced her service to me.

Looking at the spanking bench, I itch to spank her ass; for it brings her desire to the surface. She was scared at first to be spanked, until I explained the erotic feelings that she would experience. My beautiful submissive was eager for me to spank her. That night, I had so much planned, and the groans and moans, which erupted from just a spanking, ended that with a night of unspeakable passion.

I wait patiently for her to come home. Tonight is our first official night as Dom/sub in, what I deem now as our playroom. I have satin pillows in the middle of the floor, so her knees will be fine. My sub is comfortable in her skin. She requires nothing to amplify her beauty. I cannot wait to run my hands over her soft, smooth skin.

I never thought this day would come. Day in and day out, I would walk past this room, stand in front of the door and wonder when I would share this part of myself with someone. Now I wait like a kid in a candy store, jumping up and down, because I cannot contain myself. I want to rip open the wrapper of my favorite treat and splurge.

Intimacy

My Master has taught me so much about intimacy. What I thought I knew about intimacy paled in comparison to what he has shown me. There are different levels of intimacy and different ways to show and feel intimacy as well. I thought that the only way to truly show and feel a deep level of intimacy was during lovemaking. But my Master has shown me and taught me that intimacy is not just felt or shown when making love. It can be when the two of us are sitting on the sofa in our sitting room watching yet another "Tom Cruise" film. That is a level of intimacy, because my Master knows that I am a big fan of Tom and I love his movies.

Intimacy is also felt when we are lying in bed together and he is gently stroking his left hand up and down the right side of my face, and when he is stroking up and down my arms and thighs. It is the non-spoken word, which the intimacy between us deepens. I feel like I can read his mind sometimes. We can just look at each other and know what the other is thinking and what the other needs. God I find myself questioning how intimacy this deep can even be. My Master tells me, that the reason is because I was made for him and he was in turn made for me.

I love that I can be myself with him and he can be himself with me. When we are making love, I can feel a different level of intimacy. It is so profound and so much deeper when our bodies are connected together as one. When he touches me, I feel myself going up in flames. He doesn't even have to say words. Just the look in his eyes tells me everything that I need to know. I know with certainty that when he looks into my eyes he sees the same thing reflected back to him.

The level of intimacy I feel when we are in our love nest, our playroom is amplified to the tenth degree. The unconditional trust I feel when I am with him, is beyond explanation. That amount of adoration and devotion takes our intimacy even higher. I know that without a doubt, he would never hurt me. I feel that intimacy when he touches me. The way he massages his hands over my body, how he reverently touches me, as if I am a previous gift he will cherish for all time. He is so firm yet gently when we are here. Our time in our playroom is our Sanctuary.

It is more than just the flick of his wrist, when he is about to bring the flogger down upon my body. It is more than being bound to the spanking bench or bound to the Saint Andrew's cross. It is more than being tied to the bed, open for his scrutiny and his pleasure. The gift of my submission has increased the level of intimacy that I feel for him. My Master, the man I love, who is Dominant over my mind, body and spirit. He control's every aspect of my pleasure, and in doing so he fulfills me, beyond anything that I could even imagine.

His Dominance over me, giving me what I need, never judging me, is another piece of the puzzle that catapults our intimacy. When I am in need of his guidance, but I cannot find the words to express myself, he is there, patient providing me with the nudge I need. His experience and knowledge at first was intimidating. But now, I relish in it, because his experience and knowledge has given me the strength I need. I couldn't imagine my life without him by my side. I truly do not know if I would even have the strength to carry one.

I kneel here now, naked waiting patiently for my Master to enter. My legs are spread apart so that he can have a clear sight to my pussy. My back is straight and my hands are down folded neatly in front of me. My head is lowered and my eyes are cast down. I take pride in my personal grooming, because I know that he prefers it. So I have no issue with ensure that my pussy is shaven to his standards and likeness. I have no problem wearing my hair down with a little "flip" because he likes it. God I love this man and serving him, bring me nothing but pleasure.

That's way I have no issue with using daily exfoliating body gloves when in the shower or in the bath, because he loves how soft my skin is to touch. In the grand scheme of things, all that he likes and enjoys is exactly what I like and enjoy. I take satisfaction in that, because it shows the level of growth on my part, and the level of intimacy that has grown within us and our relationship. I am pulled from my musings when I hear him on the stairs. And my anticipation is about to hit the roof. Here the outside world has no bearing on us, and it cannot infringe on us.

Sloane's Threesome
By Paige Mathews

The night had finally come – the one Sloane had dreamt about, fantasized about.

Sloane undressed, stepped into the heat of the shower, and let the water warm her skin. Taking a deep breath, she stood under the showerhead, thinking about the night ahead – how the evening would progress, how the men would treat her, how Ty would respond. Sloane had talked to another couple online, found that the man who was interested in helping her achieve her biggest fantasy – help her complete the one event that she had long thought about.

Turning off the shower, Sloane wrapped herself in a towel and stood in front of the vanity. She needed to shave and get ready – thank goodness she'd already waxed the previous week. *One less thing to worry about.* Sloane was excited that Ty had finally agreed to the threesome, after months of talking to Steve, and to each other about it. There was a little curiosity on Ty's part as well – not for the sake of being involved with another male, but in watching as his wife was pleasured by another; living out her fantasy. Ty wasn't opposed to participating, yet the only thing he'd be touching was Sloane.

Sloane moved the razor up and down her legs, making sure she was silky smooth – applying a lotion as well. Nothing would be left to chance. She heard a door close as she made her way into the master closet – Ty was home. The game plan was to meet up with Steve for a quick drink, and then head up to the hotel room. Specific instructions included Sloane having to wear black lace undergarments and a short black dress – one couldn't draw too much attention to oneself. The thought made Sloane giggle. This was seriously happening.

"What's funny, darling?" Ty said, removing his tie as he strolled in to the bedroom.

Sloane turned to face her husband. "Just a funny thought. Nothing special." She walked up to Ty and wrapped her arms around his waist. "I can't believe this is actually happening tonight."

"Me either. Are you sure you still want this to happen?" he asked, sitting on the bed to remove his work shoes and unbutton his shirt.

Sloane nodded her head, a sparkle in her eye. "Yes." She paused and waited for her husband's response.

"Well, let me jump in a shower so I can get ready. Why don't you finish getting dressed?" Ty stood and pulled his blonde haired wife tight to him, placing a light kiss on her lips. "Tonight will be good."

"I know." Ty released her and stepped toward the bathroom. Sloane paused, "Ty?"

"Yeah, babes?"

"Thank you for this." Sloane smiled and dropped her eyes to look at the carpet in front of her.

"Anything for you, darling. You know that."

Ty turned and went into the bathroom, closing the door behind him. Sloane heard the shower turn on, and headed back to the closet to retrieve her black dress. She brought the dress back to the bedroom, laying it on the bed. Then she sat down next to it, directly in front of the full-length mirror that graced the wall. As she bent to slide her leg into one of her thigh-high stockings, Sloane caught a glimpse of her reflection. Her breasts peeked out slightly in the demi-lace black bustier, the matching thong situated delicately over her hipbones, and the garter belt placed to hold up her stockings. A thrill of excitement ran down her spine, awakening every nerve.

"You look amazing, and you haven't even put on the dress yet. He will have his mouth on the floor with you." Ty stepped over and stood in front of her, bending to place another quick kiss on her lips. Sloane smiled, and stood up to attach the stockings to the garter. She grabbed the dress and stepped into it, fitting the top over her breasts, praying the strapless number would stay up.

"Ty, can you zip me?" Sloane turned so her back was facing her husband. Ty walked to her, slowly running his fingertip down her spine until he reached the bottom of the zipper. Ty felt the shudder of

Sloane's body as he zipped the dress up, moving her hair off of her shoulder, and placing a playful nip on her shoulder.

"Bad boy. You have to wait." Sloane turned to face Ty, running her finger over his bottom lip. "A little longer."

"A little longer, until both of our fantasies are made a reality." Ty walked back to the other side of the room to finish dressing; putting on a pair of darkened jeans, and a black button-down shirt. He styled his hair so that it was semi-spiked in the front, then he rolled up the sleeves on the shirt so they were level with his elbows. The man stirred arousal in Sloane – that wasn't the problem. The problem was that they each wanted something more in their sex life – a little extra excitement.

The couple finished getting ready, putting the final touches on hair, perfume and attire. It was now seven-thirty, and they were due at the hotel lounge at eight-fifteen. Ty led Sloane to the Audi parked in their driveway, hand on the small of her back. Sloane spent the car ride to the hotel thinking about the events to come. Steve had stated in his last call that the couple would be pushed a little more than they had been previously – well, Sloane, at least, would be. Steve was a Dominant – thriving on total control. It was his confidence that had originally drawn Sloane to him. Ty had agreed, after multiple conversations and Skype meetings, that Steve would be the one that would assist Sloane. Ty seemed to like the man – as much as he could, knowing that his wife was to submit to Steve.

Ty didn't realize the extent of his arousal; his feelings and desire to watch his wife with another man - to participate in a threesome with her – until she mentioned it. Their sex life was decent for the most part - no complaints from either side. They just wanted more spark - something new.

Ty and Sloane arrived at the hotel at eight o'clock, and Ty handed the car keys to the valet. Taking a deep breath, he led his wife into the lounge of the hotel, settling for a seat at the bar. He quickly ordered vodka on the rocks, and Sloane ordered a Cosmo. The couple sipped their drinks in silence, the excitement of the night to come building as they waited for their host to show. Neither was sure of what exactly was to happen, when Steve would make his appearance, or how. They only knew they were to sit at the bar and wait.

Sloane sipped her drink, looking around to see if she could spot

Steve sitting somewhere in the corner, hidden, watching their reactions. But nothing - he wasn't there. Yet. Sloane switched her eyes back to the area of the countertop that was under her drink. Doubts swirled around in her head. Should they do this? They both wanted it, right?

"Stop thinking so much." A deep voice whispered into her ear; a voice that did not belong to her husband, but to the mysterious Steve. Sloane was so involved in her thoughts that she didn't hear him approach. Apparently neither did Ty, as the expression on his face showed.

"Steve." The only word Sloane could muster, as a sense of fear, unknown, crashed over her body like a wave crashing onto the beach.

"Sloane. Ty." Steve motioned to Ty, nodding his acknowledgement. "Are you ready?"

"I- um. I believe so," Sloane answered, turning to face the man.

Steve motioned to her drink. "Finish that and meet me in room 608. Here is a key card. I'll be waiting for you." As quickly as he'd shown, Steve was out of sight. Sloane turned toward Ty, trying to gage his response, his thoughts.

"Ty, you okay?" she asked, taking a long draw of her drink; nothing like alcohol induced courage.

"I'm good, darling. Are you ready for this?" Ty ran his hand over the top of his wife's thigh, hoping to calm her nerves a little.

"I think so. I mean, it's what I want, what I've waited for. I just don't know why my stomach is in knots." She looked up to meet her husband's gaze. *She could do this, couldn't she?*

"It is, but if you are having second thoughts, we can leave. We can walk away and no hard feelings. But if you want this, really want this - then this will be the chance, your opportunity." Ty ran his fingers over Sloane's elbow, calming her as he did so. Ty could see Sloane relax as she finished her drink, pushing it toward the bartender.

"Let's do this. I'm sure." Sloane stood and Ty followed, throwing enough money on the bar to cover the tab and tip.

"Alright, room 608 is waiting." The couple walked to the elevators and signaled for a car. Hitting the button for the sixth floor, Sloane knew there was no turning back now. She wanted this, and felt more relaxed now, feeling the knot in her stomach dissipate, replaced with a feeling of excitement. She glanced nervously in Ty's direction, and was rewarded with a squeeze of her hand; a small motion that calmed her even more.

The elevator halted and the doors slid open. Ty and Sloane stepped out and walked to the room, inserting the key card into the slot. Taking that first step through the threshold, Sloane and Ty entered a new world, one that had Ty already hard at the thought. The room was simply decorated in blacks and greys. The room was actually a mini suite - the bed area separated by a sitting area, complete with a sofa, armchair and television. Behind that was the king-sized bed - currently laid out with various instruments and toys: a blindfold, silk ribbons, a few vibrators, and what Sloane thought was an anal plug. Ty urged her to step forward and he shut the door as Steve appeared from the bathroom.

"I'm glad you guys came. Are you ready to begin?" Steve asked and waited for Sloane's answer.

"Yes, we are. I am."

"Good. Come here and remove your dress. Ty will sit in the chair here and watch."

The couple nodded and moved into position; Ty sat in the chair as Sloane walked to Steve's side. Steve watched as Sloane positioned herself in front of him. He ran his eyes up and down her body, over every curve that the black strapless dress snug close to.

"Turn." Steve ordered.

Sloane did as instructed, and turned her back to Steve, her eyes catching Ty's as Steve ran his fingers over her clavicle. A surge of electricity ran through her straight to her core. Ty's eyes - filled with lust - darkened as he watched his wife become aroused. Steve continued to move his fingers across the length of her shoulders to the base of her neck and spine; grasping the zipper, he slowly lowered it, revealing the delicate skin beneath. Sloane closed her eyes; the touch of Steve's fingers felt different, turned her body on differently than Ty's did.

Ty watched the scene unfold as he sat in the chair. His cock hardened the moment he watched the desire and arousal flush in Sloane's face at the touch of Steve's fingers. Thoughts flooded his mind; unable to wait for later, he wanted to sink his cock deep in to Sloane's pussy. He was brought back to reality by his wife's moans.

Looking up, he saw Steve run his finger over the barely-there lace thong that she now wore.

"Sloane, remove your bustier now." Steve's voice resonated through the hotel room. Ty's attention immediately gravitated toward Steve and Sloane. The man commanded the attention of everyone. Ty waited for the next command, holding his breath in anticipation.

"Beautiful breasts you have." Steve's hands grasped each mound, massaging them as Sloane arched her body forward, head thrown back at his touch. Steve's mouth clasped onto a nipple, drawing in the erect flesh as he flicked it with his tongue. Sloane let a moan escape her from mouth, sighing into the air. Ty shifted uncomfortably in his seat, attempting to relieve some pressure on his dick. Watching Steve suck his wife's breasts had him leaking, and aching for a release.

Steve turned to Ty. "Remove your clothes and come behind Sloane." Ty nodded, and quickly undressed, assuming the position behind Sloane. Steve ran his fingers down Sloane's abdomen, sending impulses over the woman's body. Steve was in control, and all Sloane could do was enjoy the ride.

"Sloane, turn around and get on your knees." Sloane did as commanded, positioning herself on her knees, her face level with Ty's cock.

"Good girl. Now take him in slowly. Let him feel every inch of you suck him into your wet, hot mouth."

Sloane opened her mouth and wet her lips. Steve's hand was now on her head, running down the length of her hair, urging her to continue. Sloane moved her mouth closer, noticing Ty's hands clenched at his sides. Sloane gazed up, connecting with Ty's stare - willing her thoughts into his mind. She wanted to make sure he was okay. He looked back at her, his eyes dark with desire. A short nod was all the encouragement that she needed.

Sloane opened her mouth again, and moved Ty's cock into it. Gently closing her lips around the hard shaft, she massaged the underside of Ty's dick with her tongue.

Ty moaned and a grunt escaped from Steve. Sloane smiled to herself; the ability to turn both men on was an accomplishment - even if it was small at the moment. Ty's hands grasped the sides of Sloane's head, dictating the speed and depth of her movements. Ty's fingers clamped around Sloane's hair as she continued to glide up and down his length. Ty could feel his balls tighten, and he knew he was close - something that usually took longer most nights; it surprised him that he was so close on the edge.

"Damn it, Sloane, keep that up. I'm going to come. Take it all, swallow me down." Ty's grasp tightened on Sloane's head, pulling her to him, his cock pushing to the back of her throat as he released into her wet mouth. Sloane had no choice but to swallow his come as it squirted onto the back of her throat. Ty's grip eased, and he pulled himself out of her mouth. "That was amazing."

Steve's hands descended down Sloane's arms, pulling her to her feet. "Bed, now." Before Sloane could take a step in that direction, Steve's mouth crushed down on hers; prying her lips open with his tongue, he greedily explored her mouth before pulling away. Evidence of his arousal showed in his pants. He turned his attention to Ty. "Sit at the head of the bed."

Ty nodded again and moved to the bed, sitting between the pillows. Steve led Sloane to the bed, sitting her on the edge at the bottom. His fingers ran across her erect nipples, flicking them and pulling them further. Sloane felt the wetness in her pussy, the uncomfortable ache that had started to build on the elevator had continued to be intensified from the moment she'd stepped over the threshold of the room.

Steve picked up the blindfold and placed it over Sloane's eyes. "To enhance the pleasures you are about to feel."

Sloane felt a moan escape her lips. She really was looking forward to what was to happen. She felt Steve's hands move down her arms, securing the silk ribbons around her wrists.

"Ty, take these and tie them to either side of the headboard. Sloane move your body backwards until I say stop."

Sloane moved until she was centered in the bed. Ty did as he was instructed, securing the ribbons to the bed leaving Sloane's arms extended out and over her head. She was a beautiful sight; lying partially restrained, her mind off somewhere else, her breasts exposed, the nipples erect. Ty couldn't help but touch them, running them through his fingers, mimicking the motions Steve had used. Sloane arched her chest into Ty's hands, her body demanding more contact. Steve focused on her lower half, running his hands up and down Sloane's inner thighs, stopping just shy of her apex. Ty's hands moved over her breasts, kneading and massaging them, as Steve's fingers trailed over the outside of the still in place thong.

Sloane's body tensed as Steve pulled the thong to the side, running his fingers up and through her slit, her moisture coating his fingers. The moans escaping from Sloane's mouth signaled to Ty how excited she was - a thought that increased his arousal, his cock stirring below him again. As much as he wanted into Sloane's tight pussy, he knew her ultimate fantasy was to have another man hold her down and fuck her - that was why they were there, why he had allowed all of this to happen.

Steve's voice brought Ty back to the present. "That's it, Ty, tease her breasts, suck them slowly as I fuck her with my fingers." Ty brought his mouth to Sloane's nipples as he watched Steve remove the lace thong. Steve's fingers ran up and down over Sloane's labia, before thrusting into her opening at the same time as Ty nipped at Sloane's erect peaks. Sloane's body arched off the bed, craving the attention that it desired, needed.

Ty continued to suck on Sloane's breasts, alternating between the two, and occasionally taking her mouth with a ferocity that rivaled an animalistic urge.

Steve's fingers continued in and out of Sloane's pussy, causing his dick to constrict uncomfortably against his pants. He shifted to relieve some of the pressure, as he circled Sloane's clit with his finger - one orgasm, and then he was going to sink his cock so far into her heat, she would feel it for days. The thought caused a smile to fall upon Steve's lips. He could feel Sloane's body tighten; her muscles surround his fingers, her breath turning into panting episodes. Steve increased his pace, pulling her orgasm out of her body.

Sloane felt the orgasm build. The combination of Ty's mouth nipping at her breasts and Steve's fingers hitting her g-spot as he thrust them in and out of her pussy, sent Sloane over the edge. The orgasm hit her hard as she bucked up from the bed, every muscle in her body twitching as they tightened, as Steve milked the orgasm from her, aftershocks and all. He removed his fingers, and ordered Ty to undo the restraints. Sloan could hear Steve removing his pants, and the familiar tear of the condom wrapper. The bed shifted as Steve and Ty repositioned themselves.

The calloused fingers of Steve's hands found their way to Sloan's pubis, running them over her already sensitive clit. Sloane let out a cry, moaning their names as sensations over took her body again. Sloane felt Steve line up at her core, teasing her opening with his sheathed cock. Still blindfolded, Sloane felt Ty's hands move her face toward the side, and closer to his own cock. Although Sloane desired to know what it felt like to have both men inside her at once, they had already agreed that her body and ass wasn't ready for that quite yet. Instead, Ty slid his hard length into her mouth again, whispering to her that her pussy was his later. Steve grabbed Sloane's hips, pulling her body on to his cock, impaling her. Both men moved in a rhythm opposite one another; one in, one out. When her mouth was free, Sloane's pussy was filled.

The sensations began to overwhelm her again as she tried to focus on Ty's pleasure, his blowjob. Ty's fingers trailed up and down over her breasts as Steve continued to thrust in and out of Sloane's tight cunt. The inability to see either man added to the arousal of the moment. Sloane felt herself tighten around Steve's hardness, milking his cock as another orgasm built. Ty continued to fuck her mouth with a steady rhythm, as Steve thrust in and out.

Both men were getting close as the speed of their movements increased; Ty's hands holding Sloane's head to him, Steve's fingers digging deeper into her hips, as they both released into her. A mix of moans and grunts filled the air as all three of them let their orgasms wash over them. Waiting a few moments, both men - breathless and sated - removed themselves from Sloane and, as Ty removed the blindfold, Steve made his way to the bathroom, returning shortly with a towel.

Sloane looked up at both of them. "That was amazing. Thank you so much."

Ty smiled at his wife, placing a quick kiss on her forehead. "Anything for you, darling."

Steve smiled at the couple as well. "Glad I could be of assistance. I'm going to head out. Enjoy the room for the night."

The couple watched as Steve dressed and left the room. Ty pulled the covers down on the bed and pulled his wife close to him, spooning her body. Whispering into Sloane's ear, Ty talked of his excitement at the night, and his appreciation that Sloane discussed her desires with him. "I think we might be able to make this a more frequent thing. It turned me on so much when you were taking him."

Sloane smiled to herself. "Next time, I want both of you in me."

"As the Queen wishes," Ty responded before pulling Sloane closer to him again.

A quick snicker, and the couple closed their eyes, drifting off into the sleep of afterglow.

All of the Above
By Cassandra Park

We faced forward as the casino's elevator rose. I could almost feel Pete's excitement like a vibrating energy passing between us, but we did not touch until the elevator dinged. Then I took his hand as we stepped out onto the 40th floor. I looked him up and down. He looked back at me with hungry eyes, just for a moment, and then he diverted his eyes downward.

"Are you ready, young man?" I said. His hand closed tighter around mine.

"I've been ready," he said quietly.

"I'm going to do whatever I want to you," I said.

"Oh. Yes," he said. "That's all I've been thinking about for weeks ... for months."

Last time I'd seen Pete was a year ago, here in Las Vegas. In fact, Las Vegas was the only place I'd ever been with him. Both of us had our own partners, and we lived on opposite sides of the country. We'd met a few years ago at the same fetish convention we were attending that weekend, in this very same casino on the outskirts of Las Vegas.

I missed him. He was adorable. He was 10 years younger than me, and had dark brown hair, dark eyes and lashes, firm arms and muscular thighs. And ... mm ... a butt that filled the seat of his jeans perfectly. Not too flat, not too round; firm from working out.

To most people at the convention, and to his partner, he was a top. That's how he wanted people to know him.

I treated him differently. I knew his other side. To me, he was my submissive pain slut.

As we entered my hotel room and the door clicked shut behind us, I recalled some of our adventures.

Two years ago I'd placed clover clamps on his nipples and balls, shoved him hard up against a wall and whipped him with a long leather belt, only removing the clamps after his belting.

Last year I'd caned him—everywhere. Not just on his butt and the backs of his thighs, but the front of his thighs, and his chest and nipples. I had ordered him to lie on his tummy, grabbed one of his ankles, and caned the bottom of his foot. Nothing severe—just two strokes. Then I'd grabbed his other foot. His yelps had been delicious and had sent a shiver of power through me.

Here we were in Las Vegas again, in a hotel room, at the convention. Ready for round three.

I told him to strip and then position himself facing the wall with his elbows out and his hands behind his head.

Did it make me a sadist if I was just *curious* about some people's reaction to pain and humiliation? It didn't always turn me on to cause pain, but it did turn me on that certain men would give me the power to hurt them. I picked my subs carefully. If they were too masochistic, if they didn't react, I would be bored. It was not exciting to top a bottomless pit who in the end would not respect me because I hadn't broken him. I was not out to break anyone. I was looking for mutual enjoyment.

This one was special. With Pete I *did* get turned on, partly because he looked so good as he suffered. And partly because he could take pain all over. Nipples, back, face, stomach, feet, hands, legs, butt, cock and balls. Nothing was off limits.

It was always amazing to me. But it was also a challenge. With Pete I had to get creative, as much for myself as for him. It *was* about pain. But it could never be *just* about pain.

There was something he'd said in passing last year, and had brought up once again in an email during the year. He'd told me about a female domme he'd played with who had once made him put on a women's dress during a scene.

"What did you think of that?" I'd asked.

"I liked it. It felt like I could ... I don't know ... let go," he'd admitted.

"Did you feel embarrassed?"

"Yeah ... maybe a little."

I filed it away for future reference.

"Forced Feminization" was a fetish that on one level annoyed me. It implied that it was humiliating to dress and act like a woman. On the other hand, I was fascinated by the number of guys I'd met who liked this. They were usually quite intelligent, respectful but not overly solicitous of women—by every appearance they considered women their equals in every way except physically. And they were often quite stereotypically masculine in day-to-day life. They could be the CEOs or the CFOs or the high-powered attorneys in the skyscrapers of New York, or they could be musicians or artists, talented and passionate about their craft. All of them needed a release.

For some subs, it was just about pain. For some it was pain, and giving over control, and a little touch of humiliation. I was taking a gamble that Pete would submit to a little more than pain this time around.

I hadn't discussed it with Pete ahead of time. I'd simply prepared a little package for him. He was a few inches taller than me, but he was lean while I was a bit hippy. If clothes my size didn't fit him, they'd be pretty close. I bought him new panties—and sheer ones—but almost everything else was from my own closet and drawers, stuff I was getting ready to donate or throw out because I hadn't worn it in a while. I'd also made a stop at a local Payless Shoes and picked up a pair of size 10 women's heels.

So there it was. A simple garter belt. Stockings. A little black dress. A padded bra—with a pair of socks so he could pad it further. Clip-on earrings. Lacy panties. It hadn't cost me a lot. And I thought I would have fun with this game.

"I have a surprise for you," I said, placing my hand on the back of his neck and gripping it—for nothing else than to feel the shudder run through him at my touch. "Keep facing the wall."

"A surprise?" From the side I could see him smile. "Do I get a hint?"

"Just stay in position and keep your elbows out." He adjusted his elbows and placed his feet into a wider stance for better stability. "The hint is it's something we've never done before and it's something I think you'll like."

"Hmmm," he murmured.

I lay the clothes out on the bed. "I'm going into the bathroom to change. When you hear the bathroom door close, put on the clothing and accessories I left on the bed."

"Yes, Ma'am," Pete said.

I changed into my own outfit in the bathroom.

I had purchased a men's suit, dark with thin grey pinstripes, dress shoes, a white shirt and a striped red tie. Before I dressed, I took a wide ace bandage and wrapped it around my chest, binding my breasts. I knew I didn't really look like a man, but it was a fun facsimile. I'd found a fake goatee that almost matched my hair at a costume shop. I pasted it onto my chin. I topped it all off with a fedora, and I looked at myself in the mirror and smiled. It amused me.

"Are you ready, Pete?" I called through the door.

"Almost, Ma'am," he said. "I'm having some trouble with the garters."

"All right," I said, and I came out of the bathroom.

He blinked at my appearance. "Wow!" he said. "You look ... different. I like it!"

He himself seemed a little embarrassed in his apparel, but the dress fit him pretty well. He'd stuffed the bra nicely and his boobs were rounded enough to almost look real.

I sat in the hotel room armchair. "Come stand in front of me," I said. "Next time, 'young lady,' I'll expect you to do the garters yourself."

"Yes, Ma'am." He came over. I pulled his lacy panties down, hooked his garters to the stockings and then pulled the lacy panties back up. They needed to be on the outside.

"Kneel," I told him. He knelt on the carpet in front of me, and I applied his makeup—foundation, powder, blush, eyeliner and shadow, and a dark, brick-red lipstick. As Pete submitted to this, I sensed him shaking a little.

"Are you OK?" I asked.

"Yes, Ma'am," he replied. "But no one's done makeup on me before."

"Not that domme who made you put on the women's clothes that time?" I asked.

"No," Pete said. He placed his hands on my knees to steady himself. "I did it to myself a few times," he admitted. Then, "I am so fucking turned on."

I ran my hand around the back of his head and stroked his hair. "I'm pretty excited myself," I admitted. "And you look terrific!" He closed his eyes at my touch, shivering. "Keep your eyes closed, Pete."

I pulled a wig out of my bag and put it on him, tugging it into place and using a little plastic brush to get the loose hairs in order. It was shaped in a bob, a dark, reddish brown piece. It looked great on him. Maybe it was because he was young. Maybe because I'd done a decent job with his makeup. "Okay. There you go." His hands stayed on my thighs as I worked.

"How do I look, Ma'am?" he asked, breathing heavily.

"Go see." He went to the full-length mirror across from the bathroom. I walked behind him and as he turned left, then right, looking at himself, I checked out how we looked together. I made a short man and he made a tall woman, but hey, who cared? It was Vegas. There were all kinds of freaks here.

"Ready to go for a walk?" I asked.

"A walk?"

"Yes," I said. "I want to take my girl downstairs and buy her a drink."

I knew what he was thinking. He wasn't submissive in public. People knew him as a top. What if he ran into someone from the convention? Or, God forbid, his girlfriend? My partner and his girlfriend knew that he and I played, but neither of them really wanted to know the details.

"I'm not sure about this," he said.

"Do you really think anyone will recognize us?" I said. "You look nothing like yourself."

"I don't think I look like a woman," he said, looking in the mirror again and raising his chin, inspecting himself. "I have a bit of an Adam's apple."

"I don't think I look like a man, either," I said. "I'm way too short—and I have women's hips."

"I think you look cute."

"Which proves my point that I don't look like a man—but you *could* pass for a woman."

"An ugly one!" I could see him struggling. "Do I have to do downstairs like this?"

Would it be fair of me to make him go? I knew that he would. He wanted to obey me. But would he resent me if anyone recognized him? Did I care? ... Well, of course I cared. I wanted to play with him again. I considered how to answer. It would give me a thrill to go downstairs like this. Truly, I would love to walk him around for a little while. I was not without sympathy, however.

"Are you willing to be obedient, Pete?" I asked.

"Yes..." he said cautiously. "Are you still going to beat me later?"

"Oh, probably," I said, winking. "But you might have to earn it. How about this? Since we're in Vegas, why don't we play a game?"

"Okay ... what do you mean?"

I still had some surprises up my sleeve for my young man. "Go over and face the corner. Don't turn around," I ordered. Under my suit pants, he didn't know, was a harness I'd put on earlier. I took my dildo from its case, undid my pants and inserted it into the harness. Then I kept the pants open and let my beige rubber cock stick out below the hem of my white shirt. I tossed a bottle of lube on the bed near me.

From a drawer I took out a heavy wooden bath brush and dropped it on the bed next to the lube.

I stood with my hands on my hips, tugging a little at the edge of the white shirt so he'd see my cock almost right away. "Turn around," I said.

He blinked, looked at me, looked at *it*, looked at me. "Oh," he said. "Wow. I ... hm. I didn't expect that to be part of things ... are you really going to— ?"

"I wanted to make our scene a little more interesting this time around," I said, with a wicked smile. "Are you ready to play the game?"

"Do I have a choice, Ma'am?" he said nervously. I watched him. He had not said that he would not go down to the casino with me. Nor did he say he was opposed to the strap-on.

"No, you don't have a choice," I said. Of course he had a choice. He always had a choice ... sort of.

I picked up the hotel's notepad, tore off a sheet and tore it into three pieces. I numbered them 1 to 3, then folded the slips and placed them into one of the glass tumblers, covering it with my hand and shaking it up.

"One—we go down to the casino for a drink and then come back up here and I spank you," I said. "Two—I paddle you black and blue with the bath brush. Three—you get the strap-on."

Pete watched me, seeming about to say something. He seemed very uncertain. Then he sat on the bed. "Can we talk for a minute?" he asked.

I sat next to him and held his hand. It was very surreal, looking out from under the brim of a fedora and seeing him in a dress and makeup. "Sure."

"I've been waiting all year to see you," he said. "You know I adore you and want to please you."

I waited.

"I don't *want* to choose," he said. "I want you to do whatever makes you happy. Whatever you want. Yes, I want you to beat me, but I want ... I want those other things, too." He looked at me and then anxiously away. "If this is what you want to do to me ... um ... then I want you to. I'm nervous, but I don't want to leave Vegas without exploring this." A pause. "And don't think I haven't fantasized about you with a strap-on."

"Really?" I said. "So you don't want to choose?"

"No."

"You're saying 'all of the above'?"

"Yes."

"All right," I said. "All of the above. Hm. This is going to be a fun evening."

I picked up my smart phone and turned on the camera. "Do you mind if I take a picture of you in your outfit before we go? ... just for us, no one else."

"No, I trust you," he said. "You can take a picture."

"All right, young man. " But I put the phone down on the dresser. "Hand me that bath brush." I tucked my cock back inside my pants, adjusted it downward so it was not completely obvious, and zipped up my pants. He handed me the bath brush. "This is what you want and need, isn't it?" I said.

"Yes, Ma'am."

"You don't have to be anywhere for a while, do you?" I said.

"No, ma'am."

"Good, then we don't have to rush. Bend over and put your hands on that chair," I said. "Daddy needs to spank his girl." I pulled up his skirt and tugged his lacy panties down past the garters. I gripped him around the waist tightly, holding him in place. My pain slut was going to get what he'd asked for. I started to paddle him with the bath brush, building the intensity as I went along. He tried to be stoic but after a while he finally let go and cried out. I smacked him harder and harder as he wriggled and sobbed. I beat him raw, not finishing until he had stopped fighting and was limp in my arms. Then I gave him 20 last strokes before finally pulling his panties back up and his skirt back down. I moved behind him and put my arms around him, pressing into his ass through my pants and his skirt, the cock between us.

"Just a little tease for now," I whispered. The cock pressed back against me, too, sending a craving deep within me. I was feeling such a heady rush of power. He reached back and clutched tightly at my hand. I shivered, gripped his hand for a few seconds, then got control of myself and stood up.

"Stand up, Pete. Up against that wall." I picked up the smart phone. His makeup was smudged around his eyes. His lipstick needed a touch-up already, and his wig was a little crooked. I'd redo his makeup and wig before we went downstairs, but this was the look I wanted now—dazed and disheveled. I snapped a few shots.

"Let's fix you up a little, Pete. I can't have my girl looking like a hot mess downstairs." He smiled dreamily and sat as I started to fix his makeup.

"I *am* a hot mess," he whispered, then giggled. Before I could put his lipstick on, he leaned over and kissed me, hard. "Thank you for understanding what I need," he said.

Now was not the time to get all soft and sentimental, I thought, although I was deeply touched. And horny.

"You're going to see how well I understand you when we get back up to this room," I said. "Now sit still and behave. I don't know about you, but I need a drink. I need to buy my girl a drink down at the bar, where everyone will see her squirming in her seat, thinking about what will happen next."

"You're going to fuck your girl later?" he whispered.

"I'm going to show her off, I'm going to fuck her, and I'm going to beat her again," I said softly, and felt his hand tighten on my knee at the word "beat."

I picked up the lipstick, tilted my girl's chin up, and began to reapply it to her waiting, willing lips. We were about to go public.

Puppy Gets Her Medicine
By Corrine A. Silver

He must have had a bad day. As soon as we were through the door, he told me to go to my kennel. When I didn't move right away, he swatted my butt with the newspaper and I took off at a gallop with him following me.

"Just a little bit, pet. I need a few minutes before we play." His tone was sweet, almost apologetic. I got to my box and stopped just outside it to change. Once I was in my natural state, I crawled in and curled into a loop to rest, meditating to stay settled despite the building frenzy of anticipation. He closed me in and left, turning the light out.

It was a small amount of time and my Master returned, flipping the switch. The light was so bright; I hid my eyes for a moment. But I didn't want him to think that I wasn't excited to see him, so I sat up quick, looking at him with a smile on my face.

"There's my good girl," he crooned as he unlocked my cage. When he opened the door, I stretched my neck toward him, but didn't try to get out. I remembered what happened when I didn't wait for the command.

He reached in and scratched behind my ear. His touch was heaven. I closed my eyes and angled my neck toward him, pushing into his hand. He stroked me a bit longer and then roughly hooked his fingers through my collar.

"Okay, out." With his other hand, he snapped and pointed at the floor in front of him and I scrambled to sit at his feet. "Time for Medicine."

Medicine. That's what he called it. He knew I always choked and sputtered. He kept promising it'd get better. I dropped my head, knowing I was going to disappoint him, but he cupped my chin and made me look at him as he pried my jaws apart and pushed his *Medicine* to the back of my throat.

"Be a good little bitch for me and take it." His voice was strained. I knew he was trying to make me better, but it was so hard—the pressure in my throat, the gagging feeling. It was too much and I pulled my head back, shaking from side to side. The Medicine fell out.

He looked disappointed. I had known that I was going to disappoint him again and I whined, a high-pitched sounds in the deep of my throat. I just wanted to make him proud of me, even knowing that he'd been training me like this for months and I hadn't ever done anything but let him down.

He squatted down so his eyes were level with mine and I dropped my gaze immediately. He stroked his hand over my head and said, "We're going to try again. We'll get it done, girl."

His voice was soft, encouraging even, and it made me feel a little better. I was determined to do better this time. He stood again and hooked his thumb in my mouth, pulling my jaw down. This time, I keep my eyes closed, scrunching them up. When he pushed the Medicine back against my throat, I swallowed against my gag reflex. He kept a hand on the back of my head to steady me, but murmured, "Good girl. A treat after if you take all of it."

My mouth watered. He slipped the Medicine back again, a little further this time. I struggled to keep myself controlled, but his hand was there on the back of my head to help. And I was grateful for it because I'm sure I would have pulled away if he hadn't.

For just a moment, he held the Medicine at the back of my throat. Then slipped it backward again, almost completely out of my mouth.

"Who's a good girl?" He crooned and I looked up at him, smiling stretching my mouth just a little. He slid the Medicine back into my mouth, easier this time. He held my gaze. "That's a good girl. Now, stay."

I knew what that meant. It meant stay exactly how he had put me, don't move even a little bit. So I locked my muscles in place, jaw wide, and I took my Medicine, over and over, down my throat, eyes locked on Master. His grim satisfaction, his straining neck, building to his growling curses at me. I knew what those words meant. They meant my treat was coming soon. His growl triggered my drool, like it always does now.

He held the back of my head and arched back, nearly howling with release, but then I got what I wanted, my treat. It shot hot and salty all over my tongue. I couldn't keep the smile off my face as he stood panting above me.

I have a doggy blanket on the bed that I get to snuggle into when I'm good and he pulled me up there, got me settled. "Okay, girl. Good work. Let's relax a bit."

He took his clothes the rest of the way off and snuggled into bed with me. He flicked the remote and some music turned on, low, peripheral. When he started petting my back and neck, I turned to look up at him expectantly.

But he just smiled at me. "No, honey. I think we're all done for now."

All done. Those were the words to end the scene, end the moment. I smiled, worry around my eyes.

"Bad day, honey?"

Employment Benefits
By Carrie Anne Ward

Marie had been working as a maid at Bennett Abbey for a few months now. It was a huge mansion in the countryside, close to nothing but fields. The Master was a very wealthy man. He was a man made rich by modern money, but he had old fashion values. He was undoubtedly handsome and well groomed, and Marie couldn't help but find him attractive in his three-piece suits and with his neatly sculpted mouse brown hair. However, Marie also found him very intimidating. She could see the authority in his eyes, and she feared to get on his bad side. Sometimes, when she was cleaning in the same room as the Master, she would feel his stare upon her, and she wasn't quite sure whether she liked it.

She was only 18 years of age, and this was her first job. She had to look after her family, so she worked damn hard to make sure she did nothing to fuck it up, as she couldn't afford to lose this job. It wasn't the best paid job in the world, but it was still a job, and she would do anything not to lose it, which she was pretty sure would happen soon enough.

Last week she had broken a very rare ornament, and tried her best to repair it, but she was unsuccessful in her attempts, so she decided to hide the pieces, hoping he wouldn't notice.

She was working in the kitchen today, tidying the pans away after the kitchen staff had left for the evening. She was the only one left, as she had agreed to do overtime after the Master had asked her. The open fire behind her crackled and hissed so wildly that she barely heard the Master enter the kitchen.

"Marie?" spoke the Master, standing tall and confident before her.

"Yes, Sir?" she answered in a feeble voice.

The look in his eyes made her legs wobble with worry. That was not the look of a happy man.

"Would you like to tell me where my antique vase has gone?" he asked in a steady voice.

Holy crap! She swallowed down on the large lump of fear rising in her throat. Her legs shook, and she knew this was the moment she was about to lose her job, so she spun rapidly on her heels to face the opposite direction, desperate to hide her guilt-riddled face. He stepped in close behind her as she held on to the work top surface for support from her quivering legs. He was so close that she could feel the heat radiate from him, so close that she was sure he was breaking some sort of boundary rules.

"I'm sorry Sir. I..I broke it last week when I was cleaning. I didn't know what to do. I..."

She whirled back to face him so quickly that she lost her stance and fell forward. The Master caught her in time, grabbing the tops of her arms, and planted her back on her feet. His cold eyes glared right in to hers, and all she could do was stare right back. There was no expression, no emotion on his face, and Marie had no idea what was going to happen. He still had hold of her arms, but his hands now brought with them a more powerful, bruising grip. She wriggled ever-so-slightly, to try and free herself from his grasp, but couldn't. The silence was killing her, and the longer he stared at her, the more she felt uncomfortable and exposed.

"What are you going to do, Sir? Please don't fire me, I need this job. I'll do anything," she pleaded.

He raised one eyebrow at her remark. A questioning look claimed his handsome, stern face. *What was he thinking?*

"Anything, you say?" he asked, and placed one hand on her thigh between her legs, only a couple of inches shy of her sex. She gasped at his touch. Her heart beat wildly behind her ribs, and she held onto her breath. The suddenness of his actions had her head spinning, and her body went into a frenzied state of panic. What was he doing? Was he taking advantage of her?

Suddenly he pulled her by the arm, and dragged her down to the cellar. He opened the door and stepped down the stone stairs to the cellar; it was cold and damp with an earthy smell tainting the air, Marie hated it down there.

"Two things are going to happen. In order to keep your job, you are going to be punished for your mistake, and learn your lesson, and after you have been punished, you are going to do something to make Sir happy, you hear me?" he said curtly.

"What is it I have to do to make you happy, Sir?" she choked. She asked the question, but she wasn't sure she wanted the answer.

"Be quiet and do as you're told. You want this job, right?" he asked sternly, and she nodded. "You want to make me happy, right?" She nodded again. "You find me handsome, right?" His words hit hard her, and she glared at him in surprise. She wasn't expecting him to say such a thing to her. He was right though, she did think he was handsome.

"Oh, come on, Marie. Such an innocent looking young girl you are. But I know underneath the surface there is a darker side." He stepped closer to her, towering above her, and let her hair loose from the ponytail. "You are going to pleasure me. Keep me happy, if you want to keep your job. Okay?"

She felt sick with fear. She wasn't a virgin, she had only had sex once with a boy she had been friends with at school, but Marie didn't know how to be sexual. She was absolutely petrified, but she couldn't lose this job. He was clearly using her weakness against her, and they both knew it. So, through pure fear, she nodded lightly and waited.

"Good girl. Now, remove your clothing and follow me."

She struggled to unbutton her blouse because of the incessant shaking flowing through her fingers. She tried hard to concentrate on keeping her breath steady, and she was pretty damn sure he could hear her heart pounding from within. Once she had removed all form of clothing, she walked shakily over to the wall, where he held on to a pair of iron shackles attached to a very rusty chain hanging from the ceiling. He put her wrists in to each of the shackles, and she shivered from the coldness of them on her skin. She was facing the wall, taking in long deep breaths and repeatedly telling herself it would be okay. She hadn't expected the stinging feeling of leather split across her bare bottom, and she cried out in pain from the Master's belt strike at her flesh.

Five more smacked across her bottom, when finally the Master removed the shackles and rubbed at the raw skin on her bum. She was shivering uncontrollably now, and she worried what was next. She liked the feeling of his hands on her flesh, but she tried hard to fight it. He was most definitely breaking some very personal boundaries with her, so why did she like it?

His firm hands caressed her flesh, and slid down and circled at the apex of her thighs. Then he slid his fingers inside her, and she gasped at the penetration, scrapping her fingernails down the stone wall as he moved his fingers inside.

"Someone clearly liked her punishment a little too much. Let's see what we can do about that." He grabbed her by the back of the neck, and pushed her tiny, quivering body over a wooden table, and pried her legs apart. "Are you scared, Marie?" he murmured.

"Yes, Sir," she answered with an uneven voice.

"Good."

She heard the sounds of him pull down his zipper. She closed her eyes, as she wasn't sure she wanted to see what was about to happen. "I own you now, Marie. You are mine to please and torture, whenever and however I want. Do you hear me? Otherwise, you will no longer be under my employment."

Owned? Did she want to be owned? To live this life submitting to her Master's will. Knowing that at any minute he could call on her, use and abuse her for his own pleasure. She wasn't sure of anything at that moment in time, so she agreed to his terms, regardless of what she was agreeing too. Regardless of the fact that she had just signed her life away to him, and just then, he pushed his hard, large cock into her, and she drew in a deep breath.

She was hesitant at her first but when she felt his nails prick harder into her neck she quivered and let go, accepting him fully. He pounded relentlessly into her sex, driving with such a force that it felt painful. But something was happening to her, something she had never felt before. The heat had increased somewhat, beads of sweat began to dot between her breasts and she could barely breathe. The muscles in her body turned rigid, and she felt a strange tingling feeling flourish inside of her, when suddenly an explosion rippled over her, she bucked and quivered violently. She had never felt anything so incredible in her life. She panted hard, and moaned with delight as he fucked her senseless. He hissed and continuously told her that she was his as he slid his manhood into her. He plunged one final side-splitting thrust into her, and came with a force inside of her.

She felt his cock twitch from within, his physique tighten and he grunted in satisfaction as he pulled out from her.

"Consider yourself my own personal slave," he whispered in her ear. "Once you're dressed, you may continue with your duties."

He left her there in the cellar, shuddering and in pain. He had taken her, used her for his own pleasure, and had most definitely crossed a line. She should have been upset and disgusted by him, and left the mansion there and then and never returned. But instead, she pulled on her dress and continued with her chores, counting down the seconds until the next time he claimed her, and a small smirk was trying to twitch its way in to the corner of her mouth.

Part Two will appear on my site in the near future.

My Princess
By Mia Koutras

This is the third year I've participated in Toronto's week-long International Festival.

This is the third year I've lusted after Peter, the guitarist for the Greek band that provides the live music for our dance performances—a six-foot epitome of Greek godliness himself.

This is the first time I am the Princess of the Sparta pavilion, representing Greek culture, food and hospitality in my gorgeous, goddess Athena costume. I am "Miss Sparta," hosting a huge after-party in the hall of Saint Spiridon's Greek Orthodox Church, for all the pavilions in Toronto and the media coming for interviews and highlights.

And this is the first time a man's face is buried in my tits as I'm trussed up against a fence around the corner from a church.

Good Lord.

When Peter surprised me outside the dressing room with his melodious *"Yiasou, prinkipissa,"* I knew I would follow him wholeheartedly. I had also heard the rumors about him—certain preferences that were on the edgier side of a "good time," so to speak. I didn't care, because his darker urges appealed to me, as did his confident, commanding presence. I was drawn to him. Apparently, he noticed.

As I focus on him now in the wan light, feasting on my nipples, biting and licking with abandon, he looks up at me with eyes that can entrance me with a single glance. It truly amazes me how "choice" can totally change someone's life, and how a simple walk on a moonlit night can set a person on a new path...

* * * * *

We exited the door into the humid night—it hadn't cooled down much, and considering it was late June, it was still warm outside even though it was close to midnight. We were right smack dab downtown, and the church was beside—or surrounded by—buildings from the campus of one of Toronto's three universities. Skirting the small parking lot behind the church, we walked down the pathway to a lovely sitting area with park benches and trees. Grateful for the respite from standing in my heels all evening, I sank down onto the closest bench and sighed in relief. Peter chose to stand in front of me, which meant that I had an up-close and personal view of his groin. I prayed that he couldn't see my need flashing like a beacon on my warm cheeks.

He tilted his head slightly to the side and gifted me with an all-too-knowing smile. "Are you all right, Ellie?"

I was riveted by his eyes, which looked darker now. I assumed that since it was night, then his electric blue irises wouldn't be as noticeable, but there was a full moon tonight, and I saw him clearly. Security spotlights from neighboring buildings also helped flood the area with some light. That's why I was able to see the gleam in his gaze.

"Oh, yes ... I'm fine. Just a little wired with the party and the interview I just finished."

"Here, let me rub your shoulders ... I can help you to release some of that tension."

Peter shuffled to the side and I followed suit. I sighed with contentment as soon as his hands touched my skin, and he leaned over my shoulder and winked. After some idle chitchat, he asked an interesting question, one to which I knew the answer very well. "Tell me, Ellie—what is your full Greek name? I know that there could be more than one possibility because of the short form you use."

"It's Eleftheria," I replied, shivering from his touch as his hand lingered on my neck, his long fingers resting against it intimately.

"Your name means 'freedom.' It suits you," he said warmly as his fingers slid off my neck. My skin felt bereft of his touch.

"Oh? How so?" I was curious as to how he felt that the symbolic meaning of my name suited me.

He paused as he looked at me, and that gleam I detected in his eyes earlier intensified. Then he licked his lips. Slowly.

My core clenched and my panties dampened with a rush of liquid arousal.

Holy. Shit.

He reached out for my hand, waiting patiently for my response. I didn't hesitate. I put my hand in his and he pulled me up from the bench. He tugged me close—so close that I felt the heat radiating off his body. His solid, broad, perfectly muscled body.

"Well, I've known you for a few years now, and Frances knows how ... interested I am in you," he admitted, touching my cheek with an index finger and letting it drift down to my chin.

"Oh?" I squeaked. I was secretly thrilled, but I lowered my eyes because I was afraid the hope I had made me too vulnerable. Oh hell, wait ... my best friend knew before I did?

He tucked his finger under my chin and tilted my head upward so I could look into his determined gaze. "I know that you're free with your help, you're free with your kindness, and when you feel that it's right, you're free with your heart." He smirked. "Frances also promised me that my nuts would hang from her rear-view mirror if I hurt you."

I chuckled softly. "Yeah, that sounds like her." I felt my need—insistent, demanding—a like swelling wave of desire that engulfed my senses, and I knew I couldn't mask the longing in my eyes anymore. He knew it. A seductive smile graced his pouty lips and his hand slid to the back of my neck, beneath my riot of curls, where it rested lightly but firmly. My eyes widened when I saw the passion reflected in his gaze, the color of his eyes changing to a luminous Mediterranean blue in the clear moonlight.

"Is it right, *prinkipissa*? What do you want?"

"You," I whispered, trembling in his hold.

"Good," he whispered back, and then pressed his lips to mine.

He surged forward and enveloped me in his strong embrace, crushing my breasts against the chiseled planes of his chest. My arms wrapped around his waist and I held on as my hunger for this man threatened to consume me. I shuddered when I felt his thick, hard cock pressing into my belly, straining against the zipper of his jeans. His lips were so soft, yet so insistent, and when he nipped my lips and licked at the seam of my mouth, I opened for him and his tongue swept inside. I melted into him right there, his tongue stroking and tangling with mine, stoking my desire into a raging inferno. I was burning for him.

He broke our kiss, but not our embrace, and touched our foreheads together. We both gasped for air, and we breathed in unison, our chests billowing outward so that our bodies pulsed together in rhythmic, fleeting touches.

"Ellie," he rasped, "do you want to be free ... with me? I will show you freedom like you've never experienced."

"Yes," I murmured, reaching up and snaking my hands around his neck. I tilted my face upwards, hoping for another soul-searing kiss.

He teased my lips, sipping at them as he would the rarest of delicacies, and then caught my lower lip in his front teeth. "Hang tight, baby," he crooned against my mouth. "Tonight, I'm going to make you fly."

* * * * *

We abandoned the bench and Peter led me to a shadowed area, farther away from the church, that was still touched by the moonlight. We slipped between two buildings, undoubtedly belonging to the university campus, and then he turned and cupped my cheek with his palm.

"Ellie, I want you so badly, but if you don't want this, now is the time to stop from going any further."

I understood what he needed—my clear, undeniable consent. "I don't want to stop, Peter. I want this. Please." His expression softened slightly, and his thumb caressed my cheekbone.

"What now?" I asked hesitantly, glancing at our surroundings. When I turned back to him, I noticed that wicked gleam was back in his eye.

"You, *prinkipissa mou glykia*, will leave everything in my hands. Literally." He grinned wickedly while I swooned from his endearment ... *my sweet princess*. "We're going to have some hot, sexy fun, and I promise that if you're uncomfortable with what we're doing, at any time, tell me to slow down. If you can't do something, or you're scared, just tell me to stop."

He searched my eyes, most likely watching for any signs that I might tuck tail and run. But I understood, and I smiled and nodded. He gave me a swift kiss and then pulled me towards the wrought iron fence that separated the buildings of the university campus, and I was relieved to see that it was more secluded and out of view from the church. A frisson of trepidation flashed through me, but I wasn't scared to be alone with Peter—I knew, deep down, that he wouldn't hurt me. My excitement, edged with a tiny bit of fear, was because I had a feeling that I was going to like everything he had to offer.

"Ellie, I want you to face the fence. Grab the railings and spread your legs."

A bolt of lust shocked my core. *Yep, that confirmed my feeling.*

I did exactly as he asked and fisted my hands around the unyielding metal bars.

I took one step away from the railings and spread my legs shoulder-width apart.

"Wider." The tone of his voice was different now ... it was stronger. Deeper. I stuck my ass out a little as I widened the stance of my legs. I couldn't help it—my inner naughty girl decided to show up to the party and taunt him a little.

"Mmm ... just like that. I love how your legs look, all tight and sleek, waiting for my touch. Do you want me to touch you, *prinkipissa?*"

The fact that he asked me if I wanted him to touch me—instead of grabbing and rutting on me like a feral animal—amped up my anticipation even more. My skin tingled and I almost screamed a "hell yes" at him.

"Please touch me, Peter ... I'm going crazy here," I pleaded with him.

I heard the amusement in his voice. "Don't worry, I will." And that's when I felt the rough pads of his fingers as they started at the tops of my laced sandals and glided slowly up the backs of my thighs. His hands slid under the skirt of my costume and rested on my buttocks.

"Such soft skin," he murmured. "You have a beautiful ass, but I need to see it too. Walk your hands down the railings so you can bend over more. Remember, don't let go of the fence." I went into position and noted that my back wasn't as tense like this. Then he flipped the hem of the skirt up and over so my ass was exposed. I felt the humid air caress my bared cheeks, courtesy of the nude-colored thong I had worn with my costume.

Peter was rubbing his hands all over my ass, teasing me with quick pinches and squeezing my flesh, pressing his fingers into my skin. It felt so good that I started squirming in his hands, impatient for more. Then he pulled his hands back. For a split second, I wondered what he was doing, but when I felt the impact, my brain emptied of any rational thought.

Peter just spanked my ass. *Holy fuck.* My breathing hitched, and I swiveled my neck to glare at him.

He chuckled behind me. "It's like I can actually see the wheels spinning in your head. Okay, I'm going to tell you, straight up, what I plan to do: I'm going to give you five smacks, but I'll go light on your ass for the first two. The remaining three are going to light you up, and you're going to love how the pain can turn to pleasure."

I gulped. Audibly.

He tried to reassure me. "Baby, whatever pain you feel from the spanking will transform into pleasure, if that is what turns you on. If it doesn't, then make sure to say 'stop.' I *will* respect your wishes." His eyes were glowing while he spoke to me, and then his hand was in my hair again, holding me firmly while bending down and crushing his lips to mine as if sealing his promise with his kiss. I was dazed, a little confused, but mostly surprised at how excited I felt about being spanked.

Peter hummed his approval after the first two smacks, caressing my skin and murmuring encouragement while I moaned from the tingling heat that spread across my cheeks.

The last three smacks were done in quick succession, and fire truly did blaze across my skin. Suddenly, the sting receded and the heat from my ass lit up nerve endings all over my body. My breasts felt heavy and my nipples were needy and tight. My sex was dripping and my clit was throbbing. All I knew at that moment was that I wanted his hands on me, badly, and I tilted my ass upwards, begging for his touch, while I writhed from the sensations bombarding my body.

"What is it, *prinkipissa*? What do you need? Tell me," he demanded softly, his hands pausing on my flaming buttocks in mid-stroke.

"I need you to touch me ... I need your hands on me," I managed to blurt out, even though my breathing was shallow and quick.

"Where, baby?"

"Oh God, everywhere ... please, I need to come... " I moaned, hoping that he understood my urgency.

"Shh ... I've got you, but you're not going to come yet, sweet girl. I'm not finished with you yet. I promised I'd make you fly." I felt his fingers pull my thong aside and slide into my sex, stroking the moist folds and spreading the evidence of my arousal. "Fuck ... you're so wet, baby. You love my hand on you; you love the sweet pain because you turn it into pleasure. Feel how easily I slip into you."

He pushed two fingers into my core, and my inner muscles clamped down on them immediately. I cried out at the intrusion, and when he pumped his fingers a few times, it felt so good that I protested when he removed them.

Peter laughed and plunged those two fingers into my sopping pussy again, but this time he added his thumb and agitated my clit. He was thrusting slowly, methodically, pushing me towards the pinnacle of my building climax. When I felt him brush those callused finger pads against the inner wall of my core, stimulating an incredibly sensitive spot, my legs started to shake. I didn't know if I could hold on any longer, but there was no way I was going to *stop*. I needed to reach that glorious pinnacle.

That's when Peter pulled his fingers out completely. With my chest heaving like the bellows stoking a fire, I looked over my shoulder and pinned him with a glare of disbelief and frustration that would have melted the iron in my hands. And he was completely unfazed by my obvious reaction while he stood there, basking in his power and control over me, and stared at me heatedly as he lifted his glistening fingers to his mouth and sucked them clean.

My mouth dropped open. That was one of the most erotic, sensual moves I had ever seen.

He flashed me a rakish smile. "You taste delicious, sweetness. Before we go any further, I want you to straighten up slowly, roll your shoulders once or twice, and then put your back up against the railings."

It really felt good to stretch my back, even though I struggled to get my breathing under control, and the shoulder roll helped to release the tension that had built up there. Now I just needed him to take care of the tension that built *down* there.

When I turned and faced him, my eyes were immediately drawn to his groin, where I clearly saw the outline of a massive erection trapped by the worn, light blue denim. My eyes widened—partly from shock, partly from wanton need—and my gaze snapped up to his own laser beam-like stare. The intensity of emotion emitted from his flashing baby blues was electric, and he stepped towards me. Of course, my gut reaction was to step backwards ... right up against the fence. Just where he wanted me.

I had instinctively reached out and grasped the railings again, needing something to ground me as my heart beat a wicked tribal rhythm in my chest. Peter pressed his body into mine and caged me with his arms by grasping the railings on either side of my head. He ground his steel hard cock into my belly and I gasped at the pulsating heat generated by it. He captured my eyes once again with his hot gaze, lowered his mouth and gently brushed my parted lips.

"Taste yourself, baby. *Eisai ei prinkipissa mou glykia, kai se thelo,*" he whispered against my mouth. I moaned my delight and opened to his questing tongue, which licked the outline of my lips first before delving inside. He kissed me like no one had ever kissed me before, and I was fully in his thrall as I melded with him, sharing my most intimate, female essence from his lips and his tongue. Had he said those words in English, I probably would have felt the same way, but whispering, "You are my sweet princess, and I want you," in Greek, with his genuine desire and need laced in his intonation, touched my heart and imprinted on my soul.

* * * * *

Peter broke our kiss and drew back slightly, allowing me to breathe a little more freely. Releasing the metal railings, he stepped back and scanned me from head to toe. A crooked smile teased his sexy, moist lips.

"Put your arms up beside your head so they're resting at 90 degree angles. Hook your fingers around the railings again. I don't want you to rip your pretty costume."

What? Rip my costume? My eyes narrowed into slits as I watched him advance again. Still, I obeyed, and he reached for the separate train that hung from my left shoulder. Lifting the material, he wound it around my arm *and* the railing a few times, and then secured my wrist effectively in the same manner. He tied it off by slipping the tail end of the material through one of the loops around my wrist, and then checked to make sure I still had a little wiggle room. He stepped back again and grinned triumphantly, and then repeated the same restraint on my right arm and wrist with the hanging material from that shoulder.

I was stunned, but my arousal roared through me—a blistering onslaught of heat that seared my core and disintegrated any residual doubt I may have had towards my ability to submit to Peter's dominance. Lust slammed into my brain and I tried desperately to make sense of my desires. I was tied up ... I was bound. Did I actually like this? The answer came quickly, flashing in my brain like a neon sign in Toronto's Entertainment district.

Yes.

I felt open and vulnerable, and he looked at me like a man ready to descend upon a feast and satisfy his ravenous appetite. I also felt the stirrings of pride and satisfaction—I turned him on this much, I was the one he desired above all. It was a heady feeling, powerful in its own right.

Suddenly, he dipped down and untied the laces of my left sandal, and then he quickly wound them around my ankle and the railing. He tied me securely, once again checking for a slight bit of slack. Surprisingly, he stood back up, leaving my right foot alone.

"The laces gave me this idea," he said amusedly. "When I saw you in your full costume this year, I knew I finally had to claim the gorgeous goddess for myself."

I took a deep breath and savored his words. Then I found the courage to speak. "When I first met you, I knew you were different. You have always been confident, honest and an all-around amazing man who could turn me on like a light switch. I wanted to stake my claim on you too."

I watched a myriad of emotions cross his face—lust, passion, and tenderness—and then he cupped my face, stroking my cheeks with his thumbs. "I want more than tonight, Ellie. This isn't a quick, kinky fuck for me. I don't do this with other women because, for the last few years, no one compared to you. I need to see where this goes. What do you think?"

This man had me swooning and melting every time he opened his mouth. He was going to have to scrape me up from the floor soon.

"Yes ... a hundred times *yes*! I want to see you—a lot," I exclaimed, grinning like a fool head over heels in love. I was pretty sure that I was already halfway there.

His lips crashed down on mine and our need for each other was palpable. He asserted his will into his kiss, but his reverence assured me that surrendering to him didn't mean losing myself. He had asked me first, and it was my choice. I felt respected and adored.

I had a choice.
I had power.
I had freedom.

He gentled the kiss and eventually drew back, his eyes glistening brightly, his lips pouty and moist. My lips also felt swollen from our heated kisses, but I needed more. From the look in his eyes, I believed that he felt the same way.

Peter fisted his hand in my hair again, holding tight and locking his gaze on mine. His jaw clenched briefly, and I could have sworn, even with what little light we had, that his cheeks looked flushed. Yet even in his heightening passion, he still held control.

"I need you now, baby ... I need to fuck you so badly or my dick is going to explode."

Is he asking me, or is he telling me? Does it fucking matter?

"God, yes ... please fuck me, Peter," I begged him. I was still riding high on my arousal from my spanking and his devastating kisses, and I needed release so badly from all of the erotic pressure that had built inside of me.

"First, I need to taste these." Peter reached for the drop neckline of my costume and tugged it downward, then reached into the bodice and exposed my breasts. He palmed both of them, one in each hand, plumping and squeezing my soft flesh. My beaded nipples were achingly hard, and he dipped down and sucked one, along with the top half of my breast, into his hot mouth. I moaned and panted as he suckled, rolling the nipple in his mouth and then pulling back until the taut nub was trapped in his teeth. I stifled my cry as much as I could when he bit down, but the pleasure receptors in my sex seemed connected to my breasts, and the erotic sensations threatened to overload my system. He laved my nipple tenderly, reverently, and then repeated his sensual ministrations on my other breast. He lifted his face, when he appeared to be satisfied that he had paid attention to both equally, and looked at me with awe in his swirling blue eyes...

* * * * *

"Goddamn, you're so beautiful and so responsive. I can't believe I waited this long to claim you," he admits in a low voice that makes me shudder. His half-lidded eyes are heavy with lust, and my pulse races even faster as I anticipate a joining of epic proportions. I can't believe we had danced around this attraction for three years, missing out on these electrifying feelings.

But this euphoria is so worth the wait.

"Peter, please." My voice shakes with need.

"Oh yeah, *prinkipissa mou*, I know what you want. And I'm going to give it to you—hard," he promises. His hands drop to his waist and I hear him unbuckling his belt and tearing open his jeans. He pushes them down his thighs, revealing his cock and balls. He grabs something from the front pocket of his jeans and then straightens to his full height, giving me a full view of his incredible hard-on.

My mouth drops open, almost comically, at the glorious sight of his massive erection. From what I can see in the less than favorable light, his cock is long and has a slight curve to it, stretching up towards his navel. His balls look heavy and full, and I wish I could feel their weight in my hand.

He lifts my skirt and reaches for my pussy, pulling aside the thong and stroking my outer lips, then slipping into the inner folds. He gathers some of my cream and spreads it all over my throbbing clit, making it even harder as his finger manipulates it. "Your pussy is soaking wet, and the scent of your juices is driving me crazy. Next time I'm going to lick it all up and eat you properly."

"Hurry," I plead. I'm so lust-addled from his dirty talk. Peter nods quickly and raises his unoccupied hand to his mouth and rips open the condom wrapper with his teeth. He removes his hand from my pussy—*dammit*—to sheath his bobbing cock. I almost lose my mind in a red haze of wanton lust when he tears my flimsy thong right off of me. Then he lifts my unrestrained leg and drapes it over his hip, anchoring it with his arm.

"This is why I didn't tie this one to the railing," he says smugly. And then he pushes inside me. Slowly.

Oh ... Jesus ... the overwhelming feeling of being filled with his hot, hard-as-steel cock ripples through my body. I'm bound and open, and I feel even more of the toe-curling sensations raise goose bumps all over my flesh. I can't wrap myself around him, and he uses that to his advantage as he pinches my nipples hard with his free hand. I gasp loudly as he buries himself to the hilt, and his angle of penetration provides the perfect friction for my clit.

Peter's thrusts start picking up speed, pushing me closer to the edge of bliss. He kisses me passionately, muffling our cries and grunts; our rasping breaths and vigorous skin-slapping sounds of hard fucking are the only noises that accompany the crickets and the odd car horn beeping in the distance.

"That's it, baby ... I can feel how slick your juicy cunt is, how hot and tight it is," he croons against my lips, then dives in for another tongue-tangling kiss. I feel my inner walls clench, as if my body is trying desperately to hold onto him. He breaks the kiss and gasps for air. "Fuck, I felt your pussy rippling around my cock. Dammit, I need to fuck you harder ... I need... " He trails off and hooks my trapped leg over his left arm, lifting it even higher, opening me up even more. I squeal with his shocking move because he reaches and grabs the metal railing on that side, bringing my knee right up to my shoulder. Then he reaches for another railing with his right hand, grasping it tight.

He uses the leverage to pull himself into me. Over and over he does this, pounding into me, causing me to grunt with each drive of his cock. He keeps stroking that special spot inside me, and my hypersensitive clit is screaming for release. He locks his steady gaze onto mine, and his eyes are glowing with determination. Possession. That look delivers me to brink of climax.

"Come for me, baby ... I want to see you fly. Come now!" he commands through his straining jaw.

I feel him grow impossibly harder, and then with one final

stroke, he drives in deep and grinds his pelvis against my clit. For one split second, I hover, all sensation completely suspended, and then I hurtle over the precipice into ecstatic release.

Peter hears my quick in-drawn breath and quickly covers my mouth with his, swallowing my screams of pleasure. I buck madly in his arms, but my movements are so limited because of his clever bondage that I feel like my climax keeps going on for longer than normal.

I feel Peter jerking inside me and he groans loudly, and then growls into my mouth as his body finally slows down and relaxes, fully sated from his incredible performance.

I break the seal of our lips and gasp, welcoming much-needed air into my burning lungs. "Peter, my leg," I hiss.

"Oh shit! Hold on." He releases his grip on the railings and gently lowers my leg to the ground. He pulls out of me slowly, ensuring that the condom doesn't slip off, and then he removes it, ties it off carefully and wraps it in an extra tissue he finds in his pocket.

After he pulls up his pants and tucks his spent cock away, he unties me from the fence and helps me tuck in and straighten my costume. He even bends down to retie the laces of my sandal.

"Thank God I go to yoga every week," I sigh as he helps rub and massage any tender spots. Peter looks at me incredulously and quirks an eyebrow.

"Really?" he inquires, but I see the interest on his face. Along with another spark of lust in his eyes.

"That's a demonstration for another day," I say firmly, but I tease him with my broad smile.

He looks at his watch and grimaces. "Baby, I've got five minutes to get you back to the after-party."

"Why so exact with the time?"

"Because I promised Frances that I only needed an hour of your time, and she helped maintain our privacy by covering for us if anyone asked where we were."

"Wonderful ... now my best friend knows exactly what we're doing," I grumble.

"Hey," Peter says soothingly as he reaches for me, "she can speculate, but no one will ever know how we came together tonight ... literally." He snickers and smooches me on the lips. I can never get enough of that.

"So, what if she hounds me for details like the persistent BFF she is? What do I tell her?" I ask him.

"Tell her these three simple facts," he says. Seriously. "You are *my* princess. You are *my* goddess. You are *mine*."

"Yes, sir." I reply coyly.

He growls low in his throat and his eyes gleam wickedly. He swoops in for another quick kiss. "You don't know how good that sounds," he says as he grabs my hand, gives me a knowing wink and walks me back to the party.

That's Harsh!
By Laura Antoniou
(Bonus story for the e-book edition of **The Slave**, 2010)

"Just send her into the city for the weekend, I think she won't mind a day or two off," Jimmy said dismissively, as he checked off names on the invite list.

"Hmm." Eric didn't comment beyond that abbreviated sound, and that alone made Jimmy look up to check on his lover. Raul, smooth as ever, pretended not to see the silent communication between his owners. He set down fresh glasses of iced ginger tea for them, condensation already thick from the walk to the back deck from the kitchen.

"Yeah, well," Jimmy offered with a slight shrug. Of course, she'd already had a day or two off, hadn't she, and not so long ago that everyone had forgotten it, either. "We've never had a girl here for one of these parties, and it's been ages. You know some of the guys would just die if there was actual pussy around."

"Still, it's extra help. And if we kept her, like, behind the scenes? Made her support staff…production crew? It's not like we'll have her prancing around in that tacky lingerie. And she's hardly some big titted cow, either – put enough clothing on her and she'll just vanish." Eric sketched the vanishing act with one hand in the air and snapped his fingers at their house manager. "What do you think, Raul? Can you do something with her and make her useful for the party without being the conspicuous cunt in a pack of pricks?" He grinned at his own alliteration and Raul smiled appreciatively.

"I'm sure we can do something, Master," he said. There was a slight gleam in his eye.

*****

"Tighter," he said, and Carl grunted as he adjusted the bandages.

"Ow!" Robin complained. "Now I can't breathe!"

"You're not required to," Raul said. "Now let's try the shirt."

Robin slipped the T-shirt over her head and smoothed it down over her tightly bandaged breasts. Sure enough, she looked flat – but also bandaged. The cotton bunched up over the layers of bandages and just didn't look natural or right in any way. Raul sighed.

"Know what she needs? Compression vest." Steve, aka Muscledog, was the latest addition to the household and ostensibly the reason for the upcoming party.

"What's that?" Carl asked.

"Guys wear 'em after surgery – you know, liposuction, tit sculpting. They kinda press you in, but smoothly. " He ran his large hands down his own well sculpted body. "Dude might be slightly out of shape, gets one to look better built, you know? So, get her a vest, and it'll be nice and smooth."

Raul nodded and slapped Robin on the ass. "Get one of those. Oh, and while you're at it, figure out a way to get a dick in your pants that doesn't look like a dildo. Try some balled up socks or something, and let me see my choices. And remember – you're tiny. Your dick should be, too."

"She's gonna look like she's 14 years old," Carl commented as he watched Robin head off to find a place to purchase the garment.

Raul nodded. "Some of the guests will like that, though."

"Maybe too much. How are you gonna make sure no one grabs her as a party favor?"

"Not my job. The Masters will make it clear the new boy is off limits. I mean, the *other* new boy." He winked at Muscledog who grinned happily. "This one will have them lined up."

"Life is harsh!" the bodybuilding slave exclaimed.

*****

Preparation for the party was more than costuming, though. All together, there would be 32 guests for most of a day and far into the night. There were no scheduled meals, nothing to break up the potential for sex, play or leisure time. Instead, Raul planned an ever-changing buffet of finger foods and barbeque. There would be four additional slaves borrowed from two of Jimmy's friends, just for non-sexual service. All of them would be assisting Raul with cooking and bar tending for those times when Raul would be conscripted for his Master's pleasure. "And that's another reason why I want you here," he'd said to Robin as she struggled with the number of things she had to learn in order to be acceptable. "For all this time, I worked these parties and never got to play!"

"Well...I'm not going to get to play," Robin said with a grin.

"Not my problem, sugar!"

Play was the whole point of the party. Bowls of condoms and piles of gloves and dental dams were procured, in both latex and nitrile along with bottles of several different types of lubricant and tubs of Crisco. Extra cushioned outdoor furniture was brought in, and hammocks slung from frames around the edges of the spacious acre behind the house. A sturdy steel frame was erected on one side of the pool, with bondage points, and another one mirrored it on the other side, supporting a sling of black nylon. Every whip, flogger, paddle and crop were brought out, examined for flaws and cleaned or restored as needed. Electrical toys, cupping sets, a pirate's hoard of silvery or bronze colored clips and clamps, and every strange or rarely used implement of pain and pleasure were dragged out and placed into Carl's hands. He was the one who went through the house, back deck and yard and garden and found every space where bondage points could be made, who rearranged the furniture, and oversaw the placement of spanking benches, kneeling frames and oddly shaped cages and frames. Then he erected smaller racks for the toys, so no one would have to go far to grab something for impact, torture, pleasure or penetration. Extra video screens were rented to show non-stop porn in almost every room.

The side effects from all of this preparation were laughably predictable. The tight swimsuits favored by Eric and Jimmy as the preferred uniform for their male house slaves did not hide the steady stream of erections. Robin couldn't hide her stiff nipples against the thin lycra of her running tops, either, but she did slip a panty liner into her shorts after finding herself far too wet for her own comfort. Then the Masters made things worse by commanding the slaves to torment each other.

"No orgasms," Eric commanded. "But Muscledog, I want you sucking Raul and Carl hard, three, four times a day. Raul, I want you working on their tits, I want 'em sensitive and fucking huge by the party. Carl, every morning, everyone gets 25 lashes, every night before bed, everyone gets ten on the ass with the leather paddle."

"Lashes anywhere, sir?"

"Yeah, anywhere. And you'll work on Raul's tits. Jimmy will beat you whenever he feels like it, as usual."

Carl grinned at Raul who rolled his eyes. "What about Robin, sir?"

Eric thought about that, staring at her. Robin blushed at the thought of this pre-party regimen and didn't know whether to hope she was included or hope she was left out.

"OK, leave her tits alone, last thing we need is her nipples getting *bigger*. But she gets beat on, too, every day. And she can suck Muscledog hard three times a day, too. Every morning, I want to inspect you all – I want you sore and fucking horny, not bruised or battered. Got it, fuckers?"

"Yes, Master! Yes, Sir!" They chorused.

* * * * *

Yet another addition to the list of things that are hotter in books than in real life, Robin thought as she bent over for the second evening paddling. True, she didn't even feel anything from the morning flogging on her shoulders and back, Carl didn't thump her as hard as he did the male slaves, and she had rather enjoyed the feeling of the expensive moose hide tresses. But the paddle, long and stiffened by something sewn between two layers of glossy black leather, stung as well as thumped. And much like Chris' strap, she suspected the build up of these evening beatings would be considerable.

"Don't know why they're bothering with you," Raul mused, as he tugged on Muscledog's clamped nipples. "It's not like anyone is going to see your little ass."

"Yeah, but she's got such a cute ass, I bet some of 'em will at least grab it or give her a spank over the jeans," Carl grunted as he swung.

Raul nodded. "Yeah, I can see that. OK, Dog, up here and get me hard...*again*."

Steve, the Muscledog, grinned and licked his lips. "Harsh!" he barked, before diving in.

Robin groaned as the leather paddle struck; she was right. It hurt more than it had the previous night. Her hips twitched involuntarily and she lifted one foot in the exquisite agony of arousal. Carl laughed in a good-natured way. "Could be worse, sweetheart," he said. "You could have Raul working on your titties, too, and no way to come!" He swatted her again, with enthusiasm, and she yelped.

* * * * *

In addition to the clothing, and how to lower her voice and how to walk and how to hide her hands and other tips on how to pass, somehow, as a very young man, Robin had one more thing to learn as well.

"But I know how to polish boots," she protested to Raul.

"Sure, but you don't know shit about boot blacking. You think of it as getting the boots clean – I'm talking about a sex thing here. Every morning, start with Carl, for at least two pairs of shoes or boots. And in the evening, work with the Dog and let him show you how to make it sexy. I doubt he'll be allowed to bootblack for more than a few guys here and there, and it's the perfect way to keep you busy and dressed."

It took all of five minutes for Robin to realize Raul had been right. Of course, she'd seen bootblacks working in leather bars – it seemed something that went with the masculine atmosphere of beer, leather, cigars and testosterone. And although she had some sense of the fetishism involved – leather, feet, service, kneeing in front of someone – she'd never thought of it as a particularly sexual or even sensual act before.

"No, no, don't wear gloves, that just gets in the way," Muscledog insisted.

"In the way of what?" she asked plaintively, imagining the horrors of the deep black polish getting under her fingernails.

"You gotta really feel what you're doing," he said patiently, digging his fingers into a can of saddle soap. "OK, so, you got the surface dust and dirt off with the first brushing, right? Now, we'll clean the leather. Take this stuff and just a little water, like this, and work it up to lather. Lots of guys won't need this, their leather is gonna be sharp. And really, if you have to clean 'em first, sometimes it's real hard to get a shine after. But if they're dirty, then first you cleanse…"

Then you exfoliate, Robin thought with a sigh. Or moisturize. I'm giving facials to boots. But it turned out the steps of boot blacking were similar to a facial – and why not, it's still skin, she realized. Except I don't set fire to my foundation before putting it on. Muscledog liked to ignite a can of black polish to soften it before spreading it thinly onto a boot. Raul sniffed at that practice and called it showy and lazy. But Carl liked it. "What's wrong with showy? Besides, the less she has to show she doesn't have the upper arm strength, the better."

It was useless, the boys agreed, to practice on empty boots. So every evening before she got her ten spanks with the leather paddle, she first knelt before one of them while they wore a pair of their own or one of the Master's pairs of boots, and she worked her hands into soaps and polishes and leather conditioners. She used different brushes to remove dust or to buff to a shine; she worked greasy lotions into the seams and creases of old leather. She learned when and how to bring out the mirror gloss of a high intensity shine and when she shouldn't. Then, they brought out more pairs of boots for her to learn different lacing patterns as well.

The aroma of the waxes, creams and polishes seemed to hover around her as she slid between her sheets. The sharp bitterness of the inky polishes leavened with the pine scent of the shoe grease, and under it all the faint echo of leather. Despite herself, she found it tantalizing, curling one hand up against her mouth and nose to breathe in the scents of her labor. Now, she understood why Chris' boots had that distinctive smell; he must have used some of these products. It was awful to lie there, her ass aching with the paddling, nipples erect despite not being teased by Raul's endless array of clamps and cups, and a taste of latex on her lips from the last chance every day to bring Muscledog to erection. That, at least, was easy. He sprang up at the slightest touch, and didn't mind at all that she was a girl.

Deep inside, she resented that she couldn't serve along with the rest of them. *I can suck cock!* She thought, curling up on her side. *And I know I have a tight ass, too. God, to be just another body at the party, instead of the costumed, bound up reject not allowed to do anything but polish boots. But that's what I get for belonging to a gay couple.* She signed and tried to relax, hoping she could pull it off. For all that it felt awkward, it would be her first party since…that incident with the earrings. *I want to fit in again,* she thought, her fist tight in her pillow, the scent of boot polish and saddle soap enveloping her. *I want them all to like me again. It* almost *feels like it used to be. If I can get through this and be useful and cheerful, it'll be like old times.*

Raul did as much cooking and prep work as possible even before his four assistants arrived. Two bars were set up, one inside and one out by the pool, and an icemaker and rented freezers were set up to make sure no one would lack a cooling drink when he wanted one. And of course, for all those guests, Raul, Carl and Muscledog would not be the only slaves providing sexual service or play. Most of the guests were Marketplace owners, or at least aware, plus a spotter or trainer here and there. Some of them would bring their own playthings, to use exclusively or to share. And of course, some would prefer to bottom.

"God, I hope someone grabs me to fuck 'em first off," Carl said with a groan as he got up the morning of the party. "I feel like I did when I was 13, a passing breeze could get me off today."

"We'll see what you say after the fifth one needs you to get it up," said Raul.

"At this rate? I'll say, hot damn, toss those legs around my neck, cowboy!" He stretched and grabbed the flogger hanging from the post of the bunk bed and nudged Robin with one foot. "And speaking of legs, spread 'em, sweet cheeks."

"Huh?" Robin threw back her sheets and looked up. "My…legs?"

"That's where this morning's 25 are going!" He whirled the tresses with delight and grinned at her.

Robin gasped as the first thud hit her pussy and then groaned, her head back against her pillow. Muscledog laughed and Carl did, too. "Remember, no coming," Carl said with a wicked leer. "And don't fall over laughing too hard, Dog. Your balls are next."

"Oh, man," Muscledog sighed, cupping his cock and balls for the moment. "That's…"

"Harsh," the other three slaves echoed.

* * * * *

The four service slaves showed up, and Eric had them dressed in black lycra shorts and little shirt cuffs and bowties like Chippendale dancers. They also wore a skimpy black gauze vest with "hands off!" painted on the back in bold orange letters.

"Subtle," Jimmy said, when he saw them.

"Well you know this crowd; once they start getting in gear, they'll start fucking anything that moves." Eric eyed the four men critically and then handed them over to Raul. The house manager was attired in a bright red latex jockstrap, tight around his small asscheeks, with matching bands around his wrists and ankles. Attachment rings were steel wound through with more red, and a chain half harness had been laced with long scarlet latex straps as well, and glinted in the light across his tan chest. Somehow, he managed to look as cool and elegant as always, escorting the four slaves to their service positions and showing them the day's schedule.

Muscledog, who was making his debut, wore a gleaming black latex wrestling singlet that left his ass completely exposed, and allowed his cock and balls to jut through a hole in the front as well. Long straps passed his swollen nipples and marked a lane framing his taut abdominal muscles. The only thing the scant garment did was accentuate his impressive build. He also had wrist, bicep and ankle cuffs, only his were black rubber and sported locks as well. His heavy cock was secured into a series of connected rubber rings, each one smaller than the last, a classic item of torment often called the gates of hell. Naturally fair, he had a California all-over tan, and the black latex and rubber fetish gear looked cruel on him.

But Carl was dressed in leather. The older man had a full body harness, down to the thick chrome ring around his cock and balls. The straps crossed his chest, which used to be the most brawny in the house before Muscledog's appearance, and a single strap ran down his tight stomach to the ring around his package, well hidden by something Robin had never seen before – a leather *kilt*. It was crafted of buttery soft black leather, and caressed Carl's legs when he walked. Her mouth went dry when she saw it; she'd never seen a man in a kilt in person before, and regretted that now to the core of her being. It was intensely sexy, even more so on the one man she regularly had sex with. He was the only male slave in boots, and Robin now knew every inch of his Wesco Highliners.

There was no doubt who the most beautiful man was, though. Eric was a professional model, after all. He had chosen to start the party in one of his many uniforms, this one in midnight blue leather, from the tailored breeches to the short-sleeved shirt complete with pockets and epaulets. His Sam Browne belt gleamed against his chest, his slender hips making a classic V-shape of masculinity. Under his cover, his wavy honey and platinum hair caught the light, and when he slipped on dark shades, he became a walking fetish. Robin had only been allowed to watch as Carl personally shined up the tall Dehner boots that completed the ensemble.

"If only your catalog fans could see you now," Jimmy said with a grin. He was in classic leather; chaps over jeans with harness boots on his feet and a vest over his bare chest. And he was the one least likely to change over the day; Eric had arranged several different costume changes for himself and for most of the slaves.

But not for me, Robin thought with a sigh. She felt self conscious in the layers she wore, very unsure of her ability to pass even the most cursory of inspections. After many discussions and modeling sessions, she was outfitted in Levi 501 jeans under suede chaps. A compression vest held her small breasts down to insignificance and made her catch her breath from time to time; over that, she wore a black cotton uniform shirt that looked like it came from a gas station; it even had a name embroidered on it – Rob.

"Why make up a new one?" Raul had asked when he gave it to her.

A leather bar vest over the shirt furthered the goal of making her upper body appear more masculine. She had leather wristbands that extended halfway up her forearm, and tightly laced military boots that were at least one size too big. Her feet, according to the boys, were a dead giveaway, even worse than her hands. So, she was also wearing three pairs of socks. A leather bondage belt not only threaded through the loops in her jeans, but had two locking straps around each leg, as clear a signal to guests as the "hands off" sign on the serving slaves.

Carl clipped her hair short, but not as short as she expected. "Kiddo, we expose the full shape of your head and face and people will know you're a girl from 50 feet. Instead, Eric thinks you'll pass as a sort of gothy poet kinda guy. You already duck your head about a thousand times a day; just make sure you toss your hair in your eyes a lot." And he'd snickered.

So now, she had her hair short in the back but long over her eyes and in front of her ears, styled with an unhealthy amount of mousse and gel. Her chain collar was temporarily replaced by a thick leather one, the lock dangling over her absent Adam's apple. The last stage of her transformation had been makeup, which Eric did himself. He hadn't liked Raul's efforts in the dress rehearsals. With careful, precise hands, he darkened a little under her eyes, and used a mascara brush to bring up the tiny, almost invisible hairs on her upper lip and in front of her ears. Keeping with her goth boy persona, he also gave her a little bit of liner around her eyes. His gentle touch on her face was almost unbearably intimate and tender, made more so by the memory of the back of his hand when he'd called her a thief and tore up the very foundations of her life in his household.

It was still hard to look into his cerulean eyes, despite her vows to be a good slave, patient and understanding and forgiving. But as he fussed with different touches of make up on her, she thought, maybe this *is* my redemptive moment. Maybe this really is their way of saying – well, if not that they're sorry, which she knew they would never say – maybe they were saying it was all buried in the past now. Not only by letting her stay for the party, but making sure she was disguised and included, even in this very limited way.

Still, compared to the stripped down, tightly strapped and buckled men around her, she felt short, over dressed and very, very forgettable.

Which is my job, she struggled to remember. I need to vanish. I need to be someone people will walk right by, so I can be useful and not disruptive. She had a flashback memory to her days with WISE (Women Into Sadomasochistic Expression), the lesbian SM group she had belonged to in New York. How diligent they had been in their defense of womenspace! Not only would they not attend parties with men present, they'd even argued about using a play space after a group of men had used it for a party. "What if there's…bodily fluids everywhere?" one of the officers had plaintively protested. Their fear of contamination by the mere proximity to maleness had been one of the more annoying aspects of belonging. And here was the reverse! Apparently, her mere presence as a girl, even one who could be ordered to not touch or speak to anyone all day and night, might ruin the entire party for some male spiritual twin to the …masculinaphobe? Androphobe? Whatever. The lesbian who thought boys were *icky*.

If they could see me now, she thought with a sigh. Of course, they stopped liking me when I took up with a man anyway. She cocked her head at the mirror and considered herself again. Would I have gone for me? She wondered.

Hell no, she decided. I look like an underage, clove-smoking Nietzsche-quoting piece of chicken too tiny to get noticed for anything but pretension. Complete with a tiny little dick, too.

Rolled up socks didn't work as well as they did in stories. They were too bulky and invited a touch to confirm, or they were too insubstantial and slipped out of place with the mere act of walking. Various dildos were tried, with and without harnesses and none of them suited Eric's critical eye. It was Muscledog again who came to the rescue.

Raul had picked up the item gingerly, letting it dangle between his fingers with amusement or distaste or both. "And they call this…a what?"

"Mr. Cushy," Muscledog said with a grin. "A packing dick!"

It looked ridiculous; a pale and limp facsimile of a penis, complete with a set of balls – it was short, and soft to the touch, and looked flabby dangling from Raul's slender fingers. "Why," the Latin houseman asked, making the item bounce in his hand, "would a woman – a lesbian – want to put a limp penis in her pants?"

"So she looks like a guy instead of a dyke with a huge fucking dildo," Muscledog patiently explained. "It's like…drag. Drag queens *tuck*, drag kings *pack*. Get it?"

Raul pursed his lips and nodded. Drag, he understood. He handed it over to Robin and shrugged. "Let's see if the Masters like this look better!"

Fastening it in place took more experimentation, as the heavy leather dildo harnesses in the house were far too obvious under the jeans. Robin figured it out using a pair of stockings, wound about her hips and legs, twined in such a way to keep the cock part dangling and the balls tucked up between her thighs. Once Mr. Cushy was in the right place, and her jeans buttoned over him, it was remarkable how realistic the prosthetic was! And comfortable, too, unlike a stiff dildo. Until, at the last minute, Carl came to her with a final addition.

With the ease of a man familiar with her body, Carl slipped the fat little dildo inside her cunt, and then arranged Mr. Cushy over it, tying the packing dick in place. "Jimmy thought there was no reason why you shouldn't get a little extra something today," he said with a grin. He buckled her bondage belt over everything, and set the locks with three little snaps.

"I'd rather it was your cock," Robin teased.

"Baby, me too. I could fuck six trees and a snake right now." He could, too, she thought, seeing the edge of his cock brush the kilt every time he moved. More than anything, she would love ducking under that kilt and taking him in her mouth, the scent of him mingled with the soft aromatic leather, the feel of those tall handsome boots against her naked body...

Her hips jerked and he laughed and smacked her ass, well tenderized by a week of beatings. Now, when she walked, the dildo inside her awakened the tenderness of her pussy lips as well. "Oh my God, this is going to be a long day," she said, with just the slightest of whimpers.

"Rob, my boy-for-the-day, you said a cotton pickin' mouthful."

* * * * *

"Do a good job, punk, and maybe next time, you'll get some dick," sneered the third man in her chair. Robin ducked her head and cursed herself even as she did it; dammit, Carl was right, she did bob her head down a lot!

"Yes, Master," she whispered in her lower-toned boy voice. She wrapped the rag tightly around her fore and middle finger, winding it around her hand in a firm series of anchoring twists and used it to rub and rub and rub until the spotless gleam of polish seemed to pop up on the boot. Cigar smoke floated over her head and she tried to breathe in short, shallow pants. The smoke, the heat and the labor all combined to make her feel light headed; those, plus the taste of polished boots.

The man in the chair lifted the boot she wasn't working on and planted it roughly on her shoulder. She wanted to cry out but kept it tightly inside, offering only the lowest, short grunt she could make under the circumstances. He laughed and shifted, turning his attention to a man standing next to the chair and waiting his turn.

"Leave it to Eric to grab some cherry chicken and keep him all locked up and licking leather all day."

"Yeah, well, one debut at a time. And his other bootblack isn't going to be fucking useful today, is he?"

There were two bootblack chairs, one next to each other, installed under a freestanding canopy about five yards away from the pool, situated so as to allow the man in the chair full sight of the bondage and sling frames plus the array of naked and mostly naked men lounging at the pool and Jacuzzi. Muscledog had started out working the second chair and did exactly one pair of boots before the man wearing them – and nothing else – grabbed him by the collar and shoved his face down onto the man's erection. Shortly after the man came, splattering his ejaculate all over Muscledog's chest, the newest household slave was dragged away to a sturdy beating and fucking frame that held his mouth and ass at appropriate levels.

"I guess that depends on what you mean by useful," the man in the chair said. "Getting ass raped by 30 horny fags sounds useful to me!"

They laughed and Robin felt heat rise up in her as she continued to work on the shine. Oh, God, to be strapped down and just...ganged like that! To feel cock after cock after cock, to be helpless and just completely used...

"Hey, faggot, finish up, I gotta go fuck one of your bigger brothers!" The boot on her shoulder pushed against her and she almost fell backward, but she set her teeth and nodded. "Yes, Master," she rasped, and set to work with faster movements. The speed of her arm was as, if not more important than her strength, so she had been taught. In due time, she judged the boots acceptable and lowered her head to press her tongue against the leather.

She had kissed boots and shoes before, of course. Every top she had submitted to, soft world to Marketplace, had insisted on this sign of obedience or humility at least a few times. Chris Parker had her masturbate on his boot the first night he had examined her, and then shoved that boot, glistening with her pussy juices, under her face to clean. She could still remember the mingled tastes and scents – her own lubricating wetness plus tears and that faint pine smell of what she knew now was a leather conditioner.

This was…different. Here, there was nothing to connect her personally with any of these men, no reason to think of them as dominant, or interested in her in any way, even disguised as a boy. They had nothing to offer her, other than their boots – they could not command her to perform sexually, they weren't even allowed to do more than assault her with words! But she had to bestow all of her focus and effort to please them by cleaning, polishing and yes, licking their boots, all day, if they continued to come, in two hour sessions interrupted by her enforced rest periods for food, drink and a moment of privacy to use the bathroom.

Sweat dripped down her forehead onto the boot under her lips and she moaned, licking up the droplets as they fell. The warm hide under her lips was slick with her spit and sweat and she almost slid over the surface too fast for the erotic pace she was supposed to be setting. But maybe the guest didn't mind; he was already discussing something else he wanted to be doing with his friend.

"…string his balls up with bootlaces and take turns pissing into the boot, what do you think?"

Coarse, approving laughter. Robin didn't even hear which slave they had in mind. She switched to the other boot to start licking and felt the rough thud of a kick against her shoulder. "Enough of that, asswipe, I got better things to do. Maybe you can lick my piss off the boots later!"

The two men left, and for a moment, Robin was alone. She ground her teeth again and rubbed her shoulder, and then turned to look at the vista behind her.

It was like something out of a porn movie.

Muscledog was bound tightly in layers of rope to the fucking frame, his ass getting walloped by a short, thickset man wielding a braided cat. Clamps on his already tenderized nipples were weighted with little black fishing weights swinging with every thud of the cat against his body. The bondage couldn't keep him from jerking in pain, and the wide arc of the swinging weights tugged at him mercilessly. There was a man standing over his back, just running one hand all over the muscular form of the slave, while he jerked himself off with the other hand. Luckier, perhaps, were the two men standing in front of the new slave, both of their cockheads squeezed into his mouth. Even at a distance, Robin could see the gleam of light off the spit-slicked condoms. Muscledog's mouth seemed obscenely split open, and his eyes were closed in pain, or concentration or maybe even bliss.

In the Jacuzzi, two men passed a slave someone else had brought to the party back and forth, slapping him and shoving his mouth over their nipples or under the swirling water, presumably on their cocks.

In the sling by the pool, a huge man, at least six and a half feet tall and covered with thick, dark hair, hooked one boot on Carl's shoulder and yelled something at him – encouragement? Commands? It was hard to hear over the thudding music coming from the speakers all through the garden. But Robin could see Carl moving, shifting, in response. It didn't look like he was using his cock – no. Carl was fisting the man in the sling.

Robin groaned in erotic torment and cupped a hand over Mr. Cushy, pushing the dildo inside her just enough to make it twist. She'd never asked Carl to fist her, even though she had learned to love it when Ken Mandarin was training her to take it. His hands were so big! At that moment, she would have said yes to his hands and probably been lubricated enough naturally.

Men walked in and out of the house in various states of fetishwear or completely nude. She'd never seen so many naked male bodies before, such an array of cocks. But the leather, latex and rubber were even more appealing, ranging from tiny little thongs to heavy chaps over naked asses. One man was only dressed, if you could call it that, in liquid latex, painted over his body in stripes and signage. His chest had a target on it, under the tattooed word "TOILET" in black gothic lettering.

And along with all the sex and bondage and play were men just lounging and sunning themselves in the comfortable chairs, floating on rafts in the pool, and hanging out in small groups drinking beer and cocktails, acting exactly as they might at any other backyard party. One of the service slaves fired up the grill and was finishing Raul's chipotle marinated chicken wings and chorizo, the spicy charred scent mingling with suntan lotion, leather, sweat and of course, the sharpness of shoe polish.

There was a handsome black man who must have been one of Eric's model friends, dressed in brief rubber shorts and a body harness that caressed his lithe body so elegantly he made the garments seem almost formal. He was conferring with another, younger man, with Raul on his knees before them, listening and perhaps offering suggestions. The three of them vanished into the house, the black man taking hold of Raul's collar with one hand while he walked. Raul, so calm, so strong and dependable and so very cool, stumbled after them, half on his knees, trying to keep up.

Well, he wanted to get to play, Robin thought. She groped between the chairs for her water bottle and sucked some down, lukewarm and tasting absurdly sweet in the heat of the afternoon. The acrid taste of polish and oil mingled with the water and she felt lightheaded again. How could she stand a whole day of this? And what about the night? What would happen when the sun set and there was no use for a bootblack any more? No one had ever even hinted at what her duties would be after all of this cleaning, polishing and bootlicking.

Someone smacked the back of her head and she yelped.

"No peeking at what you can't do, little boy," laughed her newest pair of boots. He heaved himself into the chair and slammed his harness boots down onto the upright supports. "Jesus, what are you, six-fucking-teen? No wonder they got you tucked away back here, these animals would fuck you to death if you were out there buck naked."

Robin nodded – and ducked her head. And then she reached up to bring his jeans up over the tops of his boots and start, once more, the only job she was allowed to do.

* * * * *

Muscledog made it back to his chair, his ass and back covered with welts and his lips already slightly swollen. Jimmy clipped a chain from the slave's collar to the base of the chair and unhooked Robin's chain, jerking a thumb at the house. "Half hour, bootlicker, then get your skinny worthless ass back here."

Robin bowed her head to the ground in acknowledgement and took a few deep breaths before trying to rise. Muscledog grinned at her as a man scrambled into the chair in front of him. "Hey, slavemeat, you guys get to use the little fag?" the man asked, bracing one boot against Muscledog's massive chest. "Unlike the rest of us?"

"Sometimes, Master! When we're very good."

"Yeah? Is he any good?"

Muscledog grinned even wider as the man twisted his boot over his already sore nipple, and he growled with appreciation. "Not yet, Master! But we'll get him in shape so he's good enough for you gentlemen, maybe the next time?"

Robin couldn't help but sigh as she heaved herself to her feet, the laughter of the guest chasing her all the way to the house.

* * * * *

The bacchanalian antics were as frenzied and erotic inside as they were out by the pool. Giant cocks and asses cavorted on the projection screen TV in the main living room, and right in front of the screen, Eric was shoving his cock down Raul's throat while the black man who had taken him inside earlier was fucking his ass. For some reason, Robin felt almost embarrassed to see this, and tried to look away, only to see a young slave, perhaps only slightly older than she looked, being trussed up to the suspension chain, his ankles locked into an impossibly wide spreader bar. Outside one of the guest bedrooms knelt another slave, anonymous in a latex hood, the word "fluffer" printed on his chest in magic marker. Two men were energetically fucking in that bedroom, the door wide open, and the sounds of spanking mingled with the grunts and groans. The slave on his knees outside the door arched in his bondage, wrists high behind his back, and licked his lips.

Past the other open doors of rooms set up for play, and past the slave's bedroom into their tiny bathroom, where she could lock the door behind her for a few minutes and take inventory.

The locks on her bondage belt were real, but the key was up

here, in the medicine chest. No one wanted to be bothered to unlock her if she needed a piss break! Not that there's much piss in me, she thought, letting what little there was go. She was soaked underneath her layers of costuming, and she stripped off as much as she could to wipe herself down with a cold washcloth. Her pussy ached with the intrusion of the dildo, and she hated putting it back in, despite the fact it needed no additional lubrication. The air conditioning and quiet time helped get her courage up to put everything back, from the dildo to Mr. Cushy to the jeans, chaps and bondage belt. The chaps were a mess, from kneeling on the grass and from the soles of boots planted on her thighs from time to time. Her shirt also bore the marks of treads. Aware of her time running out, she brushed her teeth, and ran more styling gel through her hair to keep it framing and half covering her face. The mascara, thank goodness, seemed as waterproof as its advertising promised.

Then, with a deep breath, she unlocked the door and went back down for her second shift.

* * * * *

She never could place the exact moment when the chore turned into an act of eroticism. She thought it started when a man's hand lingered as he gave a gentle cuff against her cheek in thanks for her brilliantly popped spit shine; she kissed the lingering fingers out of instinct at first and then moaned at the taste of his hand and lashed her tongue against the three deep creases in his palm. He laughed and patted her cheek, saying, "Down, boy! I know you must be dying for some cock about now, huh? Well, give those boots another swipe instead like a good boy." And he pressed her head down, where she eagerly dug her tongue against the warm leather.

That was when he dug his cock out of his leather shorts and started to lazily jack it off, watching the scenes at the pool, and occasionally jerking a boot up to command her to lick harder. The rasping of her tongue seemed unnaturally loud, as did her breathing, as she bent to the task, and she felt her hips needing to jerk in the release of pent up sexual energy between her legs. This time, there was some amount of drool mixing with her sweat as she licked.

He came on her back, and in her hair, and chuckled as he shook himself, milking the last drops.

"Keep it up kid and you'll be one hell of a cocksucker," he said. "Fuck, I'd borrow you just for my boots."

Or maybe the exact moment was when she finished off her bottle of water and realized she wanted the taste to be earthier; more like the shoe grease that evoked primeval forests and ancient loam. More like the slick surface of the patent leather stovepipe boots worn by the man in the soft leather cavalry uniform.

But without a doubt, she knew that true moment of joy; the discovery of pleasure mingled with pain, shame and delicious hunger, when the man in the ten inch Danner uniform boots planted one foot right over her button fly and ground it down over Mr. Cushy.

The jolt of near orgasm shook her like an electric shock and he grinned around the fat cigar in his mouth.

"Keep working, punk," he growled with a genial, sadistic sort of glee. And she did, her hands shaking on her spray bottle of water, the rags and brushes unsteady all of a sudden. This would hurt, too, she dimly thought, and groaned as low as she could make it, horrified to find it sounded more like a whimper.

"Nothing more worthless than slave dick," said the man, twisting the toe of his boot. "Especially little slave dicks. Am I right, cocksucker?"

Robin nodded with an eagerness to please that made her dizzy again. "Yes, Master," she rasped. She couldn't help it; the intensity made her flush from ears to toes, and she shifted her hips. The pressure on Mr. Cushy angled just a little with her awkward shift and yes! Yes! The dildo inside responded to the pressure and angled forward right against her g-spot.

The man in the chair rocked his foot, snickering, as her arms grew weaker. "I said keep working, you lazy punk-ass boot-slut. You'll never do anything but this if you don't learn to focus and make your masters happy."

It was a desperate struggle. Robin found herself almost crying with the effort to maintain her concentration on the job. What came next? Were the boots too dry? Did she spray some water, or not? Where were her rags? Where was the ball of panty hose she used for buffing?

Where are my wits, she asked herself. Jeeze, girl, pull it together! Sweat dripped down her back and over her ribcage, and the wetness of her pussy now started to seep down the insides of her thighs and along her asscrack; she felt drenched, drowning. The scent of ejaculate in her hair seemed overwhelming now, and she licked her lips tasting the salt of her own perspiration and layers of boot grease and polish.

When she managed to finish the first boot, he merely dug that one into her crotch while she worked on the second one.

She needed to come so badly that she trembled when she bent over to lick the man's sun warmed and well-polished leather. The sharp acetone smell of the edge dressing did actually make her head almost bounce against the shaft of his boot; he mistook it for affection and ruffled her hair briefly before he got up to get back to the party. "Good boot slut," he crooned, as he walked away.

With no one to take his place and no instructions to the contrary – orgasms were allowed today, in fact, encouraged unless instructed otherwise – Robin dropped one hand over her button fly, cupped her complex package and rocked forward. Almost instantly, she came so hard she saw deep colors behind her tightly screwed eyelids and her toes slammed hard into the ground behind her. It hurt; the dildo slid and rocked inside her and would not stay still, and her mouth and throat were dry despite copious drinking and drooling. "OK, OK," she muttered to herself, trying to gather her resources and focus again. I can do this. Oh, my God, but this is so…hot.

And, as Muscledog often pronounced – harsh!

* * * * *

Her second break came after a lengthy period of very little work, and when she got to the bathroom, this time she showered. Grease, sweat, come – she was just soaked like a washrag and plastered with layers of dirt and crusted bodily fluids. Sitting on the toilet seat as she dried off, she sucked down an iced sports drink, wondering why she never liked the taste before. One more shift, and then she'd have a two-hour break to eat and close her eyes for a while, and then…what? She still didn't know.

On the way out of the bathroom, she adjusted Mr. Cushy with an unconscious grab, unaware that she was swaggering just a little bit.

*****

The late afternoon shift was light, as most of the men who truly wanted their boots done had rushed the chairs early on. But a few came by, including two who had already changed clothing and boots and wanted their new pair done up right. Muscledog admitted he had only gotten to complete three pairs of boots – and what a shame, too, because he loved boots and feet and all things related to them. But his pumped up form was too much of a draw, his latex singlet stripped off by careless hands. His already well-beaten body had been brutally striped and welted by belts and whips; his tender nipples looked raw. Still, his good-natured smile never faltered, and his cock, while not hard, did manage an impressive tumescence from time to time as he was so cheerfully abused.

"You gotta feed this scrawny ass bitch more vitamins or something," the man in Muscledog's chair said, as he eased his way in comfortably. Robin almost panicked before she realized that in this case, "bitch" was derogatory for more than the usual reasons. "Protein drinks, more weight lifting, something. Christ, he's got nothing there, poor faggot."

Muscledog laughed and nodded. "We're sure workin' on it, Master. But Rob's stronger than he looks!"

"Yeah?" The man, bearded and scholarly looking despite his rubber vest and jockstrap, peered down at Robin and shrugged. "Then get him over here. Let's see how strong he really is." He lifted his feet and pointed, and Muscledog grabbed Robin by the shirt and pulled her over.

"What?" Robin started to ask, but Muscledog merely shoved her down onto her hands and knees in front of the chair, between the footrests. One heavy boot came down onto her back, resting on her left shoulder, and the other settled in on her right. Instantly, Muscledog knelt over her ass, his sculpted legs on either side of her as he leaned in to start working.

Robin gasped and planted her arms firmly against the grass. Stronger than she looked? She didn't know if she could make it through the cleaning process, let alone polishing! Indeed, her arms trembled as Muscledog rubbed and buffed and the man in the chair dug his heels into her back. The vest, shirt and compression garment seemed to do nothing to pad her against the pressure and she groaned as she struggled to keep in place.

This is yet another thing hotter in books, she thought for a moment. Being used as a footstool hurts! But then, to her amusement, she realized she as wrong.

It was hot. It was amazingly hot. With her head ducked down under the legs of one man and another man straddling her body, these wonderful smells surrounding her, the casual disregard for her feelings and even her usefulness, oh, it was one of the hottest things she'd ever done. This realization almost made her laugh, and she bit her own lip to keep silent, knowing her laugh would give her away in a second. Instead, she braced her arms and dug her fingers into the grass, struggling to keep still while she was used as a surface to clean boots on.

Perhaps it was the novelty, perhaps it was the sight of Dog's huge, muscular ass over Robin's relatively tiny, round one, the contrast between his nakedness and her jeans, but before long, they had voyeurs. One man brought over a flogger and swiped it at Muscledog's ass, and when the tails smacked Robin as well, it was hardly his fault, now was it? There was much laughter to accompany this illicit use of the off limits bootslut, and Robin tried desperately not to work her hips back for more of the sweet thumping pressure.

Muscledog had no such compunction; he worked his ass back and forth with vigor and glee, rubbing his cock up against Robin's lower back, between the shirt and the vest. "That's more action than the little punk's got all day," barked one spectator.

"Poor thing! Bet he wishes he had a hard cock up that tight little bubble butt."

Yes, yes, I do, Robin swore to herself. Oh, my freaking God, yes!

"Yeah, well, we can fuck the stud, so why's he wasting time on fucking boots?"

"Because they're my fucking boots and that's what I wanted!" cried the man in the chair. But his friends argued and pleaded; two chanted, "Fuck the stud! Fuck the stud!" and Robin felt Muscledog being jerked from her back. Then she was grabbed by the bondage belt and pulled back while Muscledog was ordered to take down the boot rests so he could kneel sideways. The man in the chair pounded his boots down on his broad back and Robin was thrust forward to take up the brushes and rags as men knelt down in the grass on both ends of her newest brother slave. Condoms were produced and slid onto engorged cocks and the cocks were shoved into Muscledog from each end and his back arched up as he took them. The furry man in the chair leaned back and chuckled.

"OK, I kinda like this view," he admitted.

The two men fucking Muscledog gave each other a high five and began to ream him with the energy and passion of men who got what they wanted after a brief struggle. Even temporary denial could be a turn on.

And as for Robin?

Her first instinct was correct – to get back to work. She dusted the grass and dirt from her hands and grabbed a brush and realized that without the narrow places to rest the boots, she would have to be careful not to knock against Muscledog's back or smear products all over him. On the other hand, she reconsidered; maybe he'd like that.

And then, in the next moment, she realized he was being fucked from two ends right there in front of her and it was the hottest fucking thing she'd ever seen. The man in front was long and curved and his cock speared Muscledog's mouth in a slow arc capped with the slave bracing himself whenever the man's balls banged against his chin. The one fucking his ass was less esthetically pleasing in his motions – he was plowing Muscledog with a mindless fury, slapping his ass and thighs with no sense of rhythm or artistry.

The savagery of the ass pounding was as much a turn on for Robin as the slow mouth fucking. Taken together, they made her drop the brush in her hand. Masculine laughter rose as she nervously gathered her supplies and tried, desperately tried, to deliver a passable shine in the midst of an orgy.

Try as she might, it was nearly impossible. Muscledog was strong and solid – more solid than she had been! But getting fucked was a terrible distraction, and when the man fucking his throat clamped down and came, the slave choked and shook and Robin wound up smearing her blackened fingers over his bruised skin. And when another man dropped to his knees in front of him and started fucking his mouth anew, Robin couldn't help but wipe at her mouth with the back of her hand. She'd never been so, so…cock hungry! In her entire life.

If the girls at the lesbian SM club could see me now, she thought again, wildly. Oh, fuck, if Chris could see me! Would he want me? Ken said he liked the younger men at the leather bars, liked to rough them up and make them cry. She remembered the image of Chris, his fist tight in Leon's long hair, shoving his face down between Chris's legs, a slight smile on the trainer's face as he watched Robin getting tormented and fucked by Gordon Reynolds, Leon's owner.

And saliva actually dropped from her mouth. She was so aroused, it hurt. When she finished the shine as best as she could, hands shoved her face forward, mashing her cheek against Muscledog's back as voices yelled at her to lick, suck, tongue that boot, faggot…

She licked. The slick sides of the boot, the curved toe, and the hot sweaty taste of Muscledog's back; it was one texture after another under her swollen, roughened tongue. She dug her tongue into the boot, feeling the man's toes under the leather, and hearing him swear.

Someone else came on her, shooting jism into her hair again.

With a soft moan, Robin came so close to fainting she thought she truly had. But it was just a blurring of time, from one moment of tasting the leather and skin to the next sharp segment of time, drawing back as the man in the chair roared for Muscledog to get his cocksucking mouth up to him. She scrambled back on her knees, getting out of the way of the crush of men around the muscular slave and crawled around to one side of the chair, trying to find her water bottle and failing. For a while, she just leaned there, feeling the thumping and pounding of the sex and her own heart.

It was Carl who came to get her as the sun set and men shifted to an informal rest period before the evening festivities took over. She took yet another shower and collapsed onto her bunk bed thinking it was the most luxurious place in the world. Naked and clean and chilled by the air conditioning, she slept two hours and gobbled an energy bar before suiting back up. She was still chewing the sweet granola when Carl came back.

"Oh, good, you're ready," he said. She nodded and was about to ask what she was going to be doing now, but he grabbed her by one arm and whipped a blindfold over her eyes.

"What are you doing?" she whispered.

"Giving you what you want, girl-fag. What you need. Now shut those pretty lips until I give 'em something to get busy on!"

He hooked a leather leash onto her collar and kept a tight hold on it, up by her throat, leading her down the hall, to what she could tell from the walk was the second guest bedroom.

"Carl, you are one good slave," said a familiar voice. Robin was sure this had been one of her customers today, one of her boot masters, but she couldn't remember which one.

"Nah, I am a bad, bad boy," Carl replied. "But tell you the truth, the punk needs a little taste, and if you want him, I guess Master won't mind too much."

"And if he does, it's your ass anyway." The man laughed and Robin was shoved to her knees, forced to crawl to him. "Oh, my fucking God, what a sweet ass little boy you got there. Are you sure he's legal?"

"Legal and hungry, Master. Shit, he can't get his hands off us, and we're just slaves."

"Just slaves, what a joke. How many guys you plow today, Carl?" Rough hands pulled her head by the hair and Robin gasped in a breath along with the thick cockhead shoved into her mouth.

"Day ain't over yet, sir." Again, rough masculine laughter echoed from two sides of her and Robin laved her tongue over the dry, flavored condom to moisten it. Mango, she thought with amused desperation. It was mango flavored, from the new tropical fruit collection they'd gotten for the party.

"Fuuuck," the man hissed, cradling Robin's head in his hands. "Hungry little come-slut, aren't you?" He braced his hands firmly and fucked deeply into her throat and she immediately gagged.

Behind her, Carl gave her a heavy handed spank on her butt. "Hey, asshole, pay attention! You know better than that! I'm so sorry, master. He is the worst cocksucker in the house."

"No...no. I like I little of this. I like choking 'em a little. Especially when they look like some high school drama club fag."

Robin did know better, she was just so turned on and shocked at Carl's little surprise that she was taken way off guard. She coughed a little, relaxing her throat muscles and when the next deep thrust came, she was better prepared. This time, she swirled her tongue along the base as he fucked forward and exhaled sharply and quickly, feeling the spongy head of the cock fit into her throat like a plug in a socket.

"Ahhhh," the man sighed. "Good boy. That's some nice long tongue action there. See, he's not that bad. Hit him again, Carl. He likes it."

Carl's heavy hands whacked her ass cheeks steadily, one heavy swat to each cheek in a steady rhythm as the guest continued to slowly fuck her face and throat. Robin didn't know what to do with her hands – when she raised them to reach for the man's legs, Carl jerked them back and folded her wrists up behind her back.

That only made things better. The combined feeling of being denied that much contact with her face fucking master-of-the-moment and the discipline of keeping her arms behind her were two terribly wonderful spices to add to this sexual mélange. She kept sucking and swiping her tongue, worked at keeping her throat open or at least receptive. When that failed and she misjudged a thrust, her chokes amused the man, and kept him going.

In the distance the party continued, hard thumping beats of the music vibrating the floor under her knees, sharp thwacking sounds of paddles and whips echoing, someone far away screaming, and through it all, that deep masculine laughter. The cock she was sucking smelled like sweat and salt underneath the cloying mango condom, and the man was wearing some kind of leather pants of shorts or chaps – she could smell those, too. And under all of that, the faintest scent of pine.

"Ahh, fuck, take that cock, you cocksucking bootslut, take me nice and deep, like you licked my fucking boots…" the man crooned to her as he ground his cock down deep enough to make her gentle choke into a stomach lurching gag.

"Yeah, fuck his throat, Master," Carl encouraged, his slaps pounding against her ass. "Let him feel it!"

The man grunted and used her head, her face, and her throat, to grind his cock close to orgasm. Then, he jerked out and stripped the condom off and fisted his cock. Robin couldn't help but gasp, and knew it sounded hungry and desperate. She could hear the moist slapping sounds and knew when he was doing and wanted so terribly to be able to taste it, to drink him down. But he did obey the rules as far as that went, and his come splattered into her hair, a few droplets snaking down her forehead and over the blindfold. Without the backyard distractions like sun and wind and all the bootblacking supplies, it was like being anointed with warm oil, the slight smell of bleach tingling in her nose.

"Heh," the man sighed, milking the rest of the come out of his dick and wiping himself off in her hair. "Worth the risk. Get him out of here before you get into trouble, Carl."

"Sure thing, master. Glad to be of service!"

* * * * *

Carl folded his arms and grinned at her while she scrubbed her hair again – for the fourth time today? Fifth? She had lost count.

"Are you going to be in trouble?' she asked him, as she rubbed self down with a towel.

"Fuck no, Rob. Think I'd really do that without permission? Eric said I could work the forbidden fruit angle on that guy, he's such a horndog for chicken." He chuckled. "You made him come faster than Muscledog did!"

Robin laughed and then coughed. Her throat was sore from dryness and that abrasive fucking. "I am exhausted," she admitted, sinking down onto the toilet seat. "And I am so horny!"

"Well, then I guess you won't mind that you're off duty 'til breakfast! Eric says we'd be pushing it to let you out there at night when things get a little, um…rough."

Robin looked up at him, amazed. "Rougher than today?"

"Yeah, well, you know…it gets late, guys get sloppy. You get some sleep, be up at five to help with the coffee and breakfast service, OK?" He patted her shoulder and adjusted his kilt. Then he flashed her another grin. "And by the way? You'll be blacking again for the guys about to leave. Expect about ten pairs of boots tomorrow morning. Then, the Masters say if any of us can still get it up when they're all gone, you're the one who has to take care of it. All dressed in your fag boy suit."

Robin sighed and rubbed her throat in expectation. If indeed the three guys could get some cocks up, she had no doubt they'd be eager. Then, she grinned and looked up again.

"That's harsh," she whispered, saving her tender throat.

Editor's Note
By Lori Perkins

I have been an editor for a number of decades now, and I love to put together anthologies almost as much as I love to read them. They are, for me, the literary equivalent of that legendary box of chocolates—and they are usually filled with old favorites and pleasant surprises.

I think you'll find that is the case with this collection.

There are 21 pieces in this book and they truly span the spectrum of BDSM fiction (and even nonfiction – there's a chapter from Dr. Charley Ferrer's *BDSM The Naked Truth* in here). There are sweet love stories of submission like Mia Koutras' *My Princess* (and she's a brand new author too!) and hardcore stories like *Dirty Girls Have All the Fun* by Lisa Horton and just about everything in between (and, yes, there's some vampire domination in here just for you!) There's even a surprisingly charming offbeat fem dom story by Cassandra Park.

This anthology brings you the work of established award-wining erotica and erotic romance authors such as Roz Lee, Cris Anson and Debra Hyde as well as newbie authors Jessica Lust, Mia Koutras and Helena Stone. And, as an added bonus, there is a story by best-selling author Laura Antoniou from her classic *Marketplace* series.

The authors and I put this anthology together on a whim like something out of a Mickey Roonie/Judy Garland film plot ("Hey, I've got a publishing company; you've got stories"), but we are very pleased with the final product.

There really should be something for everyone here – but if something's missing, we do hope you'll submit if for next year's anthology, which we expect will be bigger and exponentially juicier.

Dig in!

Lori Perkins

About the Authors

Cris Anson

Cris Anson's interest in BDSM has been evident since Ellora's Cave published her first erotic romance in 2005. More recently, her novella *No Patience* features an exhibitionist who meets her Dominant on a fetish site. In *Redemption and Glory*, her fourteenth book, two novices to BDSM learn what turns them on, but their exploration turns explosive when a second man enters their Domination and submission games. *Aaron's Jewel*, a BDSM novella featuring older protagonists, will release September 26, 2014.

Cris has given or received floggings, violet wand action, spankings and other elements of BDSM—all in the name of research, of course. Her stories and blogs are laced with her personal observations and experiences. Her books consistently receive 5-star and recommended-read reviews. Visit Cris at www.crisanson.com and read her blog at crisansonspassions.blogspot.com

Laura Antoniou

Laura Antoniou's publishing career began when she started writing gay men's smut to promote safer sex practices during the early 90's. Emboldened by getting paid to do this, she then edited the groundbreaking **Leatherwomen** series, highlighting tales of kinky women. This was rapidly followed by half a dozen other anthologies and the **Marketplace** series of erotic BDSM novels which never reached 1/10000th the sales level of the 50 Shades books, but she's not bitter. Instead, she wrote the 6th, titled **The Inheritor**, due to come out in 2015. In 2013, she turned her mind to mysteries and came out with the Rainbow Book Award winning **The Killer Wore Leather**. Now that she has achieved almost small genre success with it, she plans a sequel, to be released via Cleis. She is also the editor for **Best Lesbian Erotica 2015** and is planning many other writing and editing projects in order to fulfil a lifelong dream of actually making a living on this sort of thing. Follow her on Facebook, Twitter, Fetlife and other shady places or check her out at lantoniou.com

Gray Dixon

Gray Dixon is the *nom de plume* of erotica writer of hot, sexy stories for the adult crowd. She loves walks along the beach at sunset, a glass of wine over a romantic dinner, and a night of love.

On the serious side, she's married to her Dear Heart for many years, has three children, many grandchildren, a dog, a couple of fish, a big yard with lots of fruit trees, two cars, and a house. Ah, the American Dream as she loves to describe it. She likes a lot of different things, crafts, watching the History Channel, reality shows (not all, but some), travel, and of course writing. She's worked hard all her life in many interesting fields and enjoyed all of them, but she finally found enough time to relax and enjoy escaping into the worlds she created through her stories. She mainly writes erotica with BDSM elements, and hopes readers will enjoy the tales she weaves.

Gray Dixon can be found on:
Facebook: https://www.facebook.com/gray.dixon.50,
Twitter: https://twitter.com/GrayDixon

Cara Downey

Cara Downey is from North Preston, Dartmouth Nova Scotia in Canada. She is an avid reader of erotic romances and thrillers. Cara loves to dish on twitter and via email with her favorite authors about their current and up coming novels, and anyone else who will chime in. Cara loves to interact with readers on Facebook and Twitter and be found on twitter @cara_downey.

Dr. Charley Ferrer

Dr. Charley Ferrer is a world-renowned Clinical Sexologist and the FIRST Latina Doctor of Human Sexuality in the United States. She is the award winning author of *BDSM The Naked Truth*, *BDSM for Writers*, and *The W.I.S.E. Journal for the Sensual Woman*. She has written thirteen books on sex and self-empowerment. Doctor Charley is the founder and Executive Director of the Institute of Pleasure whose primary mission is to provide education on relationships, mental health services to women and men, and conduct research on sexuality.

Doctor Charley's advocacy on sexual health, pleasure, and alternative lifestyles has earned her the reputation as a pioneer in sexuality. She has been dubbed America's BDSM Expert for her relentless education efforts related to Dominance and submission and alternative lifestyles throughout the world; using various educational mediums such books, workshops, podcast, online workshops, and for 2014 BDSM Writers Con.

You can reach Dr. Charley Ferrer at
http://www.BDSMwriterscon.com or
http://www.DoctorCharley.com.
She welcomes emails at DoctorCharley@DoctorCharley.com

Kestra Gravier

Kestra Gravier (www.kestragravier.com) is the winner of the 2014 BDSM Writer's Conference contest with "Silver Chasings." She draws inspiration from the aphrodisia in her life. A passionate, decades long love affair. A love of cooking, and of scents. Living and loving abroad. Sexual romps beyond the boundaries of conventional society. Leather, lace and corsets. And lest you think Ms. Gravier has an unbelievably perfect life, know that she, from time to time, needs Spanx, fails to complete projects and doesn't like ice cream. All the more grist for the story mill.

Enjoy Kestra's other tales: *Encounters, Lady Elinor at Hampton Court, Silver Chasings (coming soon)*

Scarlet Hawthorne

Scarlet Hawthorne loves including elements of BDSM in her erotic romances because, as a 24/7 submissive in a DD household, she hopes to reverse the misinformation and negative stereotypes promulgated in the media. She has also published mainstream romances in a variety of genres, from paranormal to romantic suspense, under other pen names. Scarlet's upcoming release is

Deadline– a romantic suspense thriller with plenty of bondage thrown in for good behavior. Her current project is the M/M Romance, *Between the Notes*.

Lise Horton

Lise Horton writes erotic romance, and erotic fiction as Lydia Hill. *Words of Lust*, her debut novel (Carina Press, 2013), and her erotic short story, "My Master's Mark," which Library Journal called "surprisingly poignant" (starred review), is the closing story in *Slave Girls: Erotic Stories of Submission* edited by D. L. King (Cleis Press, May 2014). You can find Lise in all her naughty incarnations at http://www.lisehorton.com.

Debra Hyde

Debra Hyde is a Lambda Literary award-winning author, recognized for her BDSM novel, *Story of L*. A modern retelling of the classic *Story of O*, L updates the original tale to reflect the contemporary lesbian leather world and the women in it. She now pens the newly-released Charlotte Olmes Mystery Series, which re-imagines the famous Holmes/Watson cohorts as lesbian women in 1880s New York City just as the Gilded Age and its social and scientific advances take hold. Debra is a contributing author to the ground-breaking interactive erotic Entwined series, penning two lesbian novellas for it, *Hers* and *Provenance*. Her short fiction backlist spans over a decade of writing and will be re-released as mini-collections in ebook during 2014.

Debra is nearing her twenty-year anniversary in BDSM scene. For sixteen of those years, she was an owned submissive and although her master "aged out" of dominance in his senior years, they're still attached to each other and still playing. Devotion is ever-lasting. Visit Debra Hyde at http://www.debrahyde.comand visit her social media outlets for updates on her work.

Jennifer Kacey

Jennifer Kacey is the Award winning author – ARe top pick of 2013. She is a wife, mother, and business owner living with her family in Texas. She sings in the shower, plays piano in her dreams, and has to have a different color of nail polish every week. The best advice she's ever been given? Find the real you and never settle for anything less.

Mia Koutras

Mia Koutras lives in the Greater Toronto Area with her wonderful husband and two amazing children. When she's not working on educating students on the brilliant imagery and symbolism in Shakespeare's great tragedies, while they not-so-covertly tap away on their cell phones to make plans for lunch and after school, she's concocting story lines and character sketches in her head, just waiting for the moment to commit them to paper and hard drive. She loves using music to whip her muse into a creative frenzy, and her harder, darker tastes involve vintage Goth, alternative and industrial bands, as well as bands from the grunge and metal scene. However, Mia's creative grassroots are in the New Wave of the '80s, with a life-long devotion to Duran Duran—the "Fab Five," a band of (originally) five heart-stopping, gorgeous men who create true sensual and erotic fantasy in sound.

Her dream of writing and publishing has finally been realized, starting with her work as a freelance editor while happily toiling on several manuscripts, and she is thrilled that her first published work, "My Princess," is appearing in the *First Annual BDSM Writers Con Anthology* with Riverdale Ave Books.

> Mia can be found online at
> http://www.facebook.com/mia.koutras and
> http://www.twitter.com/MiaKoutras(@MiaKoutras)

Roz Lee

Award-winning author Roz Lee has penned over a dozen erotic romances. The first, *The Lust Boat*, was born of an idea acquired while on a Caribbean cruise with her family and soon blossomed into a five book series published by Red Sage. Following her love of baseball, she turned her attention to sexy athletes in tight pants, writing the critically acclaimed Mustangs Baseball series. When Roz isn't writing, she's reading, or traipsing around the country on one adventure or another. No trip is too small, no tourist trap too cheesy, and no road unworthy of travel.

BDSM Anthology

Jessica Lust

Jessica Lust has been writing erotica for several years for private collectors. Unlike other authors, her stories are written with a particular reader in mind. She literally interviews the individual, then creates a story based on their particular desires. Jessica writes darker more intensive BDSM novels from a first person point of you, drawing the reader into the story making it appear as if you're reading her diary and secret thoughts. If you like your romance down and dirty, you'll enjoy learning the mayhem and decadent adventures she finds herself in. http://www.jessicalust.com

Paige Matthews

Paige Matthews grew up in a small, idyllic affluent town in the western Connecticut. The town definitely did not match her personality. Staying close to home, she pursued a B.A. in Comparative English Literature from a local college and then continued on for her M.A in English Professional Writing. Paige has always had a love of reading and literature and only furthered that during her studies. During her M.A. studies, she decided it was time to challenge herself and work in a field that she had long admired and dreamt off: being a writer.

Having entered the lifestyle a few years ago, Paige writes erotica with a preference toward BDSM themes. She enjoys exploring the emotional connection and emotions behind D/s relationships. http://www.paigematthews.com

Laci Paige

Laci Paige is author of the *Silken Edge Series*. The books are a fictitious series about a group of people who are into the BDSM scene. Each book follows a different couple as they grow and learn to discover more about themselves in the lifestyle, and their relationships. *The Silken Edge* won an UP Author Award, and has hit the #1 spot twice on Amazon for Erotica. Laci's stories always end with HEA or HFN, and her husband is always a willing participant when she needs some hands-on research.

More than anything Laci enjoys spending time with her family. She and her husband support their children on the soccer pitch and off. Laci enjoys the outdoors, traveling, and of course reading and writing (and chocolate). Their family lives in Hampton Roads, Virginia where her muse comes out at night, and writes grown up stories.

Cassandra Park

Cassandra Park is a writer and editor who's been in the BDSM lifestyle for over 20 years. Her writing has been published by Ravenous Romance, Scarlett Hill, Logical Lust Publications, The Eulenspiegel Society, and Instructing Eve. Her books include *It's SUPPOSED to Hurt!* (vols. I and II) and *My First Spanking*, a short story anthology. She lives in Queens, NY, and is a coordinator for Long Island Leather N Roses, a social and educational BDSM group.

Corrine A. Silver

Corrine A Silver studied Creative Writing as an undergrad in the Midwest. After a ten year detour into health care, she started writing again. Perhaps it is due to life experience, maturity (or lack thereof), or simply an attempt at escapism...but all her writing is kinky now. And she likes it that way. She thrilled to find a thriving world of authors and readers with the same interests. She lives in the Midwest with her husband and kids.

Helena Stone

Helena Stone is Dutch and has been living in Ireland for over 15 year, where works part time in the library in Bailieborough, Co. Cavan where among other things she runs the library reading group. She will read almost anything that has words in it, and posts her thoughts on everything she reads in a reading blog.

Marie Tuhart

Marie Tuhart can't remember a time when she didn't like to make things up. Her overactive imagination comes in hand as an author. At the age of 16, she wrote her first short story and never looked back. At nineteen she wrote her first novel. Now she's a published author of seven novels and 3 short stories. Born and raised in California, after 30 years in the corporate world she retired and moved to the Pacific Northwest to write full time. When not writing, Marie loves to read, travel, and spend time with her family. Marie currently writes for The Wild Rose Press and Sybarite Seductions. Marie is an Amazon bestselling author.

Carrie Anne Ward

For many years she wrote stories in her spare time, mostly horror or supernatural, but she never felt the passion to take it further. Her love for literature at school didn't, at that point, overtake her love of Art, but as she grew older her passion for writing surpassed any other desire she had ever had.

Her love for literature over the years grew excessively (mostly erotica) and when BDSM erotic books took the world by storm, she finally found the genre in which she wanted to write. So being a real submissive, Carrie decided to take the experiences she has had and combined them with her imagination, to create a story. At the age of 33, she fulfilled her dream to become a writer by releasing her debut novel *A Taylor Made Student*, the first book of a trilogy from The Taylor Made Series.

Leya Wolfgang

Leya Wolfgang renewed her childhood love of telling stories when she took the National Novel Writing Month (NaNoWriMo) challenge in 2011. At the end of November, she finished with 50,000 words and a very good start to a novel. She has since been captured by the dominating characters of Devil You Know Kink Club™. They led her into their dark and steamy club, kept her bound to her laptop, and whipped her until she agreed to expose their kinks and their secrets. She has already published one book in the DYKKC BDSM Erotica Romance Series, has two more on the cusp of publication, and several more in development. Leya's writing has now become an all-consuming passion, often thwarted by a conservative day job that she appreciates but would abandon if she could to write full time.